Vampire League

Book IV

La Vie Dans Le Noir

Vampire League

Book IV

La Vie Dans Le Noir

by Luiza Dobrzynska

PAPERBACK ISBN: 978-1-7372486-4-4
EPUB ISBN: 979-8-2010227-8-5
✱✱✱

WRITTEN BY LUIZA DOBRZYNSKA
PUBLISHED BY ROYAL HAWAIIAN PRESS
COVER ART BY TYRONE ROSHANTHA
TRANSLATED BY RAFAL STACHOWSKY
PUBLISHING ASSISTANCE: DOROTA RESZKE
✱✱✱

FOR MORE WORKS BY THIS AUTHOR, PLEASE VISIT:
WWW.ROYALHAWAIIANPRESS.COM
✱✱✱

VERSION NUMBER 1.00

Part 1

I search for the shadow of the night, so that I can cry

"Where's the rest of your pack?" Lenore asked, entering the apartment in which the Gladiator yawned over some syllabus.

The light-haired highlander hated 'swotting up', but Conan inexorably demanded that everyone at least had general knowledge of international issues. He taught not only combat, but also anything that could prove useful.

"Never is sleeping, and Theo with Oggy got into a course for disarming explosives and have gone to have some fun in town," he said. "Gerard is training in the machine room. I bet he'll come back covered in bruises, that klutz..."

The machine room was something that, in the words of the old VASP employees, *destroyed all the newcomers*. That's what they called the training room, which was meant for exercises concerning reflexes and motor coordination. It was equipped with machinery, launching falling batons and firing projectiles – sand-filled, hard spheres that had to be avoided or repelled with a baton. At first, the rookie undergoing the training stood on the floor and then switched to the balance beam. The constructor of this device predicted different levels of difficulty, but so far Gerard could barely handle the first one.

"Oh, give him a break," Lenore said. "He's not doing bad, after all. Conan demands too much from him. Look, blonde, you're all called to gather in the general's office. I'll call Fronde, and you go wake up Never. You have another task."

"Anything's better than this damn school," Gladiator said, threw the syllabus in the corner and ran to the bedroom with relief. From there, after a while, there was a scream so terrible that Lenore literally fell from her feet. In her life, she had never heard anything as horrible as that sound. Fortunately, it quickly stopped.

"Geez," the girl grunted, getting up from the floor. "I never would have guessed that decibels could knock you off your feet. What happened in there?"

"This moron poured water on me," never said furiously as he left the bedroom. "I'm sorry, Lenore, I don't usually raise my voice indoors, but I was terrified that some flood was coming from the skies! He poured a whole bucket over me. What's this task?"

"Once you're all gathered, then I'll notify the general. He'll explain everything."

"Hopefully it's not overly tiring. After these Egyptian brawls I've had enough adventures… by the way, how did it all end?" Never looked at Lenore questioningly, all the while wiping his wet hair with a towel.

"I'll prepare a copy of the report for you, but later. For now, I have to go call Fronde."

On the way to the communications department, Lenore looked into the machine room. Gerard was sitting on the floor with a blank expression, while Conan was leaning over him, pressing a wet compress to his forehead.

"See, if you did as I showed you that baton wouldn't have a chance hitting you," he lectured him at the same time, calmly and without anger.

This large man was patient and always sympathized with the student, but was still unrelenting as an instructor. He never let anyone free from his reach until he trained them in at least a satisfactory level.

"Green-eyes, you're called to the general's office," Lenore said, struggling to contain her smile. "You'll train afterwards. Work first, pleasure afterwards."

Gerard got up, pressing the compress to his head, on which was a bump the size of a decent tangerine. Training the reflexes under Conan's eye was often painful, but he didn't complain. He knew full well that one day such training could save his life, so he trained, despite the pain.

"I have to recover before I come back here anyway," he said for his acquittal.

"In a real fight nobody is going to wait for you to recover, you have to learn to defend yourself, even when you start seeing stars swirling in your eyes!" Conan shouted towards him and called for the next student through the intercom.

Never and Gladiator were already sitting in the general's office. Never was looking through some papers, and the highlander looked at the actor with irony and advised him to go to the kitchen and grab a cold knife.

"I'll be fine," Gerard said angrily. "You probably wish that they'd smash my head, knowing you... but it's not going to be that easy. I'm letting you know that I won't be done in by some little machine."

"Ah, a shame…"

Never listened to them arguing with one ear, busy reading the report of case number 3159, that is, the one they led in Egypt. To his disappointment, there were no revelations other than those he already knew. The analysis of the hard drive did little, and the police's activity ended with several arrests, which led to the closure of the case. No one was proven guilty of murder – it seemed that the right criminals, whoever they were, escaped responsibility. Their motives also remained unclear, and the police's strange reluctance to investigate the case didn't give hope to the success in uncovering the truth.

Never finally threw the report onto the desk and looked at his friends, constantly exchanging invectives. Their eternal quarrels didn't bother him anymore, as they did at first, rather he looked at them as a circus performance and understood that in some peculiar way these constant fights serve to strengthen their friendship. It was absurd, and yet it was the truth.

After waiting for half an hour, Fronde and Oggy, who had to be pulled out all the way from the town, joined the three friends. It was only then that General Dagwood appeared, as always, impeccable and stoic.

"You're going to France," he said, putting a few tickets on his desk. "The case is mysterious and rather nasty. What happened to you, Romeo?"

"The pendulum slammed in the head," Gerard succinctly explained, without adding that he had far more bruises under his clothes than on his head.

"Ah, yes, reflex training... a difficult thing, but you have to go through it like everyone else. Grit your teeth and think of England."

"Not in my dreams. I'm a good Frenchman."

"Well, about France then, what difference does it make..." Gladiator giggled.

Gerard, wanting him to somehow prove that there is a difference, and a big one, hit him on the ankle. And since he still had iron-ended shoes on his feet, used for training in the machine room, the highlander moaned and intended to hit him back.

"You'll have time to hit each other later," the general stopped him. "There's more important things right now."

The secretary, dressed in coat and skirt, brought a tray of coffee and a plate of cookies and put the cup in front of each of us, adding a pleasant smile on top. Like most of the agency's staff, the girl had no idea how the members of the Tau Group were different from other operational agents.

"It's just camouflage," the general explained as she left, closing the leather-covered door behind her. "You don't have to drink it, just pour it into the flower pot. The palm tree will be fine."

"I'd try a sip," Theo carefully soaked his mouth in coffee. "It's not a copy of luvac, I hope?"

"What is that?" Gladiator didn't get it.

"Coffee, which the raw material is taken from the feces of an Indonesian fox," the amused general explained to him. "No need to worry, it's just Jacobs. I can't afford a copy of the luvac anyway, it costs three hundred dollars for half a pound."

"Yuck. Men are worse than pigs, they'll eat anything. Hah, they'll even pay for it!" Gladiator shook in disgust and sniffed the coffee incredulously.

"You should see how an exquisite made in Japan party loos like," Never said. "I don't have a particularly weak stomach, but when I saw a table with sea cucumbers, salted cuttlefish innards and other similar specialties, I was sick for a week."

Oggy sipped the coffee without hesitation. She liked this drink, although it clearly didn't do her any good, mainly because when she started drinking it, she lost all moderation. Now, too, after drinking her portion, she went for Fronde's cup, who did not protest. He himself could at best taste it, because Turkish coffee isn't drinkable to a vampire due to the high amounts of coffee grounds floating in it.

When the Tau Group returned from Egypt, bringing Oggy with them, the general was quite surprised, but didn't try to protest. Moreover, he was probably pleased, especially when Conan after the initial test assessed the girl's skills to be a 'strong four', which was very high.

"Oggy, slow down before you get sick, and then what will we do without you!" Never shouted abruptly and turned to the general. "Boss, what's the deal? Because I don't think we're here to discuss coffee."

"You're right. Listen, then: I'm sending you to Paris. A month ago, a certain girl's body was found there, devoid of her head. This is not the first such case, and the police don't have a foothold. This time they didn't find one either, but there's a person to hold onto instead. The girl is the daughter of Pakistani emigrants, so it was originally assumed that it was a murder done for honor. All these people need is suspicion in order to kill a woman in cold blood. Mother, sister, daughter, doesn't matter who it is."

"I know," Never shrugged with disdain. "Allah's followers are bonkers, but the Pakistanis are the pinnacle of everything. They are divided into those who can punish a woman for any reason, and those who do not need any reason. What's our job there? Let them be sentenced to imprisonment for life."

"Hold on. It seems to me that the matter is much more complicated," Theo silenced him with a hand movement and looked at Dagwood."

"It's not that simple," the general said calmly. "Everything indicates that the victim's family is not to blame in this case. Like I said, this isn't the first victim, and what connects them all is that they weren't able to find the murderer. No traces, no clues. One thing always repeats in the coroner's reports: there are no signs of rape, but death wasn't due to the cutting off of head, which is always missing to the, so to speak, full set. All the victims died of heart attacks, which is all the more strange considering that they were all young, healthy girls. The police are glad that this time they have someone to blame, but in my opinion, they are very wrong. First of, they've ignored Murphy's Law. Second, they're not connecting it with a similar series of murders which occurred some eleven years ago. And as for me... I know Muhammad Halim, we served together in the Tigers Brigade. He's a decent guy overall, and I don't believe he would have committed such a crime. Find out what's going on."

"I hate infidels. Especially Muslim," Fronde muttered with obvious reluctance, as if he were reminded of the crusades on the Holy Land. In his times, the memory of the Crusades was still alive. "Who even loves them? Maybe their own mothers, and even that isn't certain."

"You don't have to adore them, you just have to solve the case. Can you be objective?"

"I'll try," a deep sigh accompanying these words indicated that it would take great effort on his part.

"Well, great. The procurer will give you everything you need on your trip, and then you'll be going. Secret Agent Gris will pick you up from the airport and give you all the details. Do not enter into conversations with the police or the press, avoid official statements at all, because it'll come back to bite us."

"Thank you, we would never have guessed."

He could never deny himself this type of sarcasm. If he only could, he would make his boss understand that he did not need advice. And that he has already forgotten more than General Dagwood could ever learn. To his credit, Robert V. Dagwood knew about it and treated Never with respect, and had no intention of giving him any official instructions – only to outline the issue in a few sentences, leaving the Hindu vampire the whole initiative.

On the way to the airport, Gerard was still holding an ice compress to his forehead, but threw it in the trash on the plane.

"I'm going to be as tough as any of you guys," he told his friends, awakening their honest amusement. "Enough feeling sorry for myself. I'm a man, what happened, happened."

"You've almost deceived me..." Gladiator chuckled.

"I'll catch up to you guys, just wait."

"Why not, you can always try," Theo agreed with him, suppressing his laughter. "But being a man is not that simple, you have to earn it."

"I think you're trying to offend the women here. We're as good as you are!" Oggy said indignantly and approached the passing flight attendant. "Am I right, or am I not?"

"I think you are," the flight attendant said politely. "Please fasten your seatbelts, we're about to take off."

"Ughh…" Theo moaned, losing resonance and digging his nails into the handrails of the chair.

"Men…" Oggy creaked, and with real satisfaction stuck the needle of a small syringe in his hand.

When they were receiving the supplies, Dea called her to the side and handed her a small box with four such syringes, with proper, secure packaging and sterilized foil.

"Fronde is afraid of lying, as you know," she explained quietly. "One small injection and we'll have peace of mind on the plane. Truth be told, he should do some kind of psychotherapy, but so far I haven't been able to convince him."

No one knew why, in fact, Theo, familiar with modern technology and not at all its enemy, was still afraid of airplanes. He himself didn't fully know why he hasn't been able to overcome this phobia, but the background of this whole issue didn't interest him and he didn't seek to find the causes, which came back to haunt him.

Thanks to the injection, the trip passed without any awkward surprises, although Gladiator, prone to joking, as always, claimed that he sees a goblin outside the window, sawing at the left wing. This caused unexpected outrage. Theo, sleepy after receiving the medications, did not pay attention to this provocation, however, a ten year old girl sitting behind him began to have attacks of hysteria and it took a long time to calm her down. It was only after landing that she quieted down, but her father, a man named Devlin, aggressively ragged on Gladiator and demanded that airport security put this on record. Faced with a polite refusal, he decided to take justice into his own hands.

The outrage he caused ended only with the arrival of the gendarmerie, which did indeed prepare a record, but against Mr. Devlin for disturbing the peace. Only after this whole fuss ended were the friends able to look around for the mysterious agent Gris.

The airport was almost empty, the passengers spread out to nearby taxis, so they could easily spot him, even though he was sitting quite far away, casually holding in front of himself a cardboard bearing the inscription 'DAGWOOD'. They hastily finished the conversation with customs officers, signed a protocol and approached the man waiting for them. He stood up at their sight. He was very tall and very thin, not very old, but with a few gray hairs, with an elongated, not very handsome face, a high forehead and tightly protruding ears. In fact, these ears, especially unsightly, were what stood out the most.

There was something else about him – some kind of elusive similarities that made them all feel a vague association, too vague to be articulated.

"Special Agent Gris," he introduced himself, squeezing their hands one by one. He moved his eyes over them until he finally stopped his eyes at Gerard.

"Agent Tau 3," Gerard said, absent-minded, shaking his hand.

"Ah, of course, of course... One, two, three, four and this lady must be Tau 5."

"Yes, how did you know?" Oggy beamed, extending her skinny hand towards him.

"I guessed, child. Let's go, then. I parked outside the airport."

His voice also had a familiar timbre. If everyone's mind wasn't busy thinking about the earlier outrage, they would probably think about it, but for now they weren't able to.

"If I could, as I couldn't, I would show that buffoon how we handle such disputes back at the Highlands," Gladiator said ruefully, sitting down on the large seat of a Ford Passat.

"He really was a buffoon," Never agreed with him. "What do you have to do with the fact that his daughter is such a crybaby? Did you raise her? As Dea says, there are children and there are crybabies, and that's not our fault."

In general, Never didn't like children, and the thought of his own filled him with superstitious horror. He was grateful to fate for the fact that vampires are generally infertile... although a certain danger existed. He himself was the best proof of that.

"I guess you're right," Theo agreed, suppressing a yawn. "But Yanek really went too far, shouting for the whole plane to hear: *A goblin is sawing off the wing! It's about to fall off!* Where the hell did you grow up, Golden Head, in a forest?"

"No, in Tatras. Why, is there something you don't like about that?" Gladiator became defensive, ready to start the fight immediately, even inside the car.

"Golden Head... that's actually a fitting nickname. I've never seen anyone with such golden hair, not yellow, not blond or light, but truly golden. Which is interesting, since I thought that there are no blondes among you," agent Gris intervened, bringing the passat on the road and at the same time turning on the radio, which buzzed loud music.

"Among us? What do you mean by that?" Never asked coldly.

The agent smiled ironically.

"Don't play dumb, I know who you are or, or rather, what you are. More precisely: what is your diet, so to speak... but I understand that you don't want to talk about it. I don't particularly care. I'm just saying, I thought you all have black hair, or at least that it gets darker later on..."

"It depends. True, it is very rare for us to have anyone with blonde or red hair, but it happens, as you can see. And no we don't change our hair colors, what a dumb idea... unless they're dying it, they're free to do so, but Gladiator here would rather die than use such 'womanly' means of changing the appearance."

"Again, insulting the women," Oggy said.

"Be quiet, kid! Ever since you came back from Australia, you've been waving around this banner of feminism. Haven't you gotten tired of it yet?" Gerard shouted.

He had a headache again from the noise in the car and, not knowing why, lost his sense of humor. He was tormented by something unspecified, not a bad feeling, not anxiety, not regret of something lost. Perhaps it was because he was breathing the French air again, which he was no longer used to, and which he was trying to forget as something inaccessible.

"No, I haven't," she said rebelliously. "Enough with men ruling the world."

"Fronde, do something about this girl, because I can't stand her anymore," demanded the impatient actor.

"Fronde, don't you dare!"

"How about you calm down, both of you? We're not in our own vehicle," Never intervened. "We came for a reason, so let's focus on our job. Agent Gris, what do you know about this case?"

"I know everything I can," the agent said. He twisted the radio handle, lowering the volume of the noisy music. "But it's not much. It's rare for a serial killer to literally leave no traces on the corpses. The victims had nothing in common except that they were young girls without exception and that rape did not occur in any of the incidents. Race, place of residence, physical conditions, material and social status, none of that matters. In this case, it's new that the corpse was found in Paris. They were usually found outside the city, even far beyond, and this time it was the center of Paris, on the Champs-Élysées."

"Ahh, the Champs Elysees..." Gladiator hummed, stretching himself so widely that he almost broke the window with his elbow.

"If you think it's funny, that's fine. But I assure you that the elderly couple that found Maura Halim's body didn't feel like laughing, on the contrary, because the woman had a bout of hysteria and the man landed on cardiological watch. Do you want to talk to the victim's family?"

"There's no need," he said calmly. "The police bothering them is enough. If they're not to blame, the killer is still hiding among the streets of Paris, and we should be looking for him. For now, however, take us to the motel. Those locales are safer for us than exclusive hotels and we need somewhere to relax. Aside from being tired, the sun will soon rise."

"And sunlight does not serve you..."

"Well, not too much, let's say. Anyway, we prefer to sleep during the day, and then we'll begin our investigations in the evening."

The vehicle stopped in front of a small, off-the-road motel decorated with a neon sign 'Calambredin'. It was surrounded by a large parking lot with a gas station built in its depths.

"You'll be safe here," Gris said, and gave Never an insulating bag with some heavy contents. "I was told to deliver this to you. Inside you'll also find my phone number, so give me a call if you need anything. In exchange, I'd like Tau 1 to give me his phone number. I might have some extra information to share with you."

"Do you expect to have any? From where?"

"I have my sources. I'm a journalist by profession."

"Well, congratulations. That means you'll go anywhere, whether you're allowed to or not. Prepare us all the materials that you have, we'll need to look through them."

Never handed Gris a piece of paper with his number and stepped out of the vehicle. He liked motels like these, but just in case, he looked around intently and then looked at Gladiator, who simply nodded.

"No, boss. No signs of hostile emanation here. The detectors are silent as well."

Thanks to his talents, Gladiator was promoted to the 'picket' of the team, which meant that he was responsible for making sure the enemy doesn't take us by surprise. The new role was a source of pride and even conceit for the highlander, as now he felt important: the safety of the whole group depended on him. According to the division of duties, done by Conan, Never was the commander and coordinator of the team, Oggy the scout-tracker, while Fronde and Gerard the detectives. In addition, Gerard was responsible for the written documentation, Fronde for the photographic one, and Oggy for the material documentation. Thanks to this separation, their work should go more smoothly, but they haven't had the opportunity to test that yet.

The sleepy girl in the window wrote down their details and handed them keys to two rooms. They were neither pretty, nor clean, but they were enough for temporary shelter. The important thing was that no one would bother them there. They carefully covered the door, they opened the bag and, to their satisfaction, found several chilled containers filled with blood. After a thorough trip, the friends parted after the rented rooms and went to bed. They were very tired, and the temperature difference (in Poland it was about fifteen degrees Celsius, while twice as much in France) made them feel completely exhausted. Even Never fell asleep like a rock, someone who usually slept as vigilantly as a hare under balk.

He was only woken up by the ringing of the phone.

"What devil?!" Oggy shouted into the microphone, who got to it first.

"Give it here, it's not yours," Never angrily took the phone from her hands. "Is that you, Gris?"

"Can you go out?" the voice of the agent sounded in the speaker. "We've got another corpse, and if you hurry, you'll be able to impersonate my crew. The media, I mean."

Never looked out the window behind which the summer downpour was raging. The sky was covered with heavy, lead-gray clouds.

"We can," he said. "Where are you?"

"At the 14th of July street, number eighteen, will you find it?"

"Not an issue."

Never turned off his phone, sent Oggy to Gladiator's and Gerard's room, while he himself woke up Fronde, who was snoring so loud it echoed, indifferent to the surrounding noise. Moments later, the group was in full set, albeit disheveled, with messy clothes and yawning desperately. Never didn't even give them time to change clothes, so as not to waste a second. The 14th of July Street via a taxi. Once they reached their destination, they noticed a minibus with a large tricolor inscription *TV FRANCE 5*. Someone waved their hand to them from the opened door. Accepting the invitation, they entered the vehicle..

"This time, the corpse was found at the park near the Palace de la Concorde," said Agent Gris, releasing the handbrake. "The same patterns as before. There's more and more of these murders. Do you have any ideas on how to catch this psychopath?"

"Not so fast. Wait," Never answered.

He already had a vague suspicion on whether or not the killer was a psychopath, but he chose not to say anything about that yet. He had a small hope that he was wrong, so he chose to be silent.

The van stopped next to the park, where a large crowd of spectators had already gathered and several gendarmes were securing the crime area with yellow tape. Agent Gris gave Never a tape recorder with a microphone, Fronde a portable video camera, and Oggy a camera for taking photos. Gerard received a notebook, while Gladiator a sketchbook.

"Act like professionals, if you can," he advised, then jumped out of the car.

"TV 5, news program SODA," he began, approaching the highest ranking of the gendarmerie. "Could this be another victim of the elusive Head Hunter?"

"We don't know yet, we just got here..." the gendarme said, while the friends ran to the taped-off spot, trying their best to act like a typical reporter team.

On the dutifully trimmed lawn lay the body of a rather chubby, short woman, dressed in a fashionable dress, mesh stockings and slippers on very thin high-heels. The nails of her tanned hands were done with glittery nail polish, on the middle and ring fingers were gold rings. The head was gone: there was a jagged wound between the revealed shoulders. Gerard, though wanted to remain calm, screamed faintly, dropped his notebook and rushed to the side to vomit.

Others continued the documentation, not paying attention to him. Theo gave Gladiator his camera and, taking advantage of the inattention of the gendarmerie, carefully checked the nails and clothes of the hapless victim, recording his observations in a small voice recorder. Oggy photographed the sight carefully, while looking around zealously. Gladiator wrote down his observations in the sketchbook, adding crude sketches to the sides.

Agent Gris finished quietly talking to the gendarmes, gathered some accounts from the witnesses and only then approached Gerard.

"Are you going to be okay, man?" he asked with some concern.

Gerard was standing by one of the trees, bent halfway down and trying to control his nausea. He struggled to stay on his feet and was taking in air like a fish thrown ashore. His face now resembled a greenish, translucent mask of crepe paper from within which shone eyes filled with horror.

"Sorry, I couldn't take it," he whispered, trying to straighten up. "I know that it's a disgrace. I shouldn't flaunt such weakness, especially when I am what I am. But I can't stand sights like these. I don't have any bloodthirst at all."

He bent down in violent motion and vomited again on the grass. Agent Gris looked at him with compassion and sympathy, and gave him a handkerchief.

"It's clean," he said. "Wipe your mouth. Not everyone is strong enough to withstand such views. I couldn't stand it at first either, but as a journalist you have to develop nerves of steel. I'm all used to it now. Are you feeling better?"

Gerard nodded, wiping his face with the handkerchief. He was angry at himself for this cursed weakness that prevented him from matching the fortitude of his other friends, but he had no control over it. He could only hope that one day he would develop the resilience he needed.

"This again?" Fronde's voice approached from next to him. "Come on, when will you finally become a man? Get yourself together or something... it's a disgrace in front of our friend Gris."

"There's no shame in it at all," the agent said succinctly. "Better tell me if you've come up with something."

"Nev... I mean, Tau 1 is talking to Detective Frassard, who's been investigating these murders from the beginning. He just showed up."

Indeed, Never was talking to some short man with a smooth, thin face, dressed in a nice suit and well-worn shoes. He looked about fifty years old, and the dark circles under his eyes clearly indicated a few sleepless nights. After a while, Never said goodbye to him kindly and whistled commandingly.

"Excuse me, I'm not some dog to whistle at," Agent Gris said with apparent insult, but dutifully went with everyone to his work van.

"I don't know if the stuff I recorder is any good, but you have your magicians on the TV, let them put it together for you," said Never, placing the tape recorder on one of the seats with relief. "Did any of you notice anything out of the ordinary."

"I mean, I didn't see anything ordinary there," Gerard muttered, and squeezed into the corner of the van.

"Well, that's obvious."

"Leave him, Raja. You know very well that he is a lover, not a warrior," Oggy said sharply. "Not everyone is used to cruelty, like you both. Nothing's going to move you that much know."

"That's not true at all," Theo retorted. He put down the camera and rubbed his numb hand. "We also feel sorry for this poor girl, but we don't need to put on performances like he does. I guess that's what you'd expect from a former comedian..."

Seeing that the conversation is dangerously departing towards personal issues, Never considered it appropriate to interrupt them and bring it back on topic. However, he waited with that until they were all in Gris's journalist studio, where they will finally be able to get familiar with the material collected by the agent.

The way it was all developed was impressive – it really was a professional, well done job. The documents were sorted according to date, the notes were neat and clear, and the map, fixed on a cork board with designated crime scenes, had all the necessary references. Never looked at it, measuring with his fingers the distance between the locations that the corpses were found. Others snatched some old articles behind his back and argued fiercely, because everyone had a different opinion about the appearance and origin of the perpetrator.

"All right, quiet down already," said the Indian, looking at them with displeasure. "Let me tell you something that you will not find in our friend's notes: this poor woman's head was not cut off, but separated by paws armed with chiseled claws. I was able to extract information from Detective Frassard that all the victims had similar tracks. For obvious reasons, this has not been made public. Do you have any idea what kind of panic this would cause? Detectives don't understand the truth, they suspect that the psychopath is using some tool formed like the paw of some monster... though I don't blame them, but I've already seen enough to decide that this was done by something other than human."

"Some kind of werewolf?" Gris asked, raising his eyebrows.

"Excuse me," Oggy growled

"The murdered girl's name was Giselle Juverant," Never continued. "She was a prostitute. I've always felt sorry for these women, they have a disgusting job that often ends badly, and the most interesting thing is that hardly anyone cares. The police least of all."

"Just because you didn't like being in a brothel doesn't mean that everyone who works there thinks it's disgusting," Theo said ironically, putting his hands on his chest.

"Did you work in one?" he asked.

He shrugged impatiently and did not answer. There were many dark secrets in his life, and only Fronde knew some of them, but he did not reveal them either, despite the hints he sometimes made.

"She was a prostitute... so the occupation of these girls doesn't really matter either," agent Gris said with deep reflection. "Do you think that there's something we don't know about roaming around Paris? Something that will be hard to stop?"

"Well, you could say that," Never agreed with him. "Though it's probably not a werewolf, since judging by the size of the paws, it must have been really huge. Even Vishka didn't have such paws... ah, right, you don't know anything about that thing, and probably for the better."

He coughed and continued on.

"I learned that this thing bustled around in southern France before, and arrived in Paris as part of some journey. Its victims mark an interesting path, from the Ardennes to the center of the capital. I don't know where it's going, but we have to stop it. It kills once a month, right?"

"Once per lunar cycle, that is, when it's activated, so to speak," agent Gris said. "That's why I thought about werewolves."

"Right, the heads…" muttered Gerard, who suddenly had something in mind. "Maybe we're dealing with some trophy hunter like these Maori from New Guinea? They like their souvenirs."

"I thought about it, but I don't think so. If that was the case, the head would have been cut off, not ripped out. No, I doubt it's about a gruesome souvenir, although I admit that the theory is tempting. A collector would try to make sure they don't damage their trophy," Never probably wasn't fully convinced.

There was a grim silence in the studio. They still didn't know what they were going against, but the psychological portrait that painted itself more and more clearly was non-inviting at best. They didn't have that much time either. If they wanted to stop this nightmare, they had to hurry, and at the same time they had no foothold. After a long time, Never apologized to Gris and chased his entire team out on the street.

"Let's not mix the guy into this," he said. "He could have similar training, but he doesn't have the same experience as us. It'll be better to let him go to that TV station of his and work on the material we recorded. Oggy, did you smell anything strange at the park? You were right next to the corpse."

"I did. The smell was neither human nor animal, but different from the smell of werewolves. I can't define it, but I could definitely recognize it when I'll need to."

"Then let's get to work. We'll have a good walk tonight."

In fact, they didn't all have to take part in the search, Oggy herself would've been enough, but they wouldn't let the girl go by herself. Even though they couldn't help Oggy in this type of search, they preferred to at least play the role of some kind of bodyguards, especially since the killer could be hiding anywhere. The werewolf's smell remained as strong as a dog's even while in human form. Thus, the logical conclusion seemed that it would be easy to find a trace, since the smell was so specific. Unfortunately, the still dripping rain was clearing off the traces, and they could only hope that, by chance, they would come across a fresh trail.

Of course, they started with the park, using the 'circling eagle method', meaning that they swept bigger and bigger circles around the crime scene. Oggy preferred this method to others, although it was very tedious and time-consuming. As she admitted with embarrassment, she was most discouraged in this situation by the fact that the killer's scent cut off in the area that the girl's body was found. She did not find it on any of the paths, on the grass or the barks of the trees, even though it was very pronounced on the corpse itself. After all, she could clearly smell it while leaning over the girl's body with a camera, and yet it was nowhere else to be found.

She was sure that she would immediately recognize it if she stumbled across it anywhere, although finding a specific smell in the diverse fragrance mix of Paris seemed impossible. It was especially near perfume stores that the search became very difficult – Oggy began sneezing and complained that her eyes were watering. In the end, Never went into one of the nearby pharmacies and bought her some anti-allergic powders and liquid calcium for children. Oggy swallowed the pills, drank the calcium and clearly became more motivated, as it had a peachy taste, which she loved.

"I'll get to sniffing again," she promised. "Although so far we haven't gotten anywhere. There's loads of smells here, and the rain too... by the way, where are we right now?"

"Around Boulevard Saint-Germain," Gerard replied in a tired tone. "What does it matter?"

"Because I thought of something. At first, there was something about the attacker's smell I didn't like, and now I know what. And if I'm not mistaken... how do we get to the subway station from here?"

"I don't know anymore. The city's changed a lot."

"Don't worry, I'll figure it out in a second," Fronde, who always preferred simple solutions, said and jumped out on the road trying to stop the Opel combo driving past.

"Find yourself a job, nutjob!" the driver shouted through an open window, slipped past him and added gas, disappearing behind the turn of the street.

Theo froze with astonishment, and the rest erupted with irresistible laughter.

"What the hell was he talking about?"

"He probably thought you wanted to ask him for some money," he explained. "Just in case, remember that the owners of such cars are very reluctant to part with their money. The guy from the shabby fiat over the might talk to you, but forget about the fancy ones."

Theo snorted angrily and wanted to say back something snitty, when his gaze fell upon Oggy. She stood upright, sniffing as much as she could, her brown eyes moving restlessly around.

"Have you caught a trail?" he asked, forgetting about the unfortunate adventure.

"Yes and no," she said. "Have to look into it.

She went off, almost running, driven by the smell not detectable to the others. They kept up with her with slight difficulty, going so quick that they fell onto each other when she suddenly stopped near a sewer gate. Silently, she pointed her finger at it. Gladiator, who sometimes showed amazing intuition, didn't ask a thing. He grabbed the gate and snatched it with childish ease, after which the girl lowered her thin hand into the ditch and pulled out of it some strange object.

At first glance it resembled the shell of a clay pot overgrown with algae, but on closer inspection they realized that it was the bone of a skull, very fresh, still with some skin and hair. Oggy sniffed it carefully and said with certainty:

"This bone belonged to Giselle Jouverant. I would risk the claim that this part was ripped from the rest not by accident. I can smell the killer, despite the sewer smells. Any conclusions?"

Never nodded, taking her horrible trophy.

"I studied medicine," he said. "And I know that the skull would only be cracked open for one purpose: to get to the brain. This complicates the situation for us. We have a so-called Gourmet here. That's how the Devourers are called today, which are the divided into those that, well, are not picky and will eat the liver and the heart, and the other kind that we're chasing now. This thing wants brains, fresh human brains. One that was still thinking an hour ago."

"How picky…" muttered Gladiator with entertainment that was completely out of place.

"So that it doesn't carry what it doesn't need, it takes the head of the victim and takes it to its lair, where no one will interrupt its feast," Never continued, without paying attention to him. "Hence the conclusion that it is probably not incredible strong physically, at least not immediately before the attack. Although, it could just be a kind of laziness. It throws the body to the side, while the remains of the ruptured skull into the sewers, where no one will look. So, we can logically assume that we are dealing with an intelligent creature."

"Then why won't it use that damn intelligence and stop murdering!" Oggy shouted with disgust. Although she was a werewolf, she would never even consider feasting on human meat.

"Oh, it probably can't. I don't know what to think about this myself… after all, it's doing the same thing as us, just trying to survive."

"Don't be so philosophical," Gladiator spoke again. "We have to hunt down this creature, that's all there is to it. I don't know about you, but I don't care if this guy just loves the taste of human brain or can't live without it."

"Who cares about that?!" Gerard roared with fury, who, not knowing why, was annoyed by such scientific approach to the subject, and then added a few words that he didn't usually use.

"He's right!" Theo supported him and fell silent, because a police patrol appeared, coming from behind the alley. It was led by a short blonde with a bob-cut, cornflower eyes, fit and gentle, despite the uniform being slightly disorderly.

"Corporal Janine Lombardi. What are you guys doing here?" she asked sternly, shining a flashlight towards them.

Never handed her the 'sewer trophy' with grace, at the sight of which she was taken aback and stepped back.

"The grate was pulled open when we arrived," he explained. "Our friend is a marine botanist. He thought it was seaweed, and was surprised to find any here. He wanted to look at it more closely, that's why he pulled it out. It's a skull fragment."

"I can see that," the police woman carefully packed the gruesome remains into a foil bag and handed it to one of the accompanying gendarmes.

"I'll hand it to the right hands. For now, I have to write down your data and testimony," she said after a while, taking out her notebook.

"That's some luck. We'll waste a lot of time here," Oggy muttered reluctantly, measuring her with a hostile look. It didn't escape her attention that Fronde was staring at the attractive 'gendarmerie' with great interest.

"We're talking about a murder here," Corporal Lombardi sternly reminded her.

"No way! And I thought we were playing dominos," Oggy barked back

They silenced her with difficulty, and the petite female police officer recorded testimonies of each of the friends, along with the details of their documents. They weren't too happy about this, since the general directly forbade them from talking to the police, but in this situation they were without a way out. It was only then that she allowed them to leave, ordering them to testify at the police station next to Place de l'Étoile tomorrow in order to sign their testimonies.

"Why not?" Fronde said with a flirty smile. "And may we know what young miss is doing here, officer? Judging by your badge, you're not from the homicide department."

"A black panther escaped from the Zoo," Corporal Lombardi explained to him. "We received a signal that it was spotted in these neighborhoods."

"We'll help you search for it!"

"Come on, that's dangerous and stupid. Go back to your motel and leave this to the professionals."

"Well, if I'm not a professional, then I don't know who is. Oggy, you're coming with me. The rest of you, cover us. We'll find the poor cat before it gets hurt."

Janine Lombardi opened her mouth in amazement when she heard these energetic dispositions, and apparently lost her countenance. The accompanying gendarmes were also unable to find the words for such an unexpected proposition. They felt some relief since they weren't very excited about tracking a dangerous animal through the dark dark alleys and were glad that someone was willing to replace them.

"You go with them, honey," Never said to Corporal Lombardi. "When our friend finds the panther, someone has to call the main search team. I assume they have a cage?"

"I am a corporal! Yes, of course they have one... is he serious?"

"Absolutely, Mrs. corporal-honey. That guy has a peculiar gift to influence the emotions of even the most predatory animals. He used to be a trainer, and I assure you he didn't have to use any whips. Wild cats become gentle as lambs when he's involved."

Judging by the policewoman's expressions, she didn't fully believe his claims, but she no longer protested. She must have come to the conclusion that Fronde was responsible for himself, and if something happened to him, he would be the one responsible.

"There," Oggy said softly, sniffing a little and pointing the way.

Theo followed her, and at some distance the rest, trying to move as silently as possible. Oggy ran forward, driven by a smell that no one but her felt, and all the while struggling with the desire to turn into a dog. In dangerous situations, the nature of the werewolf took over, and sometimes they were unable to control the transformation. Right now, in the company of the officers, it would be awkward at best.

The sniffed out route took them through a tangle of some banned alleyways, hidden awkwardly behind the facade of modern streets, all the way to the site of a small factory, closed for two years. The buildings had already been partially destroyed, and somewhere between the protruding skeletons of the walls the panther was hiding, irritated and probably frightened by the big city.

"All right, don't do anything stupid, you hear me?" Fronde said, looking at the gendarmes. "I can handle it, but only as long as no one upsets this unfortunate animal. Miss, please call for the people from the zoo and tell them to get the cage, I'll go over there and have a talk with the kitty."

"I tawt I taw a puddy tat!" the Gladiator squeaked, mimicking the voice of Tweety from the Looney Tunes cartoons. "I did, I did!"

"Shut up," Theo muttered, plunging between the remains of the buildings.

"I could shut up," Gladiator said, looking back, "but I doubt that will change anything. Raja, does that baboon really know anything about training wild animals?"

"I think you meant buffoon," Never corrected him.

"Isn't that what I said?"

"You said baboon. It's a type of monkey with a red butt."

"Oh, then I hit the nail on the head. Well, does he really?"

The Indian looked up, as if asking the heavens for patience.

"Calm down, he could even tame you if he wanted to. You just haven't seen it in action because he rarely uses that gift. He thinks it's unfair to animals. Miss corporal, what are you standing around for? Please call for those oafs from the zoo."

"Why do you call them oafs?" Gerard asked out of curiosity. He felt like the time in this city went back to the 1960s, when he hunted in it along with his new friends, learning about the nightlife of a predator.

"Because you have to be the biggest oaf to forget to lock the cage of a wild animal," Gladiator explained to him, making an expression as if he was an expert on work in the zoo. "I mean, are you going to tell me that the kitty cat had a lockpick in its claws?"

Corporal Lombardi, not very convinced of whether what she's doing is right, reached for the radio. She had just finished her report when a deaf growl came from the depths of the dark courtyard, ending with a sharp squeak. The policewoman unwittingly jumped backwards. She didn't believe until now that these strange people actually discovered the Panther's hideout (because how would they?), but these sounds left no shade of doubt.

"She will tear him to pieces!" she shouted, terrified, nervous reaching for the holster.

"Definitely not," Never grabbed her hand firmly. "Please, leave the revolver. A wounded panther is as dangerous as the devil himself, and as long as she doesn't feel imminent threat, our friend will be fine."

He calmly patted the policewoman on the shoulder. He wasn't really as calm as he claimed to be. It's impossible to predict how a wild animal will behave, especially a wild cat, a predatory creature, aggressive and without social instinct. If it was the panther that Theo once befriended, there would be no fear, but that one died of old age a long time ago, and Fronde's gift might not be enough for this one.

A few hours later, a large cage on wheels was parked at the end of the street. It was followed by the zoo's staff with a veterinarian at the helm, as well as gendarmes who took part in the search.

"Maybe bring the whole army here, too?" Never said sarcastically, blocking their way. "At least be quiet and don't get in our way. Sink or swim, soon we'll know."

"Boss, I'll keep them in order, could always use force," Gladiator offered willingly, rubbing his big hands.

He was very disappointed when Never told him to avoid conflict. Fortunately, there was no need to 'use force' on anyone. Both the gendarmes and the zoo staff stood there silently, sticking their eyes in the dark ruins. They weren't willing to directly get involved in this matter at all.

It seemed to everyone that they've been standing there for centuries, when finally, from behind one of the half-torn walls, appeared Fronde's silhouette. He walked calmly, holding his left hand on the panther's head. The large animal walked beside him, gently moving its slender body from paw to paw and watchfully examining the area with its eyes, as golden as Never's. No one dared to move or even breathe deeply.

"Clear the way, what are you standing around for?" the Indian said, and they all moved to the sites hastily, leaving a free passage to the cage.

Theo lead the panther all the way to the opened hatch of the cage, and with a light pat on the neck, he encouraged her to jump inside. Then he closed the door and said:

"Done. You can take her back. And watch her next time, idiots."

Nervous sighs, feverish remarks and comments sounded all around, and the veterinarian, so far tightly gripping the rifle with tranquilizer rounds, grabbed Fronde's hands and shouted in a suffocating voice:

"How in the world did you do that?"

"Well, I'm not sure?" Theo calmly answered him. "I've been able to do it since I was a kid. Either way, that kitten is tamed, at least mostly, it was just scared. Give it a good breakfast and it'll forget about it all."

The veterinarian hugged him and ran to the chauffeur.

"You can talk to animals like Tarzan or Dr. Dolittle?" Corporal Lombardi asked, not taking her widened eyes off of Fronde.

"No way. I doubt that this is technically possible at all. I just know how to affect an animal's mood somehow... I don't really know how... it just happens," Theo replied with some embarrassment.

He really could not explain the essence of this phenomenon. No one could. He simply thought that this could not be explained, but was useful sometimes.

"I didn't believe you could do it. Congratulations, and see you at the police station," said the female officer, saluted and left with her people – to the quiet regret of Fronde, who hoped he could flirt with her after such an impressive feat. The friends had no choice but to take Mrs. Corporal's advice and return to the motel, so they slowly began walking towards the closest main street.

"What now? Where are we going?" Gerard asked when they came out on the busy Bassano Street, even at this hour. The night-time Pairs, illuminated by colorful neon lights, didn't motivate them for detective investigations, it instead instilled a desire for carefree fun. However, somewhere within its reach lurked a monstrous creature, and it was they who were responsible for not allowing it to harm even more people.

"We're going back to the motel," Never decided. "It's past two o'clock, and we're all tired of searching. If Agent Gris told us the truth, we have time until the next full moon. We need to divide the city into squares and start searching with the Pinkerton's system. Otherwise, we are in danger of failing completely."

"We are also in danger of hunger, since I am not convinced that we can count on a steady supply of our food here. I don't know about you, but I'm not planning on starving. Let's go hunting, before the night is over," Theo suggested.

Fortunately, Paris, although changed, still had no shortage of bad pubs, occupied by all sorts of social low-lives. They usually left the thresholds of the premises so intoxicated that, as Never said before, you could not only drain their blood, but also do an appendix operation without the need for anesthesia. They don't remember a thing anyway. It wasn't hard to satisfy the hunger without suspicion, only Gladiator had to be watched, since he easily lost control. He could then inadvertently kill the 'donor', but his friends refused to leave behind corpses.

When they finally returned to the motel, they were so tired that they only took a shower and fell asleep right lying on the beds. They only woke up in the afternoon, hungover, miserable and not able to put even a few words together for a coherent sentence. They were no longer used to blood mixed with cheap alcohol and have managed to forget how it works on their unusual organisms. As if that wasn't enough, the pub where they fed offered customers an illegal liqueur called 'Carbonet' – a strong, albeit horrible kind of wine with the addition of heroin, of black color. Customers were very happy to order them, and through their blood the 'recipient' could easily absorb a good dose of the drug without even knowing it.

They felt the consequences of its action even now, after ten sleepy hours, and could only be glad about the fact that no one took them by surprise while they were asleep. They'd be completely defenseless. Oggy, who did not drink the blood and thus avoided poisoning, did all she could and brought them some aspirin and a two-liter jug of freshly brewed tea. After this mixture, they all felt sick and took turns to occupy the toilet. After about half an hour later they stopped vomiting, although they still felt nauseous. Fortunately, their heads became clearer and they were able to talk more clearly. Agent Gris found them in this state, who was concerned that they were not present at the appointment.

"I thought that something unfortunate happened to you!" he exclaimed when they let him into the room where they spent the night.

"We're sorry that you're disappointed, but this isn't just some minor indisposition," Never said with a jeering voice, but not without his usual sarcasm. "If you want us to go somewhere with you, then you'll have to wait until we get it together."

"And that may take some time," Fronde added.

Gris sat down on the countertop, put another batch of plastic bottles full of blood next to himself, and gave them all an ironic look. It was clear that, having been educated about it through horror films, he imagined vampires in a very different way, and reality made him laugh more than scared him.

"Best do it fast," he said. "I think I've tracked down the killer, and without your help, but I won't stop him alone."

"What do you mean, how?!"

"Just like that. Well, all right, it wasn't that simple. I received a signal that the night before Giselle Jouverant's death, around the Gare de Lyon area, they found, and then took to the hospital a young man, Marc Prevost, with heart symptoms, and confusion of senses at the same time. He was terrified. Apparently, he was screaming so horribly that they had to put him to sleep."

"What was he screaming?" Gerard asked, interested.

"That's the interesting part. He screamed: *Leave me alone! Monster! You're a monster!* Isn't that curious?"

"Fronde, are you sure you're not sleepwalking?" Gladiator asked, sounding as if forcibly holding back laughter. Theo cast him a glance full of deep contempt, but he didn't indulge him.

"What's interesting is that this attack matches time-wise," Never said, thinking. "Did this man have any wounds?"

"None that could be inflicted with teeth or claws."

"So something scared him, but it didn't try to eat him. I don't think that's our Gourmet, it's something else... Which hospital was he taken to? "

"St. Lazare, cardiology department."

"Well, great. Agent Gris, please arrange for us some covered vehicle with darkened windows. We'll give him a visit. It's worth checking out."

This proposal did not cause anyone enthusiasm, but no one protested. The friends washed one by one in the shower, shaved and dressed, sipping canned blood directly from the bottles. This drink could always put them back on their feed, since blood was not only food for the vampires, but also a remedy for almost all ailments. Agent Gris watched them without emotion, but when Oggy took a piece of raw liver out of the motel refrigerator and bit her teeth into it, he stared at her wide-eyed in amazement.

"What? It's my metabolism," said the girl vaguely between one bite and another, feeling that this sympathetic Frenchman should be given some explanation.

"Oh dear gods, that's quite the attribute," Gris shook slightly.

Oggy finished the meal and licked her fingers.

"You eat raw sashimi, raw tartare, raw oysters," she said. "Why should a raw liver be something more disgusting?

"Well, if you put it that way, I guess it's less so, but I don't know if I could do that."

"No one is telling you to. But I'll tell you, before the synthesis of vitamin B, I don't remember the number, raw liver was often the only salvation for people with anemia. And Indians came up with this first, from the Shoshone tribe, actually by accident. The doctor, who was traveling in the Wild West, found out about it and took credit for the find without asking anyone about their opinion. Although to his credit, it should be added that he didn't harm any Indians in doing so, and saved many white people, mostly children."

"Well, yes, I suppose that is a certain excuse. How many times has it been that, in order to take something from the Indians, psychopaths, like General Custer wiped out entire tribes..." interjected Fronde, someone passionate about Indian culture.

"Are you done with your consultation?" Never interrupted them, buttoning up his shirt. "There is no time for wild west stories, when we have a case to solve. What about our car?"

"You can go in my passat, it has some extra blacked-out windows," Griss said, "Oh, and by the way, I'm coming with you."

"You're doing what now?"

"Exactly what I said. This is also my business, and you're in my territory."

"Insolent!" Theo called with indignation. "Know that this was my territory before anyone even thought of your great-grandmothers!"

"I have no doubt about that," Gris said calmly, "but I stand by my words."

His skinny face, adorned with a slightly eagle-like nose and ears protruding like shovels, took on the expression of resolve. It became clear that it wouldn't be easy to convince this man otherwise, and it would be better to not try at all."

"Fine," Never spoke with clear displeasure. "But you're responsible for yourself. If anything happens to you, it's all on you."

"Sounds good," Gris smiled broadly.

"Holy shit…" Gladiator muttered without lowering his eyes, but didn't add anything else. If Never, instead of getting angry, looked at the favorite child of his team at that moment, he would understand that Gladiator, who usually didn't bother with thinking, this time came up with something. And it was something interesting. However, he wasn't going to share his reflections, and since no one encouraged him to do so, the bomb should only detonate later.

For now, everyone somehow squeezed into the car and went on their way. Theo complained a little that it's too early and the sun already managed to burn his neck before he got in the Passat, but no one paid attention to him. They all know that nothing serious happened to him. The sun is not as dangerous to the undead as is commonly believed, and even a 'moth' can pass through a sunny area with minimal harm to itself, as long as it's quick enough. Fronde just loved talking to himself, and he was happy whenever he had a reason to do so.

The documents of the non-existing detective bureau, which were provided to them at the headquarters, turned out to be very useful. Without problems, they were admitted to the hospital and psychiatric ward, where Marc Prevost was transferred after cardiac examinations. The head of the unit, to whom Never showed his detective badge, shrugged his shoulders and announced:

"No more than five minutes. I don't care about your investigation, I have to take care of the patient."

"It's not like we're going to eat him," Fronde commented, thankfully quietly.

The head physician didn't, or maybe pretended to not hear him to avoid conflict. Calling the paramedics, he gave them the appropriate instructions, and then pointed the guests to the room, which acted as a visiting room. Paramedics soon brought there the young man in a state of complete nervous exhaustion and put him in a chair opposite of Never.

If it were not for the erroneous look in his eyes and the horror that still stirred his face, he could've been considered a very handsome guy – he had regular features, a complexion smooth as a girl, and long, blond hair falling just below his shoulders. He gave the impression of a local playboy, who had suffered from some strange misfortune.

"Relax," the Indian said. "I know that those you told what attacked you didn't believe you. We won't bother you too much. We are pursuing a creature that is responsible for many murders, and we believe you can help us. What happened?"

"It… it fell onto me from above," he began with a suffocating voice. "It grabbed me tightly by the hair and by the throat. Then it suddenly stopped, as if it was surprised by something… and then flew away. That's it, nothing else happened."

"I assume it wasn't a very pretty thing, if it scared you this much," Agent Gris interjected, taking a large notepad from the inside pocket of his jacket. "Draw for us what you saw."

"Good idea," Never praised him. "Sketch the silhouette of this creature, and then we'll go. We have a deal?"

The boy took the pen given to him, hesitated for a moment, and then quickly sketched a nightmarish figure resembling a gargoyle from Notre Dame: a silhouette roughly human, with a distorted face and large teeth, clawed hands and bat-wings. The drawing, perhaps was not artistically correct, but quite accurately reflected what attacked the young man.

"Thank you, kid," Never picked up the notebook. "As a thank you, I will tell you one thing: you have not gone mad and do not allow yourself to be persuaded otherwise. Miraculously, you escaped death, because what attacked you is fiendishly dangerous and never misses its purpose. But you must have realized that no one would believe you. Take back all of your previous confessions, leave as soon as possible and go home."

It was only in the car that he shared with the friends that... actually, he's at a loss.

"I know that this boy was actually attacked by something," he said, circulating the notepad. "Is it possible, however, that he had momentary hallucinations as a result of horror? Just look at what he drew there. Can the existence of such a being go unnoticed in our orderly times?"

The friends looked at the hasty, not revealing the artistic abilities drawing, one by one. It portrayed a monster as if form a nightmare. Its face resembled an old Japanese demon mask, around which was thick hair, partially covering the pointy ears. The neck was surprisingly slender, they expected a rather bullish neck. And, what surprised everyone the most, it was clear to see a woman's breasts marked on the torso. Was it a female?

"Do you think that's the same thing that killed these girls?" Gerard asked, watching the drawing not without disgust.

"What else? Do you think we have a seasonal scarecrow reunion here?" Never said sarcastically. "It would have to be a hellishly unfavorable coincidence if these things are not connected. The question is: what is this thing? I've never seen anything like it, if not counting the statues at the cathedral."

"It's a harpy," Theo said like it was the most normal thing in the world, taking the notebook from Gerard's hands.

"That's what I called my ex-wife," Gris muttered.

"A what?" The Indian asked surprised, widening his golden eyes.

"Oh, the omniscient one doesn't know Greek mythology?" Fronde mocked him. "Truth be told, I haven't heard of any of them appearing anywhere in a long time. They didn't attack people... at best grossed them out. They came in, ate everything off the table and made a mess wherever they went. That's what Epikles told me, a Greek vampire I met in the fifteenth century, but even he only knew about it from myths. He's never seen one that was alive. He was a great friend, by the way. He showed me mummified corpses, and without a doubt it was what's drawn in this notebook. Although if our enemy is a harpy, why does it murder?"

"We'll ask when we find it. If we can do it in time, that is. At least we know now what we're chasing. Let's just hope that this pretty lady doesn't have a husband who would tear us to shreds before we can blink."

„It's out of the question. Harpies are single-sex that much even I know. They're all females and they breed parthenogenetically," intervened Gerard, who, unlike Never, knew the myths of the ancient Greeks very well.

"Aren't they clever. Listen, we have a problem: If this beast is so rate, it's probably under strict protection," said Gladiator, shaking his lion-like mane.

"Oh God," Theo muttered.

"Either way, it's best that the environmentalists not to know about it. But the truth is, so what if we know what this thing is called? Are we going to call her by name? Chip chip, come here kitty kitty, or rather, harpy harpy...?"

"Shut up already, you insane pup, okay?" Never interrupted him, glad that he had someone to unload on. "It's easy for you to clown around, since you're not the one in danger! If that damn bird woman wanted to eat your brain, it wouldn't even be enough for a snack!"

"What I'm curious about is why she spared Marc Prevost. It doesn't make sense," Gerard said, biting his nails.

There was silence in the Passat. Indeed, this was interesting – the harpy attacked the young man while he was alone, caught him, and then for no apparent reason, changed her mind and flew into the darkness, not interested in the victim. This didn't fit the pattern. It can't be assumed that she didn't have an appetite, since she killed Giselle Juverant the very next night. Another puzzle appeared, perhaps needed to solve the first one, but for now it was too hard to guess.

The silence was broken by agent Gris, who, looking at his watch, issued a small cry of horror.

"Oh dear God, I'm going to be late for the studio! We're going back. Where do you want me to drop you off?"

"Maybe at Place Pigalle?" Gladiator proposed.

"Why there specifically?" Theo was surprised.

"Because the best chestnuts in Paris are there... Although Susan only loves them during the autumn..."

"What do you need them for? After all, you won't swallow even a crumb. And why are the chestnuts in Pigalle so special? I don't understand. And what does some Susan have to do with this?" Gris looked at the highlander with his eyes wide open.

"She sends the fresh portion..."[1]

"Damn it, talk like a normal person, or I'll punch you in the teeth!"

"Eh, if Dea was here, she would have gotten it right away..." highlander sighed, not bothering with explanations.

"Just ignore him," Oggy mingled in. "It's probably one of his Polish jokes that no one gets. Drop us off near Etoile, Gris. We have to visit the police station and sign the deposition, did you guys forget?"

"We might as well, whatever it is. Maybe we'll learn something while we're at it, who knows? However, I feel that we will have to return to the original plan, and this picture, contrary to appearances, will not help us much," Never said gloomily.

---

[1] Gladiator quotes fragments of the iconic Polish TV Series More Than Life at Stake, episode 11, Password.

As it soon turned out, he was right. Even though the friends now knew what they were looking for, their task was no easier. After all, they could not show random passers-by the 'memory portrait' of the hunted creature, or post prints around the city. For more than three weeks they searched Paris systematically, taking notes and speaking to dozens of witnesses, but they didn't come one step closer to their goal. The Harpy, though neither petty nor easily lost in the crowd, remained invisible. Only Oggy caught a trail of her scent sometimes, but it always lead to nowhere.

Even agent Gris, who as a journalist had 'access' to anywhere, could not help in this search. Besides, they were irritated by his company, though they could not say why and did not believe that he would be of help to them. There was less and less time, less and less opportunities, and less and less hope that it would be possible to prevent another murder. Everyone worked tirelessly – except Gerard, who was assigned a different assignment. He was going to work on a murder scheme and gather as much information as possible about the harpies. Never contacted the general several times in the hope that he would find something about harpies in the archive, but the information he obtained this way turned out to be of little value.

"I can't sleep or rest," he complained to his friends, working on the results after clearing out another 'square'. "This case is killing me. Where could that damn beast be hiding?"

"Among other damn beasts," Gladiator told him idiotically.

"Take that back," muttered Fronde reluctantly. He wasn't too keen about the thought of a larger population of harpies living in and around Paris. One seemed to be enough to keep their hands full.

"Don't be so bitter," said Gerard. "At least we know where she is not, and that's something. The area we have left to search is shrinking every day."

"It shrinks, and shrinks, and shrinks, and there's no end in sight…"

As time went on, the friends' impatience grew. They watched the moon every night as it came unsettlingly close to a full moon. They tried to guess what effect it had on the harpy, since it murders during a full moon, and it does not happen, for example, on the interlunar, but all they could think of was the new observation that the moon has a huge influence on everything that happens on Earth. However, this didn't help them, and even inexplicably intensified their nervousness with the whole situation.

Only Gerard was calm. He spent all his spare time writing papers, occasionally consulting Agent Gris, and spending a lot of time in the central library, leafing through old newspapers. It was evident that he was taking his task very seriously. Finally, two days before the expected full moon, Never called for a general meeting.

"The results of our search, dear agents, amount to nothing," he said bluntly. "We haven't found anything, no point of attachment, and time is desperately short. In fact, we can expect an attack today, because our Harpy doesn't strictly follow the lunar timetable. At least that's what our star says. Gerard, any more insights?"

"Yes. On the basis of a detailed analysis of the attack points and their interrelationships, I calculated that the next murder would take place near the Louvre or the Comedie Francais building. You know, Molière's theater. I'll explain it in a moment. Let me just add that the harpy has most likely built a nest in the Notre Dame Cathedral," replied Gerard, spreading the map with the locations of the murders on the table. Next to each was a date written in ink, along with its affinity for the full moon.

"Why in Notre Dame?" Theo asked indignantly, for some reason seeing this conclusion as a blasphemy.

"That I don't know either. Perhaps she feels safe there, or perhaps she has other reasons. In any case, look here: until now, the line connecting the various crime points has formed a broken curve with almost equal sections. The deviations are only a few meters. The murders that I have listed were committed ten years ago, and the curve of the current ones aligns with a near perfect similarity. Or rather, it would..."

"Jesus Christ, talk normally! You're wasting time!"

"For the first three it goes like curve A, but for the fourth it deviates so that the place of the fourth and fifth murders bypasses the cathedral at a fairly long distance. Curve B should, according to previous calculations, go through it. As for the variance in the possible locations of the next attack, it arose because I am not sure whether the attack on Mark Prevost should be drawn into the calculations or not. Both options are likely."

"How did you calculate all this?" Oggy shouted in surprise.

"On the abacus. Simple and accurate. But no matter how, what matters is whether it's correct."

"Let's find out," Never declared firmly.

For someone with his intellect, a quick glance at the map and notes was enough to understand that the information contained in them was accurate. He didn't have time to collect it and put it together himself, so he put the burden of this tedious work on the shoulders of the physically weak but most disciplined member of the team. Gerard did not disappoint his expectations. He did his job flawlessly and even made a final summary that Never thought he would have to do himself.

"Are we going out again?" Oggy asked without enthusiasm.

She, like the others, had sore legs from all the walking and had enough of the whole matter. It was hard to accept that the work of a detective on the screen is much more interesting than in the real world, where there are no cuts or montage scenes, and for every meter on the road you had to walk on your own feet.

"Yeaah… we should probably check out these revelations. Maybe we could save a girl who would otherwise die. We have to try."

"All right…" the girl sighed and then suddenly she felt a shudder. "Porca miseria, it's starting!"

Oggy, though of Italian descent, only spoke her native language when she felt the impending transformation into a wolf. She was doing better than ever, but that couldn't last forever, and right now, without warning, it all went out of control. After a few seconds of scuffling about, the big sheepdog came out of the dress, which it no longer needed, and, embarrassed, sat next to Fronde.

"Maybe that's even better?" Never looked at her, playing with his ponytail absent minded. "Theo, get the collar and dog documents from the bag, just in case of some kind of control. She's all good, if someone asks. The dog will come in handy, and she'll be able to rest, running on four legs instead of two."

"Four legs, good. Two legs, bad. Baaah," Gladiator said, who was in the middle of studying *Animal Farm*.

"Wow," Oggy attested

"Anyway, let's go, before Gris barges in again," Gerard sighed, folding his papers. "I'm not too convinced about that journalists…. he looks at me weird. Did he recognize me, or what?"

"Wouldn't be surprising. But well, you're right, it's best to avoid his company. He annoys me, too."

The moon was already high when the friends drove to the Moliere Theatre. After much discussion, they agreed that the attack on Mark Prevost should be included in Gerard's scheme, and therefore the Louvre area was out of the question. Moreover, from the very beginning it looked completely implausible, because the place was always filled with the Paris gendarmerie, watchmen, bodyguards and tourists.

Here, under the address of Comedie Francais, it was clearly calmer. Evening performances were canceled because of a failure of the hydraulic system, meaning that the actors would have to get to the stage by canoe, so the building was empty and quiet. The plumbers limited themselves to closing the valves and then went back home, leaving a piece of paper which said that they would return in the morning.

"Oh, and I thought that such geniuses are only in Poland," Gladiator said impressed, when he recited the note.

"Who knows? Maybe it's a Polish team?" giggled Fronde, not without malice.

The Highlander set his sights on him, but couldn't do anything else since Oggy, sniffing around nearby, raised her muzzle and barked warningly. Almost simultaneously, a broken, feminine cry roared from the dead end nearby, and then there was silence. Friends rushed in that direction, proceeded by the dog which ran at full speed, with bristled fur and raised ears, rushed by the terrible fear that they were a few seconds too late. They already knew that was the case – they smelled blood even though they didn't yet know where it was spilled.

Running after the dog, they reached a small square, overgrown with bushes, on which was a slide and two children's swings. Next to them they saw a still figure lying on the asphalt, looking black under the moonlight. Some blurred piece of darkness broke away from it when they appeared and rose, silently flying away, as if it was just a dream.

Theo knelt next to the body. As before, it was the body of a young girl, small and slender, in trousers and denim jacket. Her head was gone, as usual, the purse was nowhere to be seen, so he began to search the pockets of the murdered girl until he found a bag of documents.

"Corporal Lombardi..." he exuded, barely glancing at the identification card.

"My word," Never muttered, and Gerard felt as tears gathered in his eyes. He saw this policewoman only twice, but he could say that he knew her, and now... how could it happen that he calculated so precisely where the attack would take place and was still unable to prevent it? It was like some kind of a cruel joke of the goddess of fate.

Fronde got up from his knees when Oggy grabbed his hand with his teeth. He too could hear the distant sound of people running, though he could not boast of the same good hearing as her.

"Let's get out of here," he said quickly. "Or else we'll be arrested."

In a few minutes they reached the car and left the theatre as soon as possible.

"Where to now?" Gerard, who was driving, nervously asked, though he didn't know how he became the driver.

"What a dumb question! Notre Dame! That thing won't escape us now," Never snapped in response.

He was furious, and more than ever. What happened offended his own love, because he already believed that he would prevent another murder, especially since there were two days left for a full moon. He would later have to find out that the time period was miscommunicated, as the media had given the wrong date, and the true full moon began this very night. At this point, it all just confused him, and he understood nothing more, except that since Gerard had so precisely guessed the location of the attack, he might have been right about the hiding place of the beast, too.

Sandwiched into the corner of the car, Fronde muttered something in old-fashioned French, and his voice sounded disgusted and hateful. Oggy tugged at his feet, and Gladiator, pale, with his mouth clenched, checked the revolver and reloaded it just in case. Everyone felt lost, ridiculed and deceived by the harpy, which didn't care for all their efforts.

They quickly found themselves under the famous cathedral, silent and overwhelming with its enormousness.

"Where now? The bell tower?" Gladiator asked unsure.

"No way," Never waved his hand contemptuously. "To the Catacombs of the French Inquisition! Nobody had discovered them yet, but I know they are there. Oggy, find them."

The big sheepdog obediently moved with her nose by the sidewalk, sniffing the smell she remembered from the playground. She circled the cathedral and finally stopped in front of a bas-relief depicting an undefined saint. She looked back and barked softly. Never moved his hand over the bas-relief and apparently hit a spring, for the stone slab suddenly shifted, revealing the entrance to a dark corridor.

Without hesitation, they submerged into the darkness – their eyes penetrated it just enough for them to walk easily and not bump into anything. This mattered because the corridor was narrow and winding, branching off into numerous paths. Oggy ran along it without hesitation, however, guiding her friends to the right path, until a great hall revealed itself before them, full of medieval utensils, old and worn but still intact. In the center, on a carved table, was a split head, and beside it stood a harpy eagerly devouring the fresh brain.

But that wasn't the worst of it. Much more terrible was that, as the horrible thing swallowed the gray-white, blood-stained mass, there was an incomprehensible change in it, like in clay figures in an animated film. The wings retracted, the grayish hair covering the half-animal body disappeared, the demonic face smoothed. Gradually, as if made hastily of clay, the figure of a young woman with curly hair falling over her shoulders and a face that was not beautiful, but well-groomed and quite ordinary, appeared before the eyes of the friends.

The transformation didn't go flawlessly, at times the mouse-like fur appeared back in place of the smooth skin, the clean fingernails turned into disgusting claws, and membranous wings began to hatch from her alluring shoulders. Yet every bite she swallowed held back this regression, transforming the Harpy into an ordinary-looking woman.

The sight was so terrible that everyone was stunned, even Never, who thought he had seen everything before. The Harpy, preoccupied with her feast, noticed them only after a while, and before they had time to move, she leapt towards them with a deafening scream. It was a feint – in the last second, she turned to the side of the corridor and disappeared.

"Outside!" Never shouted.

Terrified and shaken by what they saw, they fell into the courtyard of the cathedral. Guided by a subconscious premonition, they broke into a line, encircling the harpy. She screamed again and they felt pain in their ears. Never even thought about answering her with a similar scream, but he couldn't get his voice out. Oddly enough, there were five of them in total while she was only one, but they didn't know how to overpower her or what to do next. They felt a mounting dread as they stared at that dark figure, covered in curled hair like shavings. Tensed up as if about to jump, she stood motionless, holding them in check only by the willpower they sensed in her.

"Look!" Gerard suddenly exclaimed with a strange voice, pointing to the sky. He alone retained full authority over himself, for some reason, but was too scared to do anything sane.

Everyone looked up at the same time. A swirled black mass, like some weightless tar, rolled across the sky, creating vortices and heavy waves. The moon had changed its familiar face – it was now a gloomy, dark globe, rushing towards the Earth and expanding with dizzying speed.

"Don't look up!" Never cried imperiously, miraculously recovering his voice. "She's making an illusion! This is why her victims die of fear!"

Yet despite these words, everyone, even he, trembled with fear to the core. It turned out that it was different to know and to feel, and that the subconscious mind listens to feelings more than to reason. It is unknown how this story would have ended had it not been for Oggy.

A dog couldn't be hypnotized, and no animal would ever see what is not there – and at the moment Oggy was a dog. Seeing that something incomprehensible was going on, she backed away a little, then with one leap found herself on the harpy's back, gripping her neck with her teeth. The illusion that spread around them immediately disappeared and the friends regained power over themselves.

"God damn it, this monkey has some strength," Fronde shouted, rushing to help his friend. "Yanek, help! That's enough, Oggy, we'll take care of her now."

This command was most appropriate, as the furious Oggy was about to tear the throat of the harp.

"Be careful, this is probably a species close to extinction!" Gladiator gasped out, trying to overpower the harpy, wriggling to every side and screaming.

"Don't be an idiot! If we don't stop her, then we'll be extinct!" Fronde, who usually could handle himself, this time tried in vain to bind the rampaging creature.

He still did not know whether he was dealing with an animal or a human – the harpy had already taken the form of a person, but her skin did not feel human to the touch. Fronde had the impression that he was grabbing a live suede with his hands, under which he felt incredibly hard muscles. The nails on it were not human either, but were more like claws.

Police whistles rang out from the street's direction, and four gendarmes stormed the square, lured to the back of the cathedral by the noise. Never, with his lightning-fast reaction time, immediately took out a special branch badge, which they were given in Poland. The procurer from the agency expressed the opinion that before someone has time to figure out that the badge is fake, they will have enough time to disappear. If they even try to check...

"All right," the patrol commander said at the sight of the badge. As expected, he didn't even take it. "But what the hell is happening here?"

"This lady that my colleagues are trying to tie up is the killer you're looking for," said Never, tucking a metal object into his pocket. "Her last victim is your friend, Corporal Lombardi from the police station at Etoile. You'll find her in the playground behind the Moliere Theatre, and we can show you the killer's hideout. Call in the forensic experts, they will certainly find a lot of traces. Enough to accuse her of...

"Kruca fuks, I can't hold her!" shouted Gladiator.

No one understood the content of the scream, but it was not needed because the situation was clear. The harpy broke out of the men's hands, who flew into both sides as if blown away by an explosion. She rushed at the gendarmes, who were trying to block her way, hit one of them and grabbed his service gun."

"Get down!" Never screamed, and threw himself to the pavement, hiding his head with his hands.

The first bullet, bouncing off the wall, hit the window of the cathedral wing, the second whistled right next to the Oggy's ear, which caused her to wail and drop to the ground. The furious harpy managed to fire the entire magazine before the others finally reached for their weapons. The patrol commander, one of his subordinates, and Gladiator all fired at the same time. After firing three bullets, she collapsed and fell on the slabs of the yard, releasing the stolen weapons from her hands.

"Is that thing dead?" Gerard asked in a weak voice, with difficulty daring to raise his head.

"Regardless of the laws," Gladiator replied grimly.

He got up and walked up to the woman without fear.

"Please don't get too close," the patrol commander warned him. "Reinforcement will come soon. And you gentlemen have some explaining to do."

"God damn it..." Fronde muttered to himself, well aware what 'some explaining' meant.

Fortunately, it didn't last as long as he feared, and the friends were released before dawn. The fact is that they were not suspected of anything owed mainly to a certain happy coincidence of circumstances. In the harpy's shelter, the police found a whole collection of 'trophies' – the killed beast turned out to be a fetishist in addition, which greatly facilitated the collection of evidence of the identity of the serial killer.

"Good thing it's over," Gerard said as they left the police station. "I will never in my life forget what I saw today."

"It wasn't a pretty sight," Never agreed. "At the very least we know that the harpy didn't murder aimlessly. She needed a fresh brain to retain the appearance of an ordinary woman. She chose young girls for her victims because, I'd be willing to guess, only their tissues contained the necessary combination of hormones. It was dangerous to take on her real shape, because people do not tolerate and never will tolerate what is different from them. You know, in the end it's rather sad; she wanted to be human at all costs, because she was so afraid of people."

"Go to hell with that philosophy of yours," muttered Gladiator.

"You know what, let's get drunk," Theo suggested. "The case has been settled, Maura's father will be released from custody tomorrow, and I have photographic documents for the general. We need a break with a glass of this and that."

"And for the snack, fried cerebellum in coquilles," added Highlander, making Gerard's face almost as green as his eyes.

Theo elbowed him lightly under the shoulderblade and went to the 24-hour-open store they were just passing by. Shortly thereafter, with the trunk of the car full of cans and bottles, they drove outside the motel. They really wanted to get drunk. What they saw that night shocked all of them, although they refused to admit it. After all, they were nocturnal predators, they didn't survive by being sensitive, and rather they had to have strength and resilience. That's what they tried to be, but it didn't always go that way. Now was one of those times.

They were so lost in thought that they didn't even notice that the door of their room (they rented three, but used only one of them) was open. The sight of Dei sitting on the couch was so unexpected that it took away their speech.

"You're finally here," the girl said dryly. "Four undefeated tank-men and their honorable dog[2], as Janusz Przymanowski[3] would describe it."

---

[2] A quote from the book „Four Tank-Men and a Dog", which was the basis for an iconic Polish war TV show.

[3] Janusz Przymanowski, author of the aforementioned book and the script of the TV show.

"What... Manowski?" Theo asked in a daze, almost dropping the bag with liqueurs in his arms. Without dropping his eyes from Dea, he opened a bottle of cognac and took a powerful sip from it.

"Why are you here? We managed without you, and now we're about to celebrate," said Never, looking suspiciously at the younger friend.

"Thank you, I'm glad to see you too," Dea replied. "I am not here for your pleasure, much less for mine. I came up for a very specific reason."

"Because you are a very specific person. So tell me, very specifically, what's going on. Is it about that broken tram?" Gladiator intervened, certifying a bottle of grenadine, with which he intended to prepare the cocktail 'Tequila Sunrise' for everyone gathered.

"Pour me one too. I have an unofficial order for you. I know the general gave you freedom and now you're just lounging around so you might as well work."

"Seriously? Get any other group to do it. We have been working tirelessly for the last month, we need to rest! To hell with that tram," the offended highlander gave her a tall glass filled with liquid with the colors of the rising sun.

"What are you going on about with this tram today? Whatever, it doesn't matter. Unfortunately, the other group is not an option because it is not a commission of the agency, but of Octavio," Dea took a sip and nodded with appreciation. "He called Lenore, and she came with him to me. This is an internal matter hypothetically about the organization of wimans."

"Bloodsuckers of all countries, join forces!" Gerard raised a glass and drank hastily.

"Hold on, Miss Doctor, not so fast. What's the big idea? Octavio wouldn't call because of some stupidity, I know, but we can't work for VASP at the same time and for this organization there," Theo soberly retorted.

Although he drank stew and served him a cocktail, and a full glass of napoleon, it couldn't be seen from him. He was always famous among vampires for his strong head, which was so interesting that as a person he reportedly got drunk quickly and easily, and therefore had to be very careful during friendly libations. Oggy, who has already taken human form, loudly supported his position and poured himself a drink.

Dea nodded. She herself did not seem very convinced of her mission, certainly not enough to convince others, but she tried, apparently out of a sense of duty.

"It's a nasty case," she said softly, emptying the glass to the bottom. "Does the name Amargo tell you something? Amargo Lorca?"

Friends looked at each other and shrugged their shoulders.

"Sounds Romani or something?" muttered unreliably Gladiator, without interrupting the mixing of drinks.

"It doesn't matter. What matters is who is behind that name. If I tell you it's one from Harmon's clan, will you understand?"

"Ah, damn it! Now I get it!" Never shouted in disgust. "Harmon's clan! You're right, it's going to be a disgusting job, but it has to be done, no way around it."

"I don't get it," Gerard said indignantly.

"Harmon was a madman," Theo explained to him. "All of his, so to speak, descendants are as if his clones. They kill and destroy from the very desire to do evil, real devils. Where is this Amargo?"

"Here in Paris. I even have his address. He settled in a small apartment building on the outskirts, on De Wagram Avenue. He works, if you can call it that, as a paid killer. He takes any dirty job and is incredibly effective. If we don't get him with our first shot, we're in trouble. He won't let go."

"I didn't think he would," Never muttered..

He's already dealt with the so-called 'broken blood'. It was extremely rare, but from time to time there was a vampire-psychopath, *mora*, who passed on his sick qualities. Both he and his offspring posed a threat to the people and their brothers whom they killed unscrupulously. The only salvation was the destruction of the entire contaminated line – otherwise the evil could not be stopped. Harmon was the last known carrier of 'broken blood'. He thought that all the descendants of this madman were destroyed, but now it turned out that there was at least one left. Amargo..

"We have to play our cards very carefully," he said. "We won't get anywhere acting on a whim. Give me the exact address, I'll try to get an idea at least briefly about the possibilities that the location of his headquarters will give us. You'll have to wait for me because it'll take some time. Don't do anything stupid while I'm gone, you hear?"

"No, we don't hear," said Oggy, who usually became overly aggressive after alcohol.

"Wait," Dea said. "Tell me at first how you solved the bounty hunter case, because what the general told me sounded as mysterious as it was interesting."

Fronde began explaining the just-completed incident, sipping another cocktail after each fragment, as he was still disgusted, which he had to wash down somehow. Dea listened intently to what he was saying and what the others were saying, and it was only at the end that she said:

"Wait, wait. You tried to overpower this creature without using a weapon, right? That means you don't want to eliminate it at all! Did you hit your heads or what?"

The gladiator shrugged his shoulders reluctantly.

"Well, that's right," he admitted. "We didn't want to kill her, somehow. In the end, she did it out of necessity, not out of desire. It wasn't so different from us..."

"The question is whether we had the *moral* right to kill her," Theo added.

"The question is, do you have anything in those damn heads of yours! What if she ran away from you, then what? Could you take responsibility for her next victims? I'm starting to wonder if you're fit for the job."

Never snorted contemptuously, took some shades out of his bag and went out, while the rest, closing the discussion with a change of topic, took over the tasting of cocktails prepared by their colleague. The light-haired man from Zakopane was able to prepare literally everything. Immediately after returning from Egypt, the general sent him to a bartender course because, he said, he wanted at least one staff member to learn how to make drinks. The gladiator willingly went to this training and came back very pleased, with a diploma in hand. Turns out that he has quite the talent for the job. He easily adapted the famous recipes for the use for vampires, and also invented new ones that no one ever dreamed of.

"As a bartender, you'd be famous," Dea said after a while. "You passed by your calling."

"But fortunately, not by my military calling," the highlander proudly stuck out his chest under the khaki shirt. Although he had been a civilian for a long time, he always dressed in a military manner and could not be dissuaded.

"When I was still training, every year during the conscription period I had a shake-up of eighteen-year-olds who were ready to try all possible diseases, just to get a reprieve."

"That's some dickheads," Gladiator expressed his disdain of draft dodgers very literally. "I would have sent them all to some criminal maneuvers."

"I have no doubt. But among them were actually sick people," Dea put back her glass and looked at Fronde with displeasure. "Theo, get your corpse out of this crib and go to the barber, all right?"

"Why?" Fronde was indignant.

"Because your hair is turning into braids. You look like a brush for toilet cleaning."

"Never wears a braid and so what, you have anything against him?"

"It fits the eastern beauty of Raja, but not you."

"Why the hell are you so stuck on me? Yanek also has long feathers!" Theo was clearly offended.

"But it doesn't look bad on him, but it does on you, you know? Your honest face requires a different kind of frame."

"Bullshit. If that bear can look like a hippie, then so can I. I'm not worse than him!"

"Maybe not, but it's not a competition. Yasio would look like a real man even in a skirt and a headscarf, and all you need is longer hair to look like a gay on a Pride Parade. Go get a haircut, or I'll do it myself."

Fronde jumped off the couch, threw a murderous glance at his friend, and went out, slamming the door on a grand scale.

"Oh, there he goes, he's offended now..." Dea said in a concerned voice.

Gladiator mixed another drink and handed to her with such a movement as if he was giving her anesthesia for what he was about to say.

"Well, you were going too hard on him… you know what, I like you, but there is no diplomacy in you. You're always saying whatever you want, not thinking about whether someone might feel hurt by it. Bad words don't break bones, but they can still hurt deeply, so it's best to be careful what you're racking up, especially when talking to friends. And look at that, for the first time in my life, I said something wise without anyone's help…"

"It's pretty light outside already, hope he doesn't get hurt," Oggy sighed.

She would have willingly run after her friend, but felt she had already had too many drinks, and it might be a bit embarrassing. So she comfortably stretched out on the couch, putting her head on Gerard's lap, and quietly howled like a wolf to the moon. The Actor returned it, imitating her as best he could, and for a moment they both sang in tune until the neighbors started tapping on the wall.

"People are always bothered by everything," Oggy said indignantly.

"You know what, let's sleep for a bit," said Dea. "I'm tired after traveling, and you guys are drunk."

"I'm sober as a saint," Gladiator said firmly.

Seeking to show how sober he was, he tried to pour vodka from the glass back into the bottle, but everything went to the table, and while he was at it, he knocked over the tray with empty glasses with his elbow.

"I can see that. Go to sleep everyone, now! Who knows what Never will come back with, maybe we will have to be ready for action the second he's here."

Dea knew what she was saying. Never hated waiting when he sounded the alarm. He then got annoyed and called everyone losers, good-for-nothings, May's firefighters (what he got that last term from, no one could guess). For this reason, members of his 'squad', while they were in the process of working out the case, usually slept in their clothes, and in the morning looked like they were let through the waiver.

A few hours would not be enough for a drunk person to get over what he drank. However, the three vampires and a werewolf woke up shortly after noon in a state of complete sobriety, though not without a hangover. Even Dea, who only drank a little, had a headache, possibly as a result of the attempt of the hellish mixtures that Gladiator came up with. Taking advantage of the fact that neither Never nor Fronde had yet returned, they took a shower in turn, which for centuries has been a proven way to deal with this type of disease.

Oggy, who got into the bathroom first, quickly jumped into some clothes and ran out to buy meat for herself at a nearby store. Dea was preparing aspirin for everyone, and Gerard was finishing shaving when the door slammed shut and Fronde stepped inside, proudly showing off his new haircut. Gladiator saw him first and, shouting in one breath some extremely complex curse, he retreated furiously. Stumbling on his own feet, he fell into a chair with all his weight, accompanied by another desperate cry full of surprise and horror at the same time.

The chair could withstand his weight and fell to pieces, and the highlander was on the floor, probably not even noticing it as a result of shock.

"Oh my good God!" he cried.

"Holy Jesus!" Dea exclaimed in the same spirit of Dea. "Fronde, what the hell have you done to yourself?"

"Not me, the hairdresser," Theo said calmly, very pleased with the effect he achieved. "You told me to go to the barber, didn't you? It's called dreds, and I really like it. It's the twenty-first century, I'm not going to shave my head bald all the time."

Dea's patience has finally dried up.

"Idiot, with your type of beauty you can't comb like a Polynesian because you'll scare people away! Yanek, grab him by the neck!"

"I'm grossed out," Gladiator said, but dutifully grabbed his friend in a 'chokehold'. Theo, who had never given up without a fight in his long life, shoved his elbow into his stomach, gently slipped out of control and tried to escape. Then Gladiator grabbed his legs and after a while they were both wailing around on the floor like a pair of wrestlers. Theo was more agile, but the Polish highlander towered over him with strength and muscle mass, so despite his valiant resistance, Fronde was finally suppressed and shamefully cut with the help of conventional scissors for manicure.

"Delilah!" he shouted accusingly when Gladiator finally let him go, after which he ostentatiously fell silent.

"I strongly suspect that Delilah actually cut Samson because he beat her," Dea said calmly, putting away the scissors. "Given the masculine nature in general and the nature of men in the East in particular, it could be. All it took was a shadow of suspicions for the paws of envy to go into motion. The young lady eventually had enough, and got him for good. And she was right."

The door opened again, and Oggy ran into the room. At the sight of Fronde sitting on the floor, she stood still and widened her eyes.

"Did the moles get to you?" she asked.

Theo cast an excruciating glance at her and continued to suffer in silence. Dea explained it.

"I sent him to the barber, and he came back looking like a voodoo sorcerer. I had to sort him out or else they'd be after him on the streets and wouldn't let him in a plane."

"You're lucky I wasn't here," Oggy growled with an expression that didn't bode well.

"Too bad you didn't see him, you'd even help me outm" Dea fired back.

At this point, Never entered the room, very animated.

"Listen, guys," he began, and broke away when his gaze fell on Fronde. "God damn, why does our knight look like he just went through typhus?"

"Because Dea cut his hair. Just for fun," Gladiator calmly replied, proudly shaking his own lion's mane.

"That's not true! She didn't like my new image..." Theo moaned.

Never shrugged his shoulders impatiently, went to the motel's store and returned after a moment with a cheap hair clipper. Fronde protested, but the Indian didn't pay attention to it. Maneuvering deftly with the clipper, he cut out Dea left – leaving him with a buzzcut, sure, but at least cut evenly. Cut like a rookie in the draft, Theo looked a little better, though that hairstyle, as Gladiator put it, eminently didn't suit him.

"Now it's at least bearable," Never said, throwing the clipper on the table. "Now stop being a crybaby, Fronde! It's not a misfortune that you don't look like an irritated broom. Now all of you listen to me: Amargo probably won't be expecting us. He lives on Rivoli Street, on the ground floor, apartment three. The apartment building is inhabited, so we can't use explosives because it could harm someone. I think you'll agree with me. However, with a little dexterity, we can go through the window and surprise the bastard.

"Either we surprise him, or he does us, there's no third option," muttered Gerard, who didn't like this task at all.

"If you're chickening out, then say so!" the Indian fired back at him. He himself felt bad about what they had to do, and tried to drown it out somehow.

"Let him be," said Theo, who concluded that he had enough of demonstrating his insulted dignity, since they had a job to do. "He's right, he could very well take us by surprise, just as much as we could him. We have to be prepared for that. If the guy is half as bas as Harmon, we're going to have a very tough time."

He knew exactly what he was saying. Although the vampire world is not as dangerous as it is usually described, rare immortal lunatics called *mora* give it a bad look. Such a *mora* is always a 'moth', especially sensitive to sunlight. Besides that, they're known for their incredible voracity and hatred for humanity, as well as his 'better' relatives.

Eliminating such a madman is extremely difficult. The best example of these difficulties was Harmon himself, whose sinister activities lasted almost half a century and was the direct reason for the story that vampires were descendants of Satan himself. Fortunately, Harmon had limited perseverance capabilities, otherwise he would have gathered an army of ones such as him, and a true war would have started between humans and the children of the night. The same factors that drive vampires insane seriously affect their ability to effectively transmit their genes. However, Harmon was able to solidify a few people, and Amargo was one of them. How did it work? There was one person who was sure to know about this, and it was with this person that it was necessary to consult.

"A professional killer, huh? They all work their own way. I think you're talking about S24... this code name covers, according to Interpol, an entire organization that has been around for several decades, but I have always believed that it's really just one person... or, as you say, vampire. He is very expensive, but he's reliable and hassle-free. He will kill anyone for money, regardless of gender or age. Are you saying that he is in Paris right now?"

Agent Gris looked at Dea curiously as he thumbed through a folder containing cut-outs and notes. Never, leaning his elbows on the table, studied the police reports, which the journalist certainly did not receive legally.

"He is," he said absently. "We even have an address. But we must deal with this on our own, without official factors involved. Take my word for it: this is not a human or even a vampire. He is more dangerous than animal, harpy, or ghost. He's a danger to both humans and vampires... even more so for us, because for humans he just kills whoever he was paid to kill, as for one of us, he'll kill anyone he comes across. He wants there only be to vimans like himself in the world, that is, *mora*. He must be eliminated before he can cause some serious problems.

Agent Gris raised his eyebrows slightly. Dea looked at him from under her eye, the corners of her mouth lifted for a moment in a smirk of understanding and anger, then returned to reading as if nothing had happened.

"I thought he could just create ones like him... I've heard that it's easy to become like... you guys."

"It depends. *Mora* has some inherent difficulties with this, and there is also the issue of PAS in the human genome. It's a little tricky overall. Sometimes it works, more often it doesn't, and the likes of Amargo may not be able to create replicas at all due to damage to the genetic code."

"This damage is the cause of madness for *mora*, correct?" Gris seemed to know the facts correctly. He was smart, undoubtedly, and sympathetic in his own way, but Never didn't like this peculiar sparkle in his eyes. He looked at them all like a zoologist would at some very interesting representatives of the fauna. Nothing more."

"Probably. But it has nothing to do with you, do you understand? Instead of questioning me, get on with your work," he said coldly. "You must have some kind of program to work on."

Gris smiled knowingly and remarked with some amusement:

"All morning I've been working on an interview with a detective leading the case on those murders, so now I'm free. Did you know that the body of your killer was stolen from the police morgue by an unknown criminal?"

"No!" Never turned to him abruptly, and his eyes widened. "Are you sure?"

"Maybe she was not quite dead after all?" Dea asked.

"Maybe she wasn't," the journalist agreed. "But I did not say the most important thing: the body disappeared after the autopsy. So, while this girl may not have been completely dead before the autopsy, it is difficult to assume that after the autopsy she gathered her strength and went for a walk. Don't you think?"

It was hard to disagree with him.

"What did the autopsy show?" Dea asked after a moment

"It's a classified report, but I have my connections, even to the main police headquarters. I don't have to disclose this, but let me tell you: it showed serious abnormalities in the internal structure, such as a shortened intestine (a human is long, like with herbivores) and a liver with a structure unlike anything the pathologist have known about. She resembled a Coelenterata more than anything else. The trachea was equipped with something like Johnston's organ in snakes. Since the weight of the corpse was out of proportion for its size, the pathologist examined the bones and found that they were empty except for the ends. The stomach was filled with undigested brain tissue of normal parameters, while the brain in the skull was hard, without division into hemispheres. The pathologist took the day off and is now sitting at home, swallowing lithium carbonate.

"Aww, such a delicate French puppy," Dea muttered sarcastically. "True, after such a detailed autopsy, hardly anyone will leave the morgue on their own. But honestly, what do we care now? The Tau squad did what they had to do, let the others play corpse hunters."

"Right," Never said. "We now have a more serious problem."

Yes, they did they had to hunt down Amargo, who was not expecting them, but nevertheless was an extremely dangerous target. There was something they didn't even talk about among themselves – they preferred not to talk about it, but every *mora* they heard about sharpened their senses to the limit, and it was very difficult to approach them. His sense of psycholocation was probably more sensitive than average as well, which meant problems.

"He'll detect us before we can even see him," Dea put it succinctly, and everyone knew she was right.

Amargo wouldn't have lasted that long if he didn't know how to avoid meeting other bloodsuckers. A long time ago, at the beginning of the creation of their free organization, all participants agreed on one thing: every vampire must kill a *mora* if they run into one somewhere. All in all, the opposite was also true, but it was always possible to eventually eliminate a dangerous madman, albeit sometimes at considerable expense. 'Normal' vampires towered above *mora* in only one thing – in the ability to cooperate with each other. *Mora* hated even each other, and although they had to endure „their own", there could be no question of any cooperation between two *mora*, even closely related.

From the materials collected by Gris, they did not learn anything other than what they knew. No one saw the killer, at least not one of the survivors. The route by which his employers contacted him was unknown. He always did his job flawlessly, with surgical precision. He left his identification mark on the bodies of the victims – the letter A, cut with a knife. Interpol was of the opinion that this letter meant an organization, not a single killer, as the killings with this sign first began at the end of World War 2, so, according to the detectives, it has been too long for it to be one person. However, for vampire standards, that wasn't very long...

They needed to develop a plan of action. The fact that they knew their opponent's address was helpful, but it wasn't enough. Most of all, they knew that they had to figure out everything before going into battle. Any 'whispers' on the spot were out of the question, because *mora* would have immediately understood the situation, and even though he was one and there was six of them, it was better not to take the risk. It was hard enough due to the fact that the *mora* would love to murder them all, while they treated it as an unpleasant last resort. Since Amargo, like the other *mora*, was a moth, they decided to take advantage of that and attack at dawn – moths were the least concentrated then. Admittedly, Theo and Gladiator were also 'moths', but both agreed to this sacrifice for a greater cause, as ultimately, removing a threat like a *mora* was worth a few burns. Besides, dawn was the best time for other reasons. Most people are sleeping on their sides, the police patrols yawn as they reluctantly wander the streets, and the moth will be home if it has one. He will not risk being in a strange, perhaps even hostile, place by sunrise. Of course not.

"Gerard, you'll stand on guard," Never decided when discussing the final amendments to the attack plan. "Make sure the police doesn't take us by surprise. Gladiator and I will break down the door, the rest will crawl out through the windows. Fortunately, it's the first floor. Remember: everyone attacks the moment they see this bastard. Do not hesitate and do not think twice, because all of our lives are at stake. If one of us gets hit by the other, that's too bad, they'll be fine, but if not, then… it's important to get the guy. It's important not only for us."

"Someday they'll say about us: never did so many owe so much too so few," muttered Fronde, imitating Winston Churchill's famous quote so amusingly that the others laughed.

The laughter was not entirely amusing, rather they were trying to hide their growing concern. This was the first time they had encountered a professional assassin, an assassin with abilities that most people would describe as 'supernatural'. They knew they had them too, but to a lesser extent, as they were not trained just for one purpose: to destroy. Therefore, they went into battle tense and full of bad feelings. They didn't confide in each other, but they all knew that the others felt the same way. It was not worth talking about, rather, it was necessary to put all focus on maximizing their abilities, so that Amargo doesn't even have time to realize what is happening.

*****

They were extremely careful. But it seems that they were not careful enough, or didn't take everything into account. They did not understand how it was possible for psycholocation to be this much superior, since after all, they arrived on the scene without wasting a second, and invaded his apartment like a storm. And yet Amargo greeted them with immediate fire from the Uzi, and only by an imperceptible miracle did they all go unhurt. They couldn't even see him clearly, he was moving too fast. Trained like a circus acrobat, he seemed like a man-fly, for whom the floor, walls and even the ceiling were all the same thing.

For a while, hell reigned in the small apartment. What was striking in all this, was the fact that Amargo did not say a word, did not make a sound at all. It seemed as if they were dealing with a creature not from this world. He moved quickly, avoiding being caught or shot with incredible agility. If they could just catch him and immobilize him for a moment... because hitting a target moving this fast was out of the question.

Only Never was able to grab him by the leg at one point, for which he received such a blow to the head that he completely lost balance. However, since the mora was stopped for more than a second, several bullets were immediately fired in his direction. They must have hit the mark because he curled up for a moment, but then he jumped to the window, knocking down Gladiator as easily as a chess pawn. And then he vanished. They heard Gerard's scream coming from the street, and everything fell silent.

Theo, Oggy and Dea, who immediately followed Amargo out the window, didn't see anything. Their friend was nowhere to be seen, and they were afraid to think about what had happened to him.

"Can you believe this that all this took a few dozen seconds?" Dea asked, glancing at her watch.

"Who cares," Fronda grumbled. "Why did he kidnap Gerard?"

"We'll think about it later. He kidnapped him, he didn't kill him, so that's some hope at least," she answered sharply and turned back to the car. Gladiator was already running towards them with the unconscious Never over his shoulder.

"Let's get the fuck out of here," he said as he came closer. "The whole building is already on its feet, all that's left is to wait for the gendarmes."

"Nothing in life happens like it does in movies."

"True. There, no matter how much noise you make, no one bothers you, except those who should come according to the script."

"Get in the car, guys, I'm driving," Dea ordered categorically.

This time, no one had the strength to protest against the 'female rule', which they would certainly have done under normal circumstances. However, this situation was abnormal. They suffered a tremendous defeat. They had lost one of them, their leader was wounded, and worst of all, and Amargo Lorca was now on their shoulders. They could be sure that he would not let them go. They could only hope that he would not start with the hostage.

"I doubt he'll hurt him," Oggy said as she and her friends laid the still unconscious Never on the motel couch. "At least for now. If he wanted to kill him, he would have done it right away. Faster and less hassle. I think he wants to trap us. He knows we'll be looking for our friend... but where could he have taken him?"

"We'll figure it out. For now, hand me my bag," Dea demanded impatiently.

On closer inspection, Never's injuries were more serious than she thought. The bone was damaged, the skin was cut several centimeters deep, and the Indian had not yet regained consciousness. Dea thought that no human would probably have been able to withstand such a strong blow, and that Nevers's skull, elongated as in Egyptian paintings, must be exceptionally strong, since it did not crack like an eggshell on impact.

"I'll sew him up," she said. "But this wound is less of a problem. It worries me that he hasn't regained consciousness for so long. And his irises..."

She looked Never in the eyes with a small flashlight and shook her head in displeasure.

"The left one is clearly wider. This is really bad, he might need trepanation."

"Well, then take care of it," Theo suggested.

She looked at him with obvious contempt.

"Cute. Where would I get a trepanation kit, an operating room, all the equipment and the surgeon to top it all off? I don't specialize in neurosurgery."

"It used to be that the same doctor did everything. Now you need specialization and the doctor for the left leg doesn't know what to do with the right leg. That's some great progress," Fronde grinned ironically and turned his back on her.

"I suggest we get some sleep," Gladiator said. "We won't figure anything out in the daylight anyway, but in the dusk we'll begin our search. Then we'd better be in full force. Remember: there are five of us, he is alone, and he came out as if there was no one there at all. To overpower him, we all need to be in shape."

"Why, you don't say... of course we do. If Gerard is alive, he'll get our help, and if Amargo has killed him already, then we can't help him, all that's left is to avenge him," Theo spoke more and more archaically, which showed how excited he was.

He felt guilty, though there was no way he could prevent the misfortune. Despite the suffocating anger, he lay down and fell asleep. Centuries of struggle taught him how to fall asleep in any situation, and it was a very useful skill. A certain percentage of the undead eventually begin to suffer from insomnia, because, having a feeling of constant danger from people, they are simply too afraid to fall asleep. If they are unable to break the mental barrier that prevents them from falling asleep, they die soon as a result of body exhaustion and hunger, because as a result of loss of strength they are unable to seek food. Theo was stronger. He learned to fall asleep whenever he thought he had to sleep.

They woke up before dusk. Dea, first things first, examined Never and became more concerned to see that he was still unconscious.

"It's not getting worse, but it's not getting better either," she said. "Damn it, I don't know anymore, what should I do? Should I leave him alone? It's risky..."

"I don't know, you're the doctor here," said Theo, who looked at it all much less tragically. It's not the first time that Never has been seriously injured, and yet he's always been able to cope with injuries somehow.

Someone knocked on the door. Gladiator took the safety off his gun and covered it with a towel and then nodded to Oggy to open it. Theo lined up on the other side, compressed to jump.

"Why don't you answer the phone?" Gris asked, entering the room freely.

"The one here is broken and we turned off our mobiles," Fronde said angrily. "We wanted to get some rest. What do you want here, scrounge? We're in trouble and we really, absolutely have no plans to play with you right now."

Gris, unoffended by this rather cold welcoming, looked around the room as if looking for someone.

"Where's your comrade?" he asked, looking around.

"Comrades, Agent Gris, are in communist parties," Dee said. "Tau 3 is now a hostage of our killer. We complicated the matter last night."

Gris stepped back so suddenly that everyone twitched. Suddenly he lost all his composure.

"What did you say?!" he yelled angrily. "How could you have let that happen?!"

"He didn't ask for our opinion," Gladiator muttered.

"How could you leave him in the hands of a murderer?! What kind of friends are you?!" Gris apparently wasn't able to calm down. His skinny face flushed, his pointy ears were jerky, and he seemed as if he was about to throw himself at his interlocutors."

"Shut your mouth, or people will notice..." Theo remarked, upset.

He must have been right, because after a while a woman looked into the room. She wasn't very young, but she was still very well-groomed and quite attractive.

"What happened, my dear, why are you screaming?" she asked, turning to Gris. They looked at her, surprised by such closeness.[4]

"They allowed a kidnapping, can you believe that..." the agent began and didn't have enough breath.

"Who the hell are you bringing in here? Are you going to announce our mission in the media, too?!" Oggy attacked him. "How much did you tell her?"

"As much as I had to."

"I'll write a report about you, you babbler!" roared Fronde, throwing his fists at him. "But before that, I'll kill you!"

No one knows what would have happened if the new arrival had not stood between them, separating them at the risk of her life. Theo refrained from hitting at the last minute. He never hit women, even if they deserved it.

---

[4] In France, you are only on first-name terms with the closest persons. People refer to each other with "vous" even with friends.

"Stop it," she demanded. "It won't lead to anything. What happened?"

"Don't tell her anything! It's a business secret!" Oggy screamed, clearly fighting with a great desire to turn into a dog.

Agent Gris waved his hand with contempt and nervously combed his hair with his fingers. Now he looked like a man who was hit by an unexpected disaster.

"It's no secret at all," he said in a resigned voice. "And in any case, not for the two of us. This lady is Anne Marie, my sister."

"Anne-Marie Phil, right? And your real name is Olivier Phil," Gladiator added with some amusement, which was completely out of place in such circumstances.

They looked at him with their mouths wide open. As usual, they thought of him to be the last person to show off analytical skills. Now, while looking at the siblings, everything became clear. They saw an obvious resemblance in this tall, skinny man, and in the blond woman, from whose face they clearly saw Gerard's green eyes staring back at them.

Gris nodded.

"That's right. My mother told us everything when we were adults. Since then we have both searched for some kind of contact, but so far to no avail."

"I have long guessed that, although perhaps not from the beginning," Gladiator clearly reveled in the superiority of a well-informed person, which didn't often happen to him.

Theo reopened his mouth as if he wanted to say something, and then closed it, looking at everyone with the gaze of a wounded doe and sat down on the sofa as if someone pushed him down. It was too much for him. He felt as if he it was all to make fun of him specifically.

"Well, now that that's settled," Dea concluded, "if that's how it is, you two stay here and take care of our friend, while we go back on Amargo's trail. We have to get Gerard back out of his hands no matter what."

"Do you even know where to look for him?" Anne-Marie asked. She seemed very calm, as if the whole situation did not affect her at all.

"We'll figure it out," Gladiator assured her. "We'll go back to that Ravioli Street..."

"Rivoli," Theo corrected him.

"Whatever it's called. I'll try to get in a trance there. If I catch a trail, it'll be simple."

"It would be much easier if we investigate his apartment. Maybe we'll find something that will lead us to him," Dea apparently didn't trust in Gladiator's abilities, even though she has witnessed them being used in practice.

This was understandable, since each 'sensor' has worse and better days, and its sensitivity can be disturbed by many factors. Especially by those that aren't rare in a big city.

"If the police was already in there, then do you know what we'll find? I would tell you, but I'd rather watch my language."

In the end, they decided to go to Amargo Lorca's apartment. There was always hope that the police didn't search the apartment very carefully – it turned out, however, that they were not in there at all. The gendarmerie stopped at marking the door and investigating a few residents of the building. They had no reason to believe that it was anything unusual, since there were some fights in this area almost every night, and this house was already famous for them. Amargo chose this place not without reason, amongst hooligans and other suspicious types.

"What are we really looking for?" Oggy whispered when, with all precautions, they entered the destroyed and sealed apartment through a broken window.

"Anything that may be related to our friend's current location," Dea said, and began methodically looking through all the closed drawers.

Theo and Oggy followed suit, and only Gladiator, ignoring their efforts, sat down with his feet rolled on the floor and slowly passed into a trance. He hated it – during the so-called 'scouting trance' his lungs were always paralyzed and suffered terribly, like someone going through a heart attack, but now it was not the time to complain. Gerard had to be rescued at all costs. He was one of them, and his artistic perception of the world, sense of humor and lively intelligence colored their lives. Without him it would be too sad...

Lack of oxygen stupefies the human brain, but it mobilizes the vampire's brain, brightens perception and temporarily sharpens their abilities, which is what the highlander needed. He had to 'find the way' within five or six minutes, he was not able to go any longer, although usually he managed to get what he needed within the third minute. With tracking down a human that he had already gotten to know it was usually no problem, but for other vampires, psycholocation was often helpless. A properly trained vampire knows how to cancel it out well enough that only a very strong 'sensor' can break through his protection. Gladiator was a strong 'sensor', although he was very reluctant to use his gift, precisely because of the suffering associated with entering the right type of trance. Because it wasn't just physical suffering. During its duration he felt a terrible, not comparable to anything else fear, and he was afraid of this fear more than of anything else.

"Yanek, what's wrong?! Yanek, wake up!"

Violent shaking, the strong smell of ammonia, cold water dripping down his face... Gladiator realized he was lying on the floor, and the troubled three friends leaned over him. He must have lost consciousness.

"I'm fine," he muttered weakly. "I know where they are. I was able to see the entire route... I must have overdone it this time... but it was worth it. Did you find anything?"

"Not a damn thing," Theo replied. "If you've done it for us, then get up, let's go. You're driving. And one more thing: I'll take command. It will be a purely military operation, not some nail polishing. Don't say anything, Dea, I know you're a very liberated, rebellious and ferocious woman in general, but I've had as many wars behind me as the years you've been alive, and I know these games much better. Not to mention the fact that a knight, even a former one, is obviously better in military matters than any woman."

Dea looked at him with pity.

"Did I say anything? Take command, go ahead. I want it as much as a vacation on the Devil's Island. Ah, just look at him, the knight of Pelota..." she cut off and gently jumped out of the window. She was probably a little offended, but she tried not to show it.

*****

"What are you trying to prove?" Gerard asked in a weary voice.

He stood in an abandoned garden near the suburban Rue du Faubourg Saint-Honoré, strapped to the trunk of an emaciated mulberry tree, observing his captor, who was putting on his back something which resembled a strange backpack.

Amargo looked at him and smiled. This smile was even scarier than that the whole persona of the vampire-madman. Dressed in military camo that didn't fully cover up the tattoos on his skin, his head was shaved on both sides, decorated on the top with long blue-dyed hair moving across the center of his skull. His bony face shone with ever-shifting eyes, an endlessly vicious smile was nearly stuck to his lips. He really looked like a madman.

"Do you know what this is?" he asked, tossing up a sturdy metal tube, painted dark green and attached to one side of the backpack. "This is a US Military surplus flamethrower. Contains a special flammable mixture, it's better than napalm. People can be killed in different ways. But as for my dear brothers, I recognize only the severed head and the burning, though I prefer the latter. It's an effective method, more effective than any other method widely advertised in literature and cinema. I've tried all of them."

"You are sick..."

Amargo laughed with obvious satisfaction.

"It's good fun, such hunting. Although, one like Fronde, for example, I'd like to catch alive. I've heard a lot about him. I wonder how long he would take to die, tied up to my machines. The current record is six days, but he can surely do better if even a tenth of the story about him is true. But this time I'm not risking it for science's sake. When your buddies come to save you, I will send them straight to hell. Via the express. We can watch them wail and scream together. And don't worry, there'll be enough for you, too."

"How can you be so sure that they'll come? They don't know where you took me." Gerard was clinging to his last hope.

"Oh, they'll figure it out. I'm not worried about that. I believe in the vampire intuition and I'm very rarely wrong." Amargo checked all the connections of the mechanism, and then looked at his captive with blood-curdling amusement.

Gerard didn't respond to his teasing. He was tired and hungry, his bones ached. He was tortured for almost ten hours with some strange device that he had never seen before. He sometimes had the impression that Amargo Lorca had built most of them in a moment of great boredom. The whole device was controlled remotely, so the killer simply sat in a comfortable chair, only switching the programming on a small, portable control panel. It was certainly high-end technology, although not necessarily new.

Either way, it all worked, and much better than Gerard would have liked. His torturer did not ask questions, just watched his torment with his nasty smile. He must have really enjoyed playing this game. It was a terrible experience, although the kidnapper was careful not to damage his prisoner. He still needed him alive, and he didn't know how much he could resist. Unbeknownst to him, in the very first hour, Gerard discovered a skill he never knew he had, namely the ability to suppress physical pain. It took a lot of effort, but with the right concentration, he forced his brain to release endorphins, which greatly alleviated any discomfort. His acting skills helped him hide his new talent from the tormentor so that he wouldn't realize the fact.

However, he felt sick thinking about how much he would have to endure before death would free him from the hands of the madman. In the end, it's a terrifying thing that vampires are so hard to kill... For the first time, the actor thought of death with sympathy, not as an enemy, but as a savior coming to the rescue. The situation in which he found himself was truly terrible, and, even worse, he saw no way out of it. There was no miracle, no hesitation on the part of the killer, who had everything in his power. Madness blazed in Amargo's eyes, with no trace of human emotion on his face as he prepared for the arrival of the rescue team.

Gerard thought that this time it was really the end. He lowered his head helplessly. There was nothing he could do to help his friends, who would show up and be greeted by a stream of burning liquid from a flamethrower. And he... he will witness their death in the fire before the assassin directs the nozzle of the blaster at him.

He didn't hear any sounds. It wasn't until he felt the touch of a wet mut on his bound hands that he twitched. In a heartbeat, he realized that Oggy was here, trying to carefully bite his ties off. So they came, just as the kidnapper predicted! The horror stopped Gerard's breathing when he saw three dark silhouettes that had just jumped over the garden wall. He wanted to scream, warn them, but he didn't, it was too late anyway.

The darkness of the night was illuminated by the terrifying ray of flames, buzzing from the flamethrower which Amargo was holding. Several bushes immediately caught fire, but it did not reach any of the friends who, with remarkable reflexes, escaped sideways.

"Run, run!" Mora cried with laughter that would make anyone shudder. "You can't escape anyway, the fun will simply last longer! That's even better, I love it when my prey resists before death!"

He pulled the trigger of the flamethrower again, deftly dodging Gladiator who was trying to get him from behind. Oggy ferociously bit at the hard lash in an attempt to free Gerard, while the other three did their best to get the madman's attention and at the same time avoid getting fried. Amargo was moving at an incredible speed, to which they could only react by moving at their maximum capacity. They probably wouldn't have been able to if it weren't for the fact that Fronde, anticipating such a problem, made everyone take pure sugar – a substance that works on vampires the same way as amphetamine on humans. They were aware that they would be sick afterwards, but better that than certain death.

The plan assumed switching from defense to offense only after Gerard was freed, but now they had doubts about whether they would be able to avoid the flamethrower for long enough. Vampires are more afraid of fire than humans since any kind of burning takes a very long time to heal. And when the burned area is 15% of the total area of the body's surface, they experience such a strong shock that few vampires are able to survive it. The very fact that they didn't just run away from the pursuit of the murderer with a flamethrower was a good indication of their courage.

Gerard's tight bindings finally broke, but the actor didn't rush to escape, as the plan had assumed. He fell to his knees, putting his hand on the back of the surprised wolf.

"Sorry, Oggy," he whispered. "I'm in no shape to fight or even run away. I'm afraid your sacrifice will be in vain."

"Don't give me that shit, you condemned soul," Dea somehow appeared next to him, and grabbed him under the arms. "Go back under the wall and wait. Oh, and hold on to this. If the situation is really bad, unload the whole magazine into him, but remember, only as a last resort. The thing he has on his back could explode like a bomb if it gets hit by a bullet."

She pushed a heavy Magnum 44 into his hand and returned to action just in time to confuse Amargo. The killer managed to push Gladiator to the corner of the garden and preparing to turn him into a living torch when a rock thrown by Dea hit him directly in the head. He turned around, furious, looking for the attacker, but the girl were no longer there.

Gerard gripped his fingers on the cool handgun, feeling as he returns to his usual calmness. The knowledge that he was no longer defenseless was reassuring, despite the unfortunate situation. Meanwhile, Dea whistled on her fingers twice, which told them that the hostage was freed. This caused a sudden twist in their way of handling the situation. Gladiator jumped to a wall, grabbed something, and threw it over to Fronde. He grabbed the tossed object and ominously lifted it up, right in front of Amargo. What he held was a large two-handed sword shining in the moonlight – apparently, along the way, Fronde visited a museum and took ownership of an exhibition item, without asking anyone for their opinion.

"That's how you want to play? All right!" Amargo exclaimed with a laugh. "I'll deal with you first, then with your friends. Everyone will their turn..."

He pulled the trigger of the flamethrower. Theo jumped to the side, avoiding the fiery flow, and attacked Amargo with the sword. Mora easily ducked under the slash and again turned the nozzle towards him. This time, a few drops of burning fluid fell on Fronde's shoulder, but he paid little attention to it. With a swift cut, he severed the nozzle in half and immediately afterwards pushed the flat blade towards the opponent's stomach. The push was clearly signaled, so Amargo could easily avoid it. He abruptly retreated away from the swordsman, trying to put a spare nozzle on the tube at the same time. He was good. But not good enough.

The silhouette of a wolf flashed under the moonlight. Silently, without the slightest growl, Oggy fell from behind under Amargo's knees, knocking him over. Maybe if the Mora hadn't been burdened with the heavy tank of the flamethrower, he would have been able to change the fall to a somersault, he was nimble enough. The container overpowered him, however, not allowing him to regain his balance. He fell heavily on his back. He didn't have time to do anything, Fronde stood over him with a raised sword and swung heavily, blood spouting on his face.

"Get back," Gladiator pushed him aside, unscrewed the tank valve and, throwing Gerard on his back, climbed with him on the wall.

After waiting for others to follow his example, he took out a box of matches from his pocket, rubbed one of them on the scratch and threw it in the middle of the flowing puddle of dark, thick liquid. He then jumped to the ground just before the explosion occurred. Shreds of the ruptured tank swirled all the way to the wall, the tangle of flames shot up for some good five meters and then lowered down.

"Let's get out of here," Theo said.

It was only now that Gerard realized what danger he avoided. Red spots flew before his eyes, and he fainted, all of his weight lingering on Gladiator's shoulder.

"God damn it," the highlander places his unconscious colleague in the front seat of the car, put the seatbelt on him tightly, and sat in the back seat himself. "Though, on one hand, he got what he deserved. I'll tell you in secret that my soul nearly escaped from me when that whack job started firing at us with the flamethrower. He nearly turned me into a roasted brigand. By the way, how's your hand, knight? You got hit a little, no need to play the tough guy."

Theo looked at his shoulder, visible from under the shreds on the half-burnt shirt. The burns were rather bad, but he could suffer through them – he suffered through worse injuries before, which took him months to get back to full health. In the heat of battle he didn't even notice the pain, only now did it reach his consciousness.

"I'll live," he said. He touched the burnt area and moaned slightly in pain. "Dea, you should drive, I need a rest."

"I think that's a good idea," the girl sat obediently behind the wheel. "I'll tell you honestly that when decided to grab a sword, I thought you were as crazy as this Lorca guy. Now, however, I return my respects to you. You were right."

"It wasn't about being right. I just had to have a weapon that could immediately kill the Mora, and at the same time one I'm used to. It's been centuries, but I'm still a knight, and a sword is an extension of my arm."

Oggy sat down next to Fonde and began to carefully lick his burnt arm. Theo underwent the procedure without words, putting his head on Gladiator's muscular arm. He needed a few minutes to restore his spiritual balance after what happened – that is, not even after the fact that he had to kill Amargo – but after brushing against death, which today was within his reach. If one of his reactions were a split second too late, he wouldn't be sitting in a rented car right now, he would be burning on the lawn of that abandoned garden. It wasn't the first time that he was in such danger, and every time it happened, he had to experience the fear and a feeling of danger, which he didn't feel during the action itself. Never called it 'the mental afterimage'.

"Oh, right, Never." he said. "I wonder how he's doing."

When they arrived at the motel, it turned out that their friend's condition had not changed. He was still unconscious, and the people guarding him said that he still hasn't moved. If they didn't know who they were dealing with, they would have assumed that he was dead.

"I don't like it," Dea said grimly, and began examining Gerard, who, unlike Never, quickly regained his senses.

She told him to undress to his underwear and began a methodical examination, and then bandaged the wounds inflicted by the kidnapper. Gerard passively went through these procedures, sipping blood from a bottle that Gris handed to him. The agent acted as if caring for the wounded vampires was part of his daily duties.

"What happened to you?" he asked warmly, looking with disbelief at the signs of torture on the skin of the actor.

"You don't want to know," Gerard muttered. "This bastard took me on a journey back in time to the best time of the Inquisition. Dea, be careful, damn it, my hand wants to live too!"

She snorted disparagingly.

"Don't try to lecture the doctor, okay?"

"I can see that," Gris touched the actor lightly. "What did he do to you?"

"In detail? It was some kind of electric shock device, the ends of which he placed just at the fingertips. And how did they stick there, do you know? He simply hammered them under the fingernails. The rest, as Shakespeare said, is silence. Does it look bad?"

"Better than for the one that actually died," Dea said calmly. "You'll be fine."

"Of course. It could have been worse if it wasn't for you."

He looked at the silent woman sitting next to Never, and then again at Gris.

"You're, siblings, aren't you?" he said. He looked again and suddenly his face took on such an expression that the friends were worried he'd faint again. "No, there's no way... tell me it's not true!"

"Calm down, man," Theo sat next to him, patting him on the back. "Yes, they're your kids, even though they're a little grown up, there's no reason to make a scene. Are you going to calm down or should I just go ahead and smack you in the head?"

"Fronde, you're as subtle as a waste bucket," Oggy said in disgust. "Think about what he went through today. He really wasn't ready for another shock. Gerard, close your eyes, take a deep breath and count from twenty to one."

Dea, not paying attention to this exchange, took out a tube of ointment and a narrow bandage, covered her patient's hands, smeared the wounds on his shoulders and then gave him an injection in the arm.

"This will strengthen you," she explained. "Now I'm going to take a look at Never, and you put some clothes on. Have some shame and don't parade naked in front of your daughter."

Gerard closed his eyes, trying to count down from twenty, as Oggy said, but he still felt lost. He didn't know why, but meeting his own children shocked him much more than the cases of the harpy and Amargo Lorca combined. He didn't think that Anne would tell them everything, much less that they would take it so calmly. Olivier and Anne-Marie, whom he remembered as two delightful toddlers, now stood in front of him – mature people with shiny hair, with all the baggage of a difficult life, as foreign to him as aliens from a distant start. Complete strangers. They had nothing in common.

An unpleasant feeling squeezed his throat.

"Forgive me," he whispered, not very aware of what he was saying.

"Forgive what?" Anne Marie shrugged. "It's not about forgiving or not forgiving. I didn't want to see you to hear something like that. I just wanted to look you in the eye, convince myself that mother wasn't mentally ill, that she was telling the truth. It's that easy to tell yourself: My father is a vampire. Olivier clung to those words like a drowning man onto a plank, but I always preferred to think that you were dead. I preferred if you stayed what you were. I didn't want to, and I couldn't imagine you as the child of the night, a descendant if Dracula. And yet you're sitting here now, just like on the old movies, still young, nothing changed... while I'm already an aging woman, so what are we supposed to tell ourselves?"

She touched his cheeks with her fingers, then bent down and looked so insistently into his eyes that he shuddered and lowered his eyelids. What he could read from within Anne-Marie's gaze accused him, and he had to admit, it hurt. It hurt a lot. It wasn't the first time he asked himself whether it would be better and more just if he died, just like that, dignified, like a man. He felt desperately guilty about his children who had grown up not knowing him properly and not knowing that he was alive. It felt like betrayal. For a few moments, Anne-Marie observed the game of emotions on his face, then shook her head and walked away, tapping her high heels.

"I'm rather glad you're still alive," Olivier said. "It was always huge consolation for me, a nice little secret that I couldn't entrust to anyone. Nan never believed mom, she thought she was an old maniac, but not me. Maybe I have a more poetic soul, or maybe a more open mind, I don't know. Nan has always been a sober and sane person, standing firmly on the ground. Now imagine this logical-minded woman at the time when her own mother on her deathbed tells her to swear that she will never give her father away to the vampire hunters. Think about what must have been happening in her heart."

He patted his father on the shoulder and followed his sister. Gerard remained sitting still, stunned, unable to believe what had happened. If he had analyzed his feelings now, he would say that he feels only blunt pain, some dominating grief for what has been taken away from him. He didn't see his children grow up, he did not participate in their sorrows and joys, and today they were strangers to him, who he would have passed by indifferently. He didn't even recognize his own son, and he wouldn't have recognized him still if Anne-Marie hadn't appeared, so similar to her mother. Only now was he able to recognize them...

"What are you sitting like a painted doll for?" Dea reprimanded him. "Did you think that, after such a long time, you'll see the same toddlers you played with on the beach in the fifties? You don't have any common sense."

"That's not it... it's one thing knowing that somewhere out there your children are living their lives, all grown up, and another actually seeing them with your own eyes..."

"I'll say formally," Fronde began speaking. "I propose changing our den. Maybe I'm cynical, but I wouldn't fully trust that lady. Hunters use the worst kinds of methods to convince someone to cooperate, and we can't be sure that they haven't reached Anne-Marie. Their interviews are well organized and they certainly already know that we are here, even if they don't know the exact address."

"You're in charge here," Gladiator proclaimed, and without further ado began packing his belongings. Dea wanted to say something, but changed her mind.

A few minutes later, they vacated their occupied rooms. They could do so without fear of official repercussions. Since they had already completed the official investigation, Agent Gris did not need to know where to look for them, but they were required to do everything to ensure their safety (section 36 of the internal rules of the VASP agency). Just in case, they first went to the rental company and switched to another vehicle.

"Why don't we just get out of here, take the first flight available?" asked Gladiator.

"Because we have to wait until Never comes back to his senses," Dea explained to him.

"Where are we going now?" asked Gerard, who right now would really like to just lie in a comfortable bed and forget about the world.

"Sevre. Segovia has a backup residence there..."

"He's probably kept there as a vampire showpiece model," Oggy interjected.

"...and I don't think he'll be mad if we make use of it," Dea concluded calmly.

"Let him be mad if he wants to be, screw him," grumbled Theo, at the moment occupied with observing Never's head. Something about the stitched wound bothered him and he didn't know what it was.

"Ah, I get it!" he exclaimed after a while. "This blow was struck with an object made of chemically pure silver! You can tell because the wound has taken a gray tint and looks as if burnt. That's why Raja is in such a terrible state."

"For a vampire to keep silver items in his apartment... you'd have to be really perverted," Dea was clearly disgusted, but immediately thought of something else. "If so, why didn't our detectors react?"

"Probably because we didn't even turn them on," Gladiator replied. "Am I right or am I wrong?"

He was right. They preferred not to risk alerting Amargo with a screeching detector that get activated even by 'dumb luck', as Gladiator put it. Admittedly, the thought of a vampire owning an object made of chemically pure silver could not have occurred to them.

The 'backup residence' turned out to be a small but very pretty Renaissance villa hidden among other houses. Drowning in the stream of greenery it didn't attract much attention, but soon it turned out that not everyone can get inside this cozy house. If Dea, registered in the security sensor's database, wasn't with them, they certainly wouldn't have been able to enter it.

Inside, the villa was decorated with the sublime taste of someone who didn't count their money. Any piece of furniture could have been a museum decoration, very old Persian carpets probably cost a fortune, and it seemed blasphemous to even step on them. The windows were obscured by draperies of hand-embroidered velvet, and the carved panels on the walls were a work of art of its kind. The dark interior smelled not of perfume or even aromatic oils, but of the most expensive Arabic incense, sold, as before millennia, at the weight of gold.

They felt like they were in the palace of the ancient legends of the sultan, and, reflexively, without even agreeing with each other, they took off their shoes before they entered the mosaic floor and fluffy carpets. They did not expect to find anyone inside the villa, so they froze still at the sight of a slender Asian man, with smooth as glass, braided hair. Dressed in a dark, simple outfit, like something made for fighting in the Shaolin style, he was reading some newspaper with Olympic-like calm.

"Why are you staring at me like that?" he asked, putting the magazine on an antique table. "One might think that you've never seen a vampire before."

"Bruce Lao!" Dea was clearly surprised. "But... that means... is he, too?"

"I can't believe it, Bruce! You didn't make any contact for three years, where have you been?" Theo interrupted her, delaying the explanation of her matter.

"Was I supposed to write you poste restante? I preferred to live my life. Segovia once pulled me out of an unpleasant situation and we became very friendly, so I'm allowed to stay here. And what about you? You've had some trouble, judging by the fact that you all look like a mess, haven't you?"

"Our appearance is none of your business," Dea said offended. "You yourself look like a peasant from the Ming dynasty. This braid must be to parrot Never, or is that the latest fashion amongst Asian vampires?"

"Not at all. But I think I have as much rights to it as he does," Bruce Lao walked up to the sofa on which Never lay, and put both of his hands on his head.

"A stroke in both parietal lobes and in the left temporal lobe," he said a short time later. "It's already starting to get absorbed, so at most twelve more hours and he'll return to consciousness."

"How do you know that?" Oggy asked warily.

"When I became one of you, I obtained the power to diagnose with touch," explained the Chinese man. "It's like some inner eyes that suddenly began functioning. I can place my hands on the wounded spot and know what the ailment is and at what stage, as if I can see everything. More interestingly, I not only have zero medical training, I don't even have any inclinations in that direction."

"The PAS factor. It can sometimes give such abilities, although most often it causes physical deformities. I could feel it in your blood," Fronde said, nodding seriously.

"Too bad I don't have it, I could use such an ability," Dea muttered with jealousy, which she tried in vain to hide.

"Even if you had it, instead of a diagnostic ability, you might have just grown scales. Only ten percent of people with PAS, who underwent preservation, don't look like a demon of Goya afterwards."

"Why Goya?" Gladiator asked.

"Because he was a little messed up and saw various things. Although it's still nothing compared to Salvador Dali, for example..." Fronde explained to him, and they both began discussing things that were the inspirations of poets and artists.

"Have you been here long, Bruce?" Oggy asked friendly, not interested in this topic.

"No," he replied. "Actually, I just wanted to relax here a bit. I was in Paris before that, cleaning up after you guys."

"What do you mean, clean up after us?" Gladiator was outraged, interrupting his discussion with Theo. "Give me a break, descendant of the great Mao."

Bruce Lao didn't pay attention to his anger. He walked slowly through the room, looked out the window, and sat on the window sill.

"It is what it is," he said. "Who do you think cleaned up the remains of the harpy from the police morgue? How could you let humans do an autopsy of an inhuman? After all, the main commandment of our organization is: Protect the secrets of the inhuman world from the eyes and ears of man. In general, the way you handled this matter calls for fury from the heavens."

"Hold on, why would that be?" Fronde exclaimed. "What were we supposed to do when she threatened the environment, and nearly twister our necks? If it wasn't for the police, we could've been in a poor situation."

"She didn't just fight for herself..." Bruce said slowly.

"You knew her!" Dea exclaimed, her eyes widening.

"I did, but I didn't know you were tracking her, otherwise I could have prevented the misfortune. Alkis didn't tell me anything, and I highly doubt that she wasn't aware of a bunch of crazy vampires and a werewolf in a dress looking for her. Either way, maybe she didn't want me to get involved, because who would take care of..."

He paused, then breathed deeply and finished:

"Alkis entrusted me with her greatest treasure, her child, Athalia. She was during another pregnancy and couldn't take care of her properly. During pregnancy, she had to prey on brains, because not only could she change her appearance, but her baby could have been born in human form. Unfortunately, it will no longer be born..."

"We didn't know that," Gerard whispered after a while with guilt. "We knew nothing, we went in blind. I understand her motives, but do you think she had the right to kill these girls?"

"I don't know," Bruce shrugged. "I don't study the law. But I know one thing. Every expecting mother who already loves her baby is willing to kill to protect them. Alkis was no exception. She wanted her children to be able to live among people, not hiding in the shadows, to have control over the transition from harpy to human form, and vice versa. This was made possible by this grotesque ritual during every full moon. But it's not magic, of course, it's biology. I don't blame you for what happened... you didn't know anything, and you still didn't want to kill Alkis, I know it. You tried to capture her, and then the police arrived."

"If she hadn't panicked and tried to communicate with us instead, then maybe..." whispered Theo, biting his fingers. What he heard shocked him deeply, and he did not know how he could cope with the guilt.

"Maybe this, maybe that," Bruce sighed with sad resignation. "It's hard to predict all the consequences of your actions. However, in the future, remember that not everything is as unambiguous as it seems. And before you start the next investigation, contact WVO. It's an abbreviation. World Vampire Organization."

"Why don't we know anything about it?" Fronde became alert. "Somebody creates a new organization, only for the chosen ones? Who the hell?"

Bruce smiled softly.

"It doesn't matter for now. Don't be surprised that you haven't been informed about anything so far. You work for humans. Not for hunters, but nonetheless... humans."

"That seems logical," Dea admitted.

"There's nothing wrong with it, if you have wisely chosen those for whom you sacrifice your freedom. They are also different: better, worse, wiser and stupider... there's even ones like General Dagwood among them, who has an incredible, for an average human, super-consciousness. Yes, I know you work for VASP, and this agency was created by Robert v. Dagwood. We know everything about him. I admit that he is great, and his son inherited from him the ability to see further than the tip of his nose. Most people don't have that ability and they don't want it at all. That's why we're careful."

He paused. His slender, dreamy face remained elongated and cloudy, but his eyes relaxed. It was clear that, unlike many other vampires, he wasn't bothered by the fact that he was learning of 'secret paths' all by himself, without his mentor's supervision. He effortlessly found himself in a world full of dark connections and traversed it his own way, without needing help from anyone. It was hard not to respect him.

"What are you going to do now?" Dea asked after a while. She may not have looked touched, but she was also shaken by one element of what Lao said. "What are you going to do with Athalia?

"What do you think? Nothing extraordinary. I will raise the poor, orphaned harpy like my own child, away from you and anyone who may harm her. I'll teach her and protect from any danger. If you try to get close to her, even by accident, I'll kill you, no matter how much I owe you. It's not a threat, just a warning. I won't let any harm come to Athalia, not from you, not from anyone in the world. Is that clear?"

"Clear as day," Gladiator replied.

Even he was subdued enough that he didn't try to initiate a shouting match, which he probably would in other circumstances, upon hearing a similar threat directed at his team. It happened very rarely.

Lying on the sofa, Never sighed deeply and weakened. His eyelids shuddered, his mouth parted slightly, and after a while his whole body was gripped by a short spasm. Friends rushed to him, but the Indian was again immobile and did not respond to any stimuli.

"See, he's starting to regain consciousness," Bruce said calmly, watching them with the observer's cold indifference. "I've seen cases like this, and not just once. Soon he'll be muttering under your ears again. Well, I'll be leaving now. Don't take it personally, but I'm already sick of your company."

He got up and left the room. They heard him close the door to the garden as he left, and then everything went quiet. They remained alone, with their guilt. Only Dea seemed unfazed. Moreover, she had no reason for a moral hangover, since she didn't even take part in the harpy hunt.

"His pulse has increased," she said, examining Never carefully. "The irises are starting to react to light. He'll be fine."

"I hope so," Theo muttered.

He was not entirely convinced, but he began to feel hopeful. Never was, after all, the toughest 'lash' he knew. He survived things that no average vampire would've been able to, so even getting hit in the head with an object made of silver might not have been strong enough to kill him. With the known allergy to chemically pure silver, such an injury would be fatal to most vampires, but probably not to him.

"Okay, so we're going to stay here until Raja is all better," he said. "We'll hide the car, and I don't think anyone's going to find us here, are they?"

"Probably not," Dea agreed. "Segovia has a freezer with goods here, so we can withstand it for a while. Although Oggy..."

"We walked past the local store," the werewolf interrupted her. "I'm sure they have some raw meat. I'll just go and buy myself some."

"There's no need for that," Gladiator said. "When you were buying alcohol at that night market, I took a visit to the meat department. I have four pieces of beef and loin in my bag, wrapped in foil."

"Did you steal it?" Dea asked sternly.

"I refuse to answer that question," the highlander said with dignity.

"The answer is clear anyway. Someday we'll all get caught because of that mania of yours!"

"If the honorable lady does not like my company, she could have stayed in Klewki, no one asked her to come here."

"All right, all right," Theo interrupted them, seeing that the doctor was preparing for a verbal fight. "Let's leave the quarrels for a time when we have nothing else to do. In the meantime, let's make ourselves at home here and allow ourselves this short holiday, not disgusting each other with pointless quarrels."

"Tell her that," said Gladiator, and then sat ostentatiously in the largest armchair.

"Too bad Segovia isn't here," Dea sighed. "He would shut that dumb face of yours in no time. I hope you didn't steal anything else?"

"Me? Almost. Just a small radio with headphones, two wigs and a Barbie doll."

The doctor stared at him.

"I give up," she said after a moment and sat down helplessly in the other chair. She picked up the newspaper left by the Chinese man.

"A Barbie doll?" Gerard repeated incredulously. "What do you need that for?"

"A kleptomaniac will steal not what's useful, but anything they can get their hands on," Oggy explained to him.

"They're writing about the fire at Rue du Faubourg Saint-Honoré here," Dea said. "They didn't find Amargo's body or anyone else's."

"Maybe he burned to ashes?" Gladiator raised his pale eyebrows in a sign of vague interest.

"Or he ran away. Fronde screwed up," muttered Gerard.

They were too tired to think about it now. They needed rest, not more puzzles.

There was a rustle outside the window, then the rain started hitting against the glass. The smell of damp earth, blooming jasmine and grass entered the room. The silence of the stylish interior, the sounds of the downpour and the soothing atmosphere acted on their tired minds like a drug.

"What if we delayed our visit to the agency a little?" Theo suggested, trying out the sofa covered with silk cushions. He stretched out on top of it with a satisfied sigh.

Gerard, who was just sliding the heavy curtains by the windows (it wasn't long until down), agreed with him silently.

"What if we didn't come back there at all?" Gladiator muttered sleepily, resting his head on the cushioned armrest.

There was silence again. Everyone thought about how to respond to this suggestion, while listening to the steady rustle of rain outside their cozy shelter. They remained silent, until they finally fell asleep – something they deserved after all these experiences, and at last they could feel truly safe for once.

Part 2

Nobody Leaves Here Alive

One of Fronde's hidden charms was that he was able to play the accordion. He learned that skill relatively recently, during his occupation, for the purposes of the Resistance. Apparently, he received such an order from the command, but Never thinks he did it out of his own initiative. He played it quite well, with equal ease performing Frenching waltz as Russian folk tunes and music a little more serious, although the latter Dea had doubts about and complained that it was 'completely blasphemy'. This small talent was helpful in integrating the Tau group with the rest of the team. At first, the friends kept in the shadows, not knowing how to treat other employees of the agency, but eventually began to appear at integration events, where they quickly appreciated Fronde's musical skills. Encouraged by people, Theo played waltz, songs by Edith Piaf and folk tunes, and since he also had a soft-toned voice, pleasant to the ear, he also sang.

"Once you get tired of working for the agency, you can just earn money singing on the sidewalk. "Dea commented pungently, though she still enjoyed listening to the music.

The general himself also appeared at integration events. In fact, they were rarely parties in the full sense of the word, rather quiet public meetings with a glass of grog, a small treat and... music. This time, however, it was an evening organized only for vampires working at the agency, or as they were called in their immediate surroundings, vimans. From time to time they liked to meet exclusively in their own company, talk without inhibitions and drink what they wanted to without fear.

General Dagwood, as an 'initiated one' and, more importantly, liked by the employees, attended such meetings and talked about life stories on equal with others. And there was what to talk about, because the general was on the front lines of World War II, and then in Korea and Vietnam, and he had immense hatred for wars. As he himself once said, it's not even because of how monstrously stupid they are, not worthy of the intelligent creatures that people like to consider themselves. He hated them for turning ordinary, decent people into monsters, next to whom a vampire would seem harmless.

"War enslaves the mind," he said, sipping on a glass of whisky in between sentences. "It's like a living, intangible and hellishly vicious intelligence. It hurts both those involved and uninvolved, and changes those it even brushes against. No one remains the same afterwards. However, wars will continue until people learn to think for themselves, because then they won't allow themselves to be dressed in the same rags and rushed like a flock of sheep into the slaughterhouse. And then let the dictators go after each others' heads if they so desire."

"That would be a sight to see," Gladiator agreed with him.

"King John II the Good challenged Edward III to a duel, but he did not accept the challenge. If he did, maybe there wouldn't have been a hundred-year long war..."

"Then there would be a different time. In your times, someone was always fighting with someone, and no one saw anything wrong with that. It was our time that gave rise to a race of people who see the senselessness of such cruelty," said Conan, who – contrary to his name and massive build – was not combative at all.

Lenore, sitting beside him, smiled mockingly and added:

"And yet our Terry likes to romanticize these times so much... he loves killing, though he doesn't admit it."

"No, because it's not true. I don't like killing at all," Theo said. "It's a terribly unpleasant thing. But I think sometimes a person has to kill, and it is what it is."

Oggy nodded at him with a dog's growl and stuck out her tongue as far as it can go towards Lenore. Even while in human form, it was always of unprecedented size and she didn't brag about it usually. Not to mention, lately it caused her some problems because it turned into a dog's tongue during inappropriate moments and she had a lot of difficulty talking at that moment – but when she wanted to stick it out to someone, the effect was really something else.

"There is a saying: don't judge anyone for what they did during war," Tygier said. He sat at the table and mixed the gin and plasma absent-minded, adding some vanilla sugar to it. "I used to be very offended by it, but now I realize that war causes a kind of mental illness on both sides and that in fact it can turn the best people into sadists."

He coughed slightly. Lately he has been bothered by a dry, nagging cough, which was all the stranger because, in general, the undead don't get sick at all. Dea wanted to examine him, but Tygier gave any excuses he could to avoid it. Moreover, he was convinced that something was simply stuck in his bronchus, some small foreign body, which wasn't too rare of a thing. In such a scenario, the vampire might have to deal with it for months before they manage to remove the bothersome particle.

"And when did you realize that, general?" asked Never, addressing Dagwood with a subtle irony. Although he himself was half-English, he didn't like England or its citizens because of his Indian mother.

The general did not pay attention to this irony. He sat in his chair, with his head leaning against the wall and his eyes half-closed, as if looking into old memories.

"It was back in Vietnam," he finally said. "I think you already know that it wasn't a picnic. I was already offered to join the agency before, because in truth it was already being formed during the Second World War, but I didn't take on the offer. I was so stupid. All I knew was that I was close to madness. I bragged loudly to my team that nothing affects me anymore, and I truly believed that. Until one day. I was coming back from the division headquarters, and an artillery shell exploded very close to me. Two wheels and the radiator immediately went out in the jeep, but nothing happened to me, so I went out and called for help through the radio. And then I saw that the shell killed a dog – just an ordinary, emaciated mongrel that probably managed to escape before they managed to eat him. You wouldn't believe it, but something in me snapped at that moment. Me, who saw atrocities of all kinds, death and torture of my own men, sat next to this dog and cried as if I had lost someone closer to me. That's how they found me. Then I was transferred to the reserves due to battle exhaustion, and then I found myself at the agency. And that's all."

Everyone thought about that story. For a while there was silence, then Fronde played some melody and began to sing something that was difficult to understand even for those who knew French well. There was something familiar about these words, but no one could understand what. It was not only the rhythm of the poem, which seemed familiar, but also the words, which were somewhat understandable, that aroused some distant associations. Only Gerard Phil figured it out and called out:

"That's a poem by Francois Villon!"

"You got it," Theo said with a smile. "Ballad of the Hanged. He had talent, that poor deviant."

"Did you know him?"

"I did. He was my friend."

"No shit," Lenore said with disdain. "Villon was born in 1431, and you were fatally wounded in 1369. Isn't that too big of a spread?"

Fronde smiled again, showing the charming pits in his cheeks, which would have made him look like a pretty girl dressed as a guy if it weren't for his height."

"And did I say that I met him as a human?" he asked. "No. I met Villon when he was banished from Paris. He was thirty years old, while I have been a vampire for over ninety years at the time. He joined me because, in truth, he had nothing to do with himself."

"And?"

"And, nothing. We didn't wander together for long, but Francois was already in the last stage of tuberculosis and he didn't last long. The long months in prison, which he spent in a cold and humid dungeon, took a big toll on him. It was strange that he even had the strength to accompany me for a few more months."

"Did he know who you were?" Tygier was interested.

"Not initially, but he quickly caught on. This unfortunate loser, a tramp from love and a criminal by chance, a little bit of a thief and a little bit of a pimp, was not stupid."

"How did he react?" the general asked. "It's not every day a person learns that a fellow traveler is a vampire."

"Did he want you to solidify him? I mean, he knew he was terminally ill," Gerard joined.

"He did," Fronde admitted, "but I didn't want to. So I put my hands on his shoulders, and I told him: *My good companion, may you not know that you friend upon death shall be condemned to eternal fires of hell? Even if centuries he spends in joy, by right my Soul is Satan's property, and will ultimately be delivered unto him, for eternal despair and torment.*"

"Is that the dumbest thing you could have thought of?" Never asked with umbrage.

Fronde shrugged his shoulders and reached for a glass.

"Well, how was I supposed to convince him?" he said reluctantly. "He wasn't fit to be a vampire, and even if he was, I didn't have the ability to solidify anyone yet. I only got it half a century later, but I couldn't use that argument because he just wouldn't believe me."

Someone knocked on the door which opened after a moment, revealing the pleasant face of Dagwood's secretary.

"General, there's a call for you on the third line," she said and then immediately disappeared.

She never stayed in sight longer than necessary. Marjorie really looked like a typical silly blonde, but she was an exemplary secretary: she did all her duties quickly and carefully, and made sure that the boss saw her only when necessary.

The general returned a dozen minutes later, visibly moved.

"You won't believe what happened," he said. "I got a call from the police station in Klewki. Dea is in custody on charges of assault and battery."

"They arrested Dea? For what? And she just let them? There's no way!" questions and shouts sounded out.

"They didn't want to tell me on the phone. I'm going there. Fronde, Conan, come with me. We can't allow her to be in custody because, first of all, she's our colleague, and second, she is one of the vimans, and it's better that no one examines her too closely."

Never snorted nervously and poured himself a cocktail. He had long since crossed the line, but he had no clear intention to stop, as long as he was still able to keep himself on two feet.

"I knew that sooner or later one of us would do something stupid and cause you trouble," he said openly. "But I never thought it would be Dea... she is so level-headed..."

The general waved his hand and left, taking with him Fronde and Conan. He chose them because they were the most sober. Conan drank little at all, and Fronde, busy with the game, didn't really have time to, so he didn't abuse the drinks. Fortunately, it was already after dark, since both of them were 'moths' and couldn't tolerate sunlight.

When they came back, it was almost midnight.

"And?" Tygier asked them who, along with others, was waiting for their return, curious about the news.

"A damn ruckus, that's all," Fronde said, throwing himself onto the sofa. "Dea went to the disco in town and met some guy that she took a liking to. And then that son of a bitch added something to her drink, they call it date rape drug, it's a real plague on parties nowadays. Well, if I had a daughter I wouldn't let her near those places. This thing doesn't work on us as it does on humans, but it does make us a little stunned. Dea got a bit dizzy, but when the guy was trying to take off her panties, she... well, you all know her. She immediately sobered up and gave him such a beating that the rascal was put in the hospital, in intensive care."

"And that's why they arrested her?! That's ridiculous!" Gerard exclaimed with scandal. Although he had lived in Poland for some time, he still couldn't get used to some things.

"Unfortunately, that's just how it is in Poland," Gladiator sighed sadly. "But that the lady also had to do it herself... were there no men around at the disco or what? If I was there with her, this bastard wouldn't even need the hospital anymore."

"How could they have known? I mean, he didn't do it in plain sight, not to mention that Dea didn't call for help, and instead immediately gave the bastard a smack in the face."

"The general bailed Dea as his employee, while I learned that officially our agency is a center for public opinion research and personal data processing. No one here knows what we're really doing," Theo concluded, pouring himself a drink.

"Of course they don't. Did you think we would just put up a sign at the entrance which reads: *VASP Agency, Center for Paranormal Research?* Just imagine how much they'd bother us about what we we're doing in here then," Lenore snorted.

"Are there no leaks? Not even gossip?" Oggy asked in disbelief.

"They didn't find any leaks. There are always rumors, but we have a method for that. We ridicule or discredit whistleblowers, and that's where it end. In Poland it always rumbles from all the latest gossips, so one less or one more doesn't change anything. Moreover, the average Pole is much more concerned about what's on their own plate than, for example, what floats in the plate in the sky. That is why placing the agency in Poland was decided to be the best strategic decision," explained Tygier.

"Well, let's drink to that," Never said, raising a glass.

The next day, the friends overslept shamefully. They left morning lectures on the practical meaning of the Coanda effect, language course and training in the boiler room, in general appeared in the hall only after eleven o'clock in the morning. But no one paid attention to it, everyone seemed to have thoughts that were more important. Using this, they also decided to skip the rest of the lectures and went to the medical center, where Dea sat in front of a turned off computer and flipped through some script with a gloomy expression.

"Hey there, tigress," said Fronde, kissing her on the cheek. The girl muttered in response something vague. She seemed downbeat and that had to be fixed.

"You done that bastard in good, I hear," Gladiator said admiringly, sitting at her desk (which, as everyone knew, she hated).

"He'll think twice before doing such a thing next time," Oggy added.

"I don't think there will be a second time. I think I gave him some permanent damage," said Dea. "Yasiek, get your ham off my table! Anyway, who cares about that pervert? Let the police worry about him. Do you know what's up with the agency's computers? From the morning they've said that we're not allowed to turn them on, and no one will explain to me why."

"We don't know anything," Never said. "We were asleep. Yesterday, when you went to the disco, we were drinking and talking to each other, and we left a little. We just got up recently."

"I'll go look for Conan," Fronde said and disappeared outside the door. Perhaps he wanted to explain why he wasn't at training this morning, or maybe some other thing with him – for a week now Conan has been giving off mysterious expressions and was promising a surprise *in your style, Fronde.* Poor Theo hated expectations and always wanted to know everything in advance, so he suffered this hellish torture, unable to get any details out of Conan.

"What was that about computers?" Gladiator asked, reluctantly coming off the table.

"I don't know. Dagwood visited me this morning, forbid me from turning the thing on, and left. So now I'm just sitting here, because what else can I do? I have no idea what happened, but apparently this ban applies throughout the agency until further notice. Someone must be bored."

"No, they're not bored," the general entered the office, not knocking as usual. "We have a serious problem. Dea, does your Fronde believe in the existence of computer viruses?"

Never laughed when he heard the question.

"He doesn't even believe in the existence of regular viruses," he said. It was true – Fronde did not believe what he did not see with his own eyes and had his own opinion about most of the phenomena occurring in the world.

"We have a hell of a problem. Someone gave us some new type of virus that mimics chess gameplay. To disable it, you have to win the simulation, and I don't have a single good chess player here. I hear that Theo is good, is that true?"

Never scratched himself at the base of his braid and wrinkled his forehead.

"Well, he's not Kasparov," he said unconvinced, "but he has a good head on his shoulders. I think he's the best you'll find for this issue. What happens if he loses?"

"Our system will fall. He better not lose. That would be a disaster. Where is he?"

"He went to see Conan, probably wants to bore him talking about that surprise of theirs..."

The general waved impatiently and wanted to leave when the door opened with a bang, and Theo, beaming, ran inside like a bomb.

"Do you have any idea?! Conan is organizing auditions to a wrestling group!" he shouted and stopped, slightly extinguished when his gaze fell on the general. As former military, he respected the highest ranks, as did Gladiator.

"Ah, yes," Dagwood said indifferently. "I should have organized something like that a long time ago. I'll explain it later. And in the meantime, Tau 2, with me, I have a very important task for you."

"You're going to be saving our computer system," Oggy added.

"Me?" Fronde was terrified. "I don't know a thing about computers! Not a damn thing!"

"You don't need to," the general took him by the elbow and pushed him into the corridor, and Gerard followed them with Oggy. They were both very curious about what the computer virus looks like, one that mimics chess gameplay.

When Theo realized that no one required him to interfere with the program, only to move the figurines on the screen, he calmed down and sat down at the keyboard, over which the image of a standard chessboard flickered. The roles of pawns were played by smiling emoticons, the figures had more traditional shapes.

"Bring me some of the goods here," he demanded. "And the key is that I can close the door from the inside. Let no one even dare disturb me, else I might mess up."

After getting what he wanted, he really did lock himself in the room, unceremoniously throwing everyone out the door.

"I wonder if he can handle it," the general muttered with some doubt. He decided to use Fronde's help not because he believed in his genius, but because he had no choice. The agency had several chess players, but they played quite mediocrely, and Fronde has already managed to deal with each of them.

"You should put some trust in him," Oggy said. "He really knows how to check mate."

"I hope so, because otherwise we will need years to get back from out losses. All our business, all the documentation is in the computers."

"I always knew it was idiocy to pack everything into a virtual space," Lenore said, walking down the corridor, and handed the general a letter. Lenore, though a modern vampire, was a strong opponent of computers. She believed that, on the whole, their spread would do more harm than good, and had reasonable arguments for believing so.

"You're probably right," the general said submissively, "but we can't be waving torches around while everyone else has halogen lamps."

He tore the envelope open and began to read. When he turned to the contents of the letter, his face became more and more sluggish. He regretted that he couldn't use the computers right now, but after some thinking, he decided to use a more old-school method of communication to contact the sender, and went to the communications area. Although only the emergency phones worked – as others had a connection to computers and at the moment could not be used. Though it was a good idea, because Robert W. Dagwood preferred that no one register his conversations.

Despite the emergency, the agency kept working nearly the same as always, so the Tau branch went to daytime lectures on the law. Dea didn't want to go. She said that the only law she cares about is her right to peace and quiet, but contrary to her words, she did not give in to a blissful rest, but closed herself in the laboratory. She was going to do an analysis that she didn't need computers for, fortunately. Tygier remained in the solitary cells of the patient's ward since the morning, as he had gotten a severe fever last night. It was as unusual as the cough that tormented him, and this time Dea categorically drove him to bed. She was very worried, especially since Lambdon had recently lost weight and complained of constant fatigue. So far, he has been able to successfully escape proper examination, but that morning he felt so poorly that he came to her office out of his own volition. Not that he was terrified, but he was worried for sure. Dea told him to lay down on the bed, drew his blood for tests and went to work. She was immediately struck by one thing – an absurdly low number of white blood cells during the morphology. She has never seen anything like this in a vampire, of whose incredible health is nearly inappropriate, given the number of diseases that afflict the general population.

"There is something wrong with you, but it'll take me a while to understand what exactly. The main problem is that I cannot get help from professional laboratories, and I have to do everything myself," she said openly to Tygier, who only shrugged his shoulders. He was restrained and indifferent, unlike how he used to be, as alive as the spark of Lambdon.

Only late in the evening did all the friends gather in the apartment assigned to the Tau ward. They had already found Fronde lying on the couch watching the match.

"Did you take care of that virus?" Never asked while sitting next to him.

"I did. It was less difficult than I expected, but a little... well, it was only when I remembered Lapinsky vs Zukertort in 1904 that I realized how I should play this game correctly. Subscribing to the chess monthly magazine paid off. However, I have to admit that it was a little exhausting."

"You are not used to mental labor, that's true. Did you tell the general?"

"I did. He thanked me, but he's acting strange..."

"He got a letter," Oggy interjected. "He read it and then called somewhere and looked very concerned. He also ordered Marjorie to call team Beta to join him."

Using her canine hearing and sense of smell, Oggy always knew best what was going on at the agency. By nature, she was very curious about what was happening around her, which made her eavesdrop and observe everything that could be eavesdropped and observed. As she confessed in a conversation with friends, she knew that these were very ugly habits, but at the same time, very cognitive. She kept the Tau branch well informed.

"Let him be concerned, who cares," Never shrugged his shoulders. "In any case, having an agency as VASP on your head is not a joke. Conan, what's that about some wrestling group?"

Conan, who had just entered, sat down in a chair with a sigh.

"Here's the thing," he began. "Once upon a time, the agency needed cover for scouts traveling to different countries. Since wrestling is popular in the United States and in many European countries, it was decided that each of the agency's branches would train several agents with suitable builds, who, going to competitions or training camps, would be able to collect information without attracting anyone's attention. The system worked, and some of the wrestlers so selected even rose to prominence. Now I need to train two or three as such at our place, I just don't know who."

"I volunteer!" exclaimed Gladiator.

"Me too," Theo held up two fingers without getting up from the couch like a student asking for permission to speak.

"That's to be expected," Gerard muttered, who didn't seem all that interested. He never liked sports which revolved around heavy clashes, his entire artistic soul rebelled against them.

"I don't know... The general would have to agree... You're both moths, so there might be a certain difficulty with that. In general, wrestling groups are for humans," Conan said hesitantly.

"But that's discrimination! Racism!" pompously exclaimed Fronde.

"As if you're so tolerant...! You are a racist yourself! And who recently talked about how stupid those people in Africa are?" Dea asked ironically, waving her cocktail glass with her fingers.

"Because it's true," Theo insisted. "They keep complaining about how bad the white man is, and then they sit back and wait for the terrible white man to feed them, give them water, dress them up, heal them, cover them with all sorts of goods and even apologize. And when you tell them about the need to protect the environment on which their lives depend, about the endangered species that they recklessly hunt, you're suddenly talking in Chinese. There's nothing you can say that will reach their dull, hairy heads. What else would I call them?"

"Don't you think they are owed something for their time of slavery?" Gerard asked.

"First, you should decide who to blame: the whites who bought what was on sale, or the blacks who sold their fellow countrymen, nay! Often even fellow tribesmen."

"I think both are to blame," Conan said amiably. "But what was and what was not is not on the register. I don't know why I should be responsible for my great-grandfather who had a plantation and who fought against the abolitionists in the Civil War? Moreover, he did not leave any family fortune, because the Yankees set fire to both the plantation and the buildings. To be precise, I would like to add that then most of my great-grandfather's slaves died of hunger, because there was no longer a 'vile and cruel master' to feed them, and they could not cope on their own."

"So you support that kind of system?"

"Of course not. That was the result of social development at that time, and instead of fighting and destroying, after liberation, the slaves should have been granted the status of free workers and should have been allowed to continue to work, not for the shelter and food, but for money. Meanwhile, the Yankees had freed them, destroyed the places where they could make a living, and they still didn't give a damn about their efforts. It did more harm than good. The same goal could be achieved by economic and political means, perhaps twenty years later, but at little cost compared to the cost of the civil war."

"And thus the culture of the world would suffer: *Gone with the Wind* would not exist," Fronde finished for him…

"Go to hell," Dea snorted.

There was a short silence, in which there was only the rattle of the shaker and the agitated voice of the sportscaster gasping for breath from his own speech.

"What about Tygier?" Never asked at last.

"He's in bed with a fever," Dea replied grimly. "I've never come upon such symptoms before. I've done the morphology, got stupefied by the number of leukocytes and, just in case, set the cultures. Though how am I to know if it'll even do anything? I've never heard of bacteria that like our blood. All the more since I know that cultivation on our blood is impossible. And yet there they are."

Gladiator handed her a full glass, took an empty one and sat down next to him.

"It's not myeloma, is it?" he asked carefully. "Never nearly died of that. Please, call Stasiek, he knows about this stuff."

"It's definitely not that. I already called your brother, the symptoms don't match. They are also not suitable for asepsis... this is a rare blood disorder that, with all the signs of sepsis and necrotizing fasciitis, does without any microorganisms. Although it temporarily makes the vampire look like a decomposing corpse, it is treatable. Except for the two exceptions, so far no diseases have been found that could infect our kind. I suspect that Tygier is suffering from a third kind, and this is disastrous for us, because we have to act blindly. We do not know how much time he has left and what can help him."

"Maybe it's nothing particularly dangerous?" Oggy consoled her.

"I sure hope so... I am beginning to have unpleasant suspicions, and hopefully they will remain unconfirmed. I'll tell you more about it tomorrow."

Everyone considered this explanation sufficient, and the conversation turned to something different.

The next morning, Conan would not let them sleep in. He woke them up at six in the morning and rushed them to training as if there was a fire. He had to get some additional instructions from the general as he had never forced them to do so before. It could have been some kind of test, an exam, but it was more like regular training, only rigorous. Conan, usually patient and understanding, this time didn't shy away from harsh words and shouts. It was only when they couldn't catch their breath that he allowed them to sit down and rest, and then they looked at their watch and found that the devilish training had taken six full hours.

"Conan, you Cimmerian goon, did you fall on your head?" Gerard asked, breathing heavily. "Maybe a sadist like from an American movie has awaken inside of you? Ugh, I can't..."

"Just get back on your feet and you can," Dea, who had just entered, advised him. "How are they doing?"

Conan handed her a notebook in which he noted the results of his assessments.

"Could be better," he said, "but they live up to their standards."

"Okay," Dea flipped through the notebook and returned it to him. "Now line up for me, roosters, and head to my office."

"What for?" Gladiator groaned slowly.

"For tests."

"If you wanted to see me naked, just ask. No need to make excuses," Theo chuckled and looked at his friend cheerfully, and she looked at him coldly.

"How fitting for you," she said. "Have you noticed that you are far from the standard of male beauty? Go ahead! We don't have the whole day!"

"What do you mean? What else do you want to learn about us?" Never asked reluctantly.

"We'll meet tomorrow and I'll explain everything to you. But today you need to be patient."

Muttering reluctantly, the friends rushed to the doctor's office, accompanied by Oggy, very offended that no one wanted to examine her in particular. However, Dea only cared about the vampires. She examined each one individually, finally drew some of their blood, and only then allowed them to return to their chambers. They were finally able to wash up and eat something, because Conan had left them no time for their morning breakfast. It seemed that now they can do whatever they felt like, but suddenly that turned out to be false. Gerard, who wanted to go to the city, returned disappointed and announced that he was forbidden from leaving the base.

"What the hell does that mean?!" Never shouted and flew out the door like an arrow. He returned after a while, already collected and calm.

"That's just for today," he said, "general's orders. The guards tried to explain it to me, but they don't know anything themselves. But I know that Dea isn't doing tests on just us, but everyone else too, so it might be related."

"What if this is just an excuse to eliminate us?" Oggy whispered.

Never shrugged and slung the braid over his back.

"Don't you think it crossed my mind? There is such a possibility, albeit a small one. I don't think Dea and Conan would be involved in that... although, of course, we can't rule that out completely. So we should be ready for any surprises."

He lifted the seat of the sofa and pulled out a flat drawer from under it. Inside were several small dark metal pistols which looked like toy guns, and a dozen spare magazines. Never distributed them to everyone present.

"Put them in the back, under the waistband of your trousers, and cover them with your shirt," he instructed them. "We can only use this as a last resort, so wait for my command"

"What can we even do with such a toy..." Gladiator grimaced, in whose huge hand the pistol seemed ridiculously small.

"With this toy, you can shoot as many people as with a huge magnum," the Indian said coldly. "And it's much easier to hide."

"How did you get this stuff? After all, weapons are prohibited on the base," Oggy gazed admiringly at the deadly instrument that had been handed over to her. She didn't know where to hide it until she finally slipped the small object into her dress' pocket.

"I have my ways. I don't trust people, that's how I'm still alive, and since I don't trust people, I choose to protect us. Just in case, you know... I swear by the great Brahma, every night I examine every wall and corner in here, checking for bugs, because it's better to keep our eyes open than to regret not to later."

"Rather smart," Fronde agreed with him.

"So what should we do?" Gerard asked helplessly.

"The only thing we can. We'll watch TV, read a book..."

"Play some chess..." Theo finished for him and took out a chessboard from the drawer. "Come on, are you picking white or black?"

"White, I guess," Gerard sat down across from him at the table and they began a game that Oggy followed with the interest of a thoroughbred fan. She was supposed to be next in line. Gladiator turned on the TV, and Never sat down next to him on the sofa with a book in his hand. They all seemed calm and relaxed, but deep down they were all ready to act immediately. Not that they fully believed in a real threat... but life has taught them that the unexpected happens to them almost as often as possible. They preferred to be prepared for the worst.

However, no one disturbed them that day. It would seem that the agency forgot about them. No one knocked on the door, no one entered, no one even called the internal telephone. This calm irritated them more than any confusion. So much so that they locked the door and everyone but Oggy stayed awake all night with a sense of undefined danger. As a result, in the morning everyone was tired and gloomy. After a short discussion, they decided not to leave their apartment until they received an official summons, and then all leave together. After drinking the morning canned blood, everyone, including Never, felt so sleepy that, alerting Oggy, they lay down and fell fast asleep. They slept until noon when they were awakened by a rattling intercom. Never, who at first jumped up with a pistol in his hand, regained consciousness, put down the weapon and switched the device to reception.

"What's happening with you guys? It's the third time I'm calling," Dea's displeased voice came from the speaker. "Everyone to the conference room, now."

"Okay, give us a minute. The Indian muttered, yawning violently."

As soon as they could, they tidied up and went into a small room that the agency called, slightly exaggerated, the conference room. There, Dea was waiting for them, accompanied by Conan and the general. All three had very serious expressions, although this did not appear to be due to what they silently suspected.

"I called you here to report your test results," Dea began as they sat down at the table. "As you all know, Tyger has been ill for a long time. I didn't know what was wrong with him, because he did not allow himself to be examined. Currently, due to a significant deterioration in his health, he allowed me to do so. To be honest, I was scared by the results of his tests, so scared that, after consulting with the general, I examined all the employees of the agency, and most of all you guys. Why you in particular? Because Tygier's disease can affect anyone, and, unfortunately, possibly all of our blood. This is no joke, my friends. It turned out that there is at least one virus that can feed on our blood. That is, HIV."

"What do you mean?" Fronde didn't understand.

"Tygier has AIDS," Never said, his eyebrows arched in one line. "We don't know how he got infected, but you have your suspicions, don't you?"

"That's right. I would advise you to be as careful as possible when using suspicious sources for our food. Best not to get it from dubious sources at all, but that can be difficult, for example, during field operations. Besides, there is the problem of the entire population. We have to warn as many as we can, that AIDS is dangerous not only for humans, but also for ourselves."

There was a silence, broken only by the hum of the ceiling fan. The news were not just bad – they were downright tragic. This meant that everyone was in danger, because no vampire could be sentenced to just plasma from a blood bank.

"Wait," said Gerard, "if it was all as you say, there would be an epidemic among the Vimans. After all, AIDS was not last year's invention. They've known for many years that such a thing exists and, unfortunately, is quite popular in some circles."

"Good point. The problem is, we don't know how many of us are HIV positive. In this base, none of us, but all over the world? How do you do a comprehensive study, because many vimanas are not affiliated at all and it's difficult even to judge how many there are? Dea slowly shook her head and looked at her notes. "But you're right that Tyger's case may be unique." It could be a specific vulnerability or condition that we don't know about yet. But to figure it out, it will take me a lot of time and money. There is a series of lab tests to be done, and you have to help me."

"Now? Because it seems that general has a task for our crew..."

Robert W. Dagwood nodded slowly. It seemed like he didn't want to talk about it, but he had to.

"I received a strange notification," he said. "It's about the appearance of some extremely aggressive stinging insects in the vicinity of Bratislava. I sent the Jota crew there, but they've gone missing. The whole squad. I have not received any messages from them other than the standard report that they have arrived at the site. Finally, I asked a friend from Bratislava to check what was going on. He found no trace of them. I sent Beta's squad to look, and an hour ago the liaison officer called me: they found Commander Jota in the police morgue. He was killed with a wooden stake driven into his heart. Nothing is known about the rest of the squad."

There was silence. The friends silently looked at each other and only after a long time, Never said:

"I guess we didn't foresee this..."

"The hunters found us," Theo added. "And since we work for VASP, they decided that the agency is all vampires. It's all because of us."

"Slow down, Fronde. Nobody is saying that it's your fault. We have enemies, too, because many of our investigations have already resulted in jail time. The fact that Agent Briscoe was treated like one of you proves nothing. This could be a trick, so you don't know which direction to sniff in. It could be a coincidence. We don't know anything for sure yet. You yourself understand that you are the most suitable team to investigate this outlandish case."

"Of course, General. But it would be better if we lived away from the agency, regardless of the outcome of the investigation. Otherwise, we could attract so much trouble to you and your team that you'd never get back up from it."

"Come on, don't you think you exaggerate sometimes?"

"Not this time," Never interrupted. "He's right, but we'll discuss it another time. Right now we need to get down to business. Bratislava, right?"

"The area of Bratislava. The village of Bertholdan. Right next to it is a branch of a certain institute, which officially works with pesticides, and unofficially, God knows what. We suspect the aggressive bugs came from this institution because they have never been seen in these areas before. These are not bees, wasps or hornets. They look a bit like wasps because they are slender and not too large, but their stripes are red rather than black, and their wings are dark brown. They fly in flocks and attack people and animals. So far, they have had two deaths and dozens of them seriously ill. We tried to contact the institute, but they're not answering, as if they died out. On the other hand, we know that the staff did not abandon it. Agent Leland handed me a code this morning that shows the institute is likely to be co-funded by an organization called Nuntia."

"Oh," Auggie muttered, looking pointedly at her friends.

They haven't mention Nuntia to the general before, so he had no idea what his agents were now facing. This message, along with information about how Agent Briscoe was killed, made up a coherent whole. Nuntia was even more ruthless than the Van Helsing Institute, and worse, its members held on to the worst kind of fascist ideas.

"Is there something I should know?" the general asked coldly, looking at the members of the Tau squad. Their excitement did not escape his attention.

"I don't know if you should," Never spoke calmly, "but for us this is very important information. We'd like our equipment and then we'll be on our way."

"We're going there to fight wasps? Did I understand correctly?" Gladiator asked.

"Seems like it. Now they're making us play exterminators, what a disaster," Theo muttered in displeasure. He tried to imagine what the deadly insects look like, and what he imagined was not reassuring. As a lover of horror movies, he was very familiar with *The Swarm*, and now that he was about to face the same threat as in the film, he felt uncomfortable.

"I'm afraid of insects," Gerard warned them all.

"You're afraid of your own shadow," Dea snorted nervously.

"Not true," the Frenchman said, insulted, "I'm just not in support of unnecessary risk."

"If you think about it, any risk is unnecessary," sighed Conan. "Since human life is supposed to be the highest value..."

Fronde looked at him with deep pity but said nothing. He still couldn't understand how Conan, a big lump of muscle, who could knock down an ox down with a single punch, was actually a pacifist and hated violence. He would have fit much better with the 'flower children' than with this agency, but fate played a trick on him, putting in his way a certain mentally disturbed vampire. As he once told in his own colorful way, that vampire was Shabati, an Indian of the Ogellala Sioux tribe. His name meant 'Hard Stone', but Shabati was not really a tough warrior like his tribesmen, but he had what Conan called, "a good dose of cuckoo, and sexually unclear inclinations." The blue-eyed, dark-skinned giant with raven hair must have appealed to him, because he 'stuck' to him in a way that wouldn't accept any objection and accompanied him everywhere. Conan, somewhat despite himself, liked 'that Indian' and eventually couldn't live without him. Only then did he realize how much trouble he got into when it was too late. Shabati performed the 'solidification' via an extremely rarely used method called 'the indirect graduation method'. This method was often effective even against individuals with innate resistance to the process, but hardly any vampire knows how to use it. So Conan became a vampire, though he neither wanted it, nor strove for it, nor was he even aware of what he was becoming. When it was finally clear, he had no choice but to accept the facts. But his gentle disposition could never change.

***

When in Bratislava, friends learned that the 'case' had at least two aspects: a mysterious insect and a private museum, which was located in a medieval castle under the city and had clear connections with the laboratory in Bertholdan. Agent Leland, who came after them, spoke reluctantly and scantly, but still the Tau branch found out that the museum was *haunted*.

"What a riot," Gladiator laughed. "What are they keeping there? A skeleton cracking its chains or some conventional ladies in white?"

"Laugh all you want, blonde, but the situation isn't funny at all," said Leland. "I'm not superstitious, I don't believe in much of what I see, let alone something that's so elusive, but this museum has something. Some nasty aura. No one will stay in it for any money overnight, moreover, you don't need to watch it then. The thief who broke into it was found in the state of a burnt mummy. The pathologist ruled out self-immolation because the body was almost charred, but, interestingly, the clothes were intact, and the mosaic floor on which this unlucky man lied was not even reechy. Another, who broke into the thing a month later, was also found dead in the morning. He looked seemingly intact, but his guts were crushed to one mass and the bones looked like they were crushed by capers despite no external damage. There was a third, and this one really confused the pathologist. He didn't look so bad at first sight. They were just surprised that the body was so hellishly hard after death, but nothing more. Well, not much to go on. Before they cut him, they already knew he had died in immense suffering, judging by the body's position, clenched fingers and his mouth wide open. Then it turned out that in his blood vessels, instead of blood, there was molten lead. The condition of the vessels indicated that it was initially liquid. It was even found in the capillary retina. There were no more people willing to try and collect the exhibits."

"What exhibits?" Oggy asked.

"From different eras. We have already analyzed the case from this point of view, but none of them are cursed, at least no one knows anything about it. We made standard measurements, there are some deviations from the norm, but small. The only thing that is really unusual, yet captivating, is that in this building the compass loses orientation. The needle whirls around the axis and cannot point in any direction, even when you get the magnet closer to it. We don't know what's in there."

"How is this ferocious museum associated with Bretholdan?" Never asked.

"The keeper is also on the list of employees of the research institute to which this station belongs. It may have nothing to do with it... or everything to do with."

After that note, there was silence in the car. Everyone tried to imagine a mysterious evil that could turn human blood into molten lead or destroy it in a different but terrifying way, and they all at once felt chills. They have stumbled upon things that were inexplicable before, and they could already tell how dangerous it was. They couldn't imagine that a person could be associated with dark forces and still survive. The conclusion was clear: if the museum's keeper, an employee of Nuntia, was really part of what was going on there, he may not be human.

"What about the Jota team?" Gerard finally asked, breaking his silence.

"We don't know. Maybe they vanished in thin air, fell under the ground, got kidnapped by aliens... make your choice. We didn't find any trace of them."

"Maybe the people in that lab know something?"

"Maybe. I'm set to meet with them today, so I'll go and sniff around. What are you going to do?"

Gerard looked expectingly at Never, who saw his gaze and shrugged his shoulders.

"We'll see," he answered vaguely. He chose not to say much in front of Leland, whom he had seen for the first time. He must have understood that because he didn't say a word more. It was only when they arrived near the village that he asked:

"Where do you want me to drop you off?"

"Here," Never said. "Go to the lab, we'll talk later."

The exiting party took a good, watchful look around. In the distance was the background of even more stretched hills of the castle-museum, the village was much closer, and everywhere there was suspicious peace and quiet. The day that recently began was heavy and foggy, harmless to vampires, although probably not very pleasant for humans.

"All right," the Indian spoke, with a rather uncertain tone of voice. "Gerard and Oggy, come with me to the museum. Fronde and Gladiator look around the village, and then meet with Leland. Keep in contact through phone, meet tomorrow morning, at this point."

He pushed several boulders scattered around the meadow in one place, creating a kind of cubist flower.

"What should we look for?" Fronde asked.

"Anything unusual. You have a set for collecting samples in the haversack, although I don't know if you will come across anything worth collecting. Take notes."

"I'll try. And you take care of Oggy," Theo fixed the haversack, the belt of which was annoying his shoulder.

"I can take care of myself," the girl growled. She was very unhappy that she wasn't going with Fronde, but with Never, but she wanted to hide it from the male part of the band.

It just so happened that when they split into two groups, Theo and Gladiator went together. Maybe it's because they complemented each other considerably – if one of them missed something, the latter would surely notice. If someone came up with an idea, the other immediately understood how to implement it. Despite the constant quarrels, the cooperation between them worked perfectly. Now, in truth, they did not expect any sensational discoveries, but, crossing the border of the village, they realized that something was wrong. The village was quiet, except for barking dogs and cackling of chicken. From time to time, some cow mooed, but they couldn't hear any people around.

"It's so quiet here," Fronde said, adding, after a while, "too quiet. You know, I've always wanted to say that."

"Stop playing around. It's all really damn suspicious. Look there."

Theo looked in the direction pointed to him, and saw two women lying on the side of the road. Both were unconscious and did not react to anything. A little further, behind one of the houses, lay the third, next to whom was a bucket, from which all the fresh milk has already poured out.

"Odd. Like something took them by surprise," Gladiator muttered.

They began methodically searching the village. They entered houses, broke into yards and found people everywhere, dead or unconscious. Those who had not yet completely lost consciousness seemed drunk, although they had no smell of alcohol – they were mumbling something helplessly, stumbling about until they fell down, losing consciousness. Some, either stronger or less ill, were aggressive and looked like they've been overtaken by madness. Attempts to calm them ended the same – after a short, fierce struggle, they lost consciousness and no longer came back to it. The friends drove them home, took them to the bed, dumped food on farm animals that loudly demanded morning feeding... The worst thing was milking cows that their owners didn't have time to finish milking – they had to do it themselves because they started mooing louder and louder, and something had to be done about it. The rural mongrels, barking at the strangers, they released from their chains. They didn't know when their owners, at least those who still lived, will recover, and it was better not to leave the poor animals restrained.

"They'll eat the chickens and ducks," Gladiator said, but did not protest when Front took off the the dogs' collars.

"Let them. At least they won't starve to death," Fronde replied.

It was noon when they could finally relax a little, after taking the people off the streets and yards and looking into every house in the village. It was a rather thriving village, akin to a small town equipped with everything you need. There was a an inn, a club-cafe, three stores, a pharmacy and a clinic, whose staff, however, found themselves helpless in the face of a mysterious illness, which took them all by surprise.

"What in the hell is happening here?" Gladiator scratched his head, looking at it all with growing confusion.

"It's funny, but I think I can feel the faint smell of acetone everywhere," Fronde muted. "Some chemical weapon? No way, I didn't hear about one. Did you?"

"They didn't say anything during training. Either way, I don't smell anything. You know, I'm going to call Dea," Gladiator, convinced it was the right choice, grabbed his mobile phone.

Theo, not wanting to disturb him, went aside and completed the notes. He didn't like voice recorders. Even an ordinary pen was already too modern for him, but at least it created more convenience than pen and ink, he had to admit it. The medieval knight was not the enemy of progress, but sometimes insisted on such ridiculous trinkets as ink and goose feather, which he still used until recently.

"What did she say?" he asked, seeing that the friend turned off the phone and approached him with a strange expression.

"That it doesn't fit together. But never mind that. It gets worse. The whole area was surrounded by a sanitary cordon about an hour after our arrival. Not even mice will slip through. Scientists from some central institute are supposed to come here tonight, I didn't catch which one. And in the meantime..."

"In the meantime, let's go see agent Leland," Theo interrupted him. "He's probably on that research station right now. He said he'd meet with someone there."

He yawned involuntarily. He didn't sleep at night, the day passed while working, and the coming twilight will also not bring rest. He knew this well and accepted it with resignation."

They went outside the village, where there was to be a research station behind the garden line. The day was still overcast, but the rain was still not coming, which is why Gladiator noticed that one of the cherries growing nearby has a strange color. Intrigued, he came closer and after a while called his companion. The sight was indeed peculiar. The bark of each tree was covered with insects sitting next to each other, and on top of each other, the very strange wasps mentioned by the general. From afar they looked like fluffy, multicolored upholstery on a gray bark, in some places they hung in large clusters, like bunches of dried grapes. They weren't moving, they were dead. Nowhere was there any trace of pesticides, and it was very difficult to find an explanation for this collective death. Looking around, the companions saw that there were several dead birds and rats on the ground, apparently stung to death by wasps, before the latter covered the tree trunks, waiting for the end of their existence. Theo tipped a few dead insects into sample boxes, taking extra care to avoid touching their stingers. He'd rather not take the risk.

"This is getting weirder and weirder," he said. "Maybe we'll find someone who can explain all this at that station."

The search for a branch of the institute took them some time. It was out of sight, rather reminiscent of some economic complex, with only a small sign on the door that read *Fertilizer Research Station*. The door itself, moreover, looked ordinary only from afar. Nearby, it was clear that they were massive, heavy and locked with a keypad. Next to the control panel was a call button, but it was just a dummy – the bell did not sound, the button fell dead. They tried to look through the windows, but they looked like Venetian mirrors, transparent only one way and behind the wall for greater security.

"It looks like Lenin's mausoleum," Gladiator giggled, but he was interrupted, because someone nearby moaned suddenly, apparently hearing his voice.

They both rushed in that direction. Behind the corner of the building, nearly against the wall, lay agent Leland. His chest was pierced through with a wooden stake – it was evident that it was made specifically for this purpose.

"Sapristi!" Fronde shouted furiously on this sight. He knelt on the grass and raised the head of the wounded man.

"Why didn't you tell me that you were vampires?" Leland whispered with difficulty.

"Does that matter right now? We want to help. Tell me what you know," Theo took the handkerchief out of his pocket and gently wiped the agent's face.

Leland had clearly gathered his last strength, but his voice refused to obey him.

"This place," he whispered, "you have to get inside… Listen, Tau 2… Ludolphian…"

"What?" Theo asked, not understanding anything, but Leland's head fell inertly on his shoulder.

"He won't tell us anything else," he pressed his fists to his pockets, and looked around nervously. "What was he talking about?"

"How would I know?" Fronde carefully put the agent's body on the grass and got up. "Probably some cure for this plague. Is that why they killed him? Someone probably didn't want people to recover. We have to deal with this ourselves, Yanek, because no one will come to us through the sanitary cordon. If it turns out we're not resistant to this disease, well, adios, pal."

"Now, don't fall into paranoia. Apart from Tygier, none of us have ever been infected with anything," the highlander said soberly. "This was no accident. Better call Never and ask for this ludolphian. Maybe it can be bought at a pharmacy, then it will be delivered by helicopter to the village and we can save at least a few people."

Theo pulled his cell phone out of his pocket. He still couldn't get used to the invention and was pretty distrustful of it, but even he had to admit that it was a huge help, especially when the team had to separate as they did now.

"He turned off the phone, or he's out of range," he said after a long time. "He's not answering. I'm going to call Dea, she has to know something."

He gently put in the number and breathed a sigh of relief when he heard the girl's voice.

"Hey, girl," he said warmly, "I need a little help. Tell us what ludolphian is, what it treats and whether it can be obtained without a prescription."

There was a silence on the other end. Then Dea sighed heavily.

"I don't know why I'm still surprised by your coastal ignorance," she said with resignation. "I should be used to it by now, and here I am constantly surprised..."

"Oh, come on," Fronde said offended. "How am I supposed to know what all the drugs are called when I'm not a doctor... that's your job."

"Ludolphian, must mean the ludolphian number, not a type of drug," Dea explained to him patiently. "That's what they used to call the number pi."

"Pi?"

"Yes, three and fourteen hundredths with a hook. You must have heard of it, though fleetingly! According to some reports, it was already used by the builders of the pyramid of Cheops. What do you need with it?"

"I have no idea. Agent Leland said with his dying breath that it would help us with our task, although I can't find figure out how we could use that to cure anyone or even get to the laboratory."

"Ah, that's simple. The value of pi must be the password," Dea said dismissively.

"Perhaps... in that case, gratias Dea, and talk to you later."

Fronde turned off the phone and headed towards the lab building. Gladiator was there, still looking around alarmingly, but he didn't see anything. The building itself was also quiet, as if for years abandoned and only the corpse of the guard in the cabin by the barrier indicated that until recently it was buzzing with life. The encryption lock in the door blinked with a red LED, waiting for password input.

"A six-digit password," said Gladiator, looking closely at the panel, "what did Dea say?"

"That the password is the value of the pi number, but that's only three digits."

"Not really. 3.14159. The number of pi doesn't seem to want to end in a convertible way at all, but these are the first digits. I remembered it from lectures on military courses, because you know, pi is useful for calculating this and that..."

Fronde looked at him with reluctant admiration. This boy was able to surprise everyone, even him, even though he didn't try to.

"Will you come with me?" he said, "I don't demand that from you. We don't know if this virus is not dangerous to us either, and if it is, then we really may not be able to recover."

"Eh, come on, you're exaggerating. Remember once and for all, my dear, that a Polish highlander isn't scared of any disease. He'll drink half a litre, down it with beer, and he'll be fine."

Gladiator carefully inputted the code into the panel, whistling Mozart's *Turkish March*. After a while, a green LED broke out and the door opened silently. From inside the lab approached the smell of chemicals and decomposing corpses. The friends went inside, looking around intently and holding tasers, ready for an emergency, but no one seemed to be attacking them. Only two people survived from the entire team of this small research station: an elderly lady in a white putt and possibly an 18-year-old cleaning lady. They were both in the hallway, in a deep coma. Others also fell where they stood – in the studio, in the social room or in the bathroom.

"Terrible," Theo commented. "As one detective, who led the case of a serial killer, once said, a few more corpses and I'm really going to start losing my patience."

"Better just keep quiet, okay? Your sense of humor is starting to be unbearable, even for me."

"If you had experienced as many major epidemics as I did, you would have been more resistant. Well, let's go, we need to get to the computers before we both die from this smell."

They opened doors to more rooms, finding bodies in almost all of them. This small station had as many as five separate laboratories, and in one of them they stumbled upon a cage with a trembling monkey. She was not much larger than the average Pekingese. She had black legs, a dark brown back, a long tail, a flat face, and a puffy white 'hairstyle' of long, coarse hair that resembled a lion's mane. At the sight of people, she began to jump around the cage, emitting joyful squeaks and beaks.

"Poor thing!" complained Fronde. He opened the cage, and then the monkey literally jumped into his arms, wrapping her arms around his neck in a human gesture. She snuggled up to him and said something in her monkey dialect.

"Chicks are sure into you, huh?" Gladiator said sarcastically. "What are you going to do with her now?"

"What else? I'll keep her. Experimenting with such wise and sensitive beings is a scandal. In general, I believe that experimenting with animals is the same as experimenting with humans. It is a crime."

"If Louis Pasteur, your compatriot, by the way, thought the same way as you, we would still be trembling in front of rabies. Do what you want anyway, but let's finally find some computer."

The computer room was open. Another corpse lay on the keyboard of one of the modern Hyundai, a screen with an open program flickering above it.

"He was writing to someone," said Gladiator, lifting the deceased from his chair. "But I don't know the language."

"It's Hungarian," Theo closed the letter and began typing one of the agency's closed addresses. "It will be easier for us this way."

He pulled his handy notes out of his pocket and checked what he was told to do. Despite completing the course, he knew little about computers, and Oggy explained to him in detail, point by point, how to operate the computer so that Rick Lemony, the leading computer scientist at VASP, could get the data he needed. While doing so, he collided with a piece of paper that fell to the floor, right at the feet of Gladiator.

"What is it?" the highlander was surprised, picking up the paper.

The curved letters drawn by someone's trembling hand clearly stood out against the white background, forming only one word: *Caxap,* followed by an exclamation point. Theo studied them for a long time, frowning in surprise, but he couldn't figure it out. Only Gladiator slapped his forehead with a laugh.

"It's in Russian!" He exclaimed: "Sahar! Sugar. That I didn't immediately understand it. I sure have a brain..."

"You have a brain? I thought it was just muscles."

"Look at this smartass. And I myself heard Dea say that what's under your skull looks like a well-baked cauliflower."

"Dea is a pessimist. Okay, sugar. But why did this guy think it was so important?"

Gladiator shrugged helplessly. Now they both wanted Never to be with them, whose above average intelligence would surely cope with this mystery.

"Are they poisoned with sugar or what? Did someone give them strychnine?" he tried guessing after a while.

"No, I don't think so," Theo shook his head, "but something tells me it's a damn important clue. Sugar... is there a sugar-related disease?"

"Yeah, diabetes. A person suffering from it poisons themselves with sugar not processed by the enzymes of the pancreas. Even I know that, but I'm not a caveman like you."

"If so, then you should have figured out the link between sugar and this mysterious disease, but this caveman did," Fronde muttered, and called Dean on his cell phone.

"Can we seek advice from Mrs. Doctor?" he asked.

"Stop fooling around, just tell me what you found," she replied dryly.

Fronde informed her of the situation discovered at the institute and the conclusions that a mysterious note suggested to him. There was silence on the other side, as if Dea wondered if her interlocutor could draw any meaningful conclusions at all.

"That may even be plausible," she said slowly, "I haven't heard anything like it, but... Is there anyone alive?"

"Yes, two people."

"We have no time to lose. Look for glucose for intravenous infusions. There is a pharmacy in the village, break in if necessary. Based on symptoms that I have never been described, coupled with what you just told me, we are dealing with an overproduction of insulin, not a deficiency. In other words, with the drop in blood sugar of our patients. There are no viruses or bacteria that cause these symptoms. I mean it hasn't happened yet. Get your samples as they could be priceless. And hurry up, these people need to raise their blood sugar as quickly as possible!"

"Are you absolutely sure? What if you're wrong?"

"If I'm wrong, you're killing the sick instead of helping them."

"Good perspective."

"Stay calm. You must take the risk. Contact me as soon as you have the glucose."

"Where the hell is Never?" thought Theo, turning off his cell phone.

Now he would give a lot for the company of the crazy Indian. He felt the same helplessness that always gripped him in the face of huge epidemics. Then he watched as hundreds and thousands of people die before his eyes, while him himself, untouchable, and circled between them like a vulture. He could not help them, although he tried awkwardly – and it was little consolation that at that time doctors could do a little more than he, a layman. Even recently, relatively recently, as it happened at the beginning of the twentieth century, the epidemic in Spain took the same losses as smallpox and plague in the past. A long-lived vampire experienced indescribable fear at the mere thought that someone could artificially create a disease, and then infect the population with it. During the Korean War, he read about how the Americans transferred typhus and other diseases to their enemies – and although Jackie the Liar explained to him that it was just hostile propaganda and that epidemics among Koreans were the result of war, malnutrition, and poor hygiene, the grudge remained. Theo didn't like Americans.

"Well, no time to waste," he sighed, catching Gladiator's expectant gaze, "let's get to work."

It was easy to say... there were only three apparatuses in the pharmacy. They had to reconnect with Dea, who patiently explained to them step by step how to administer glucose intravenously. By the time they finished this work, it was already getting dark, and time was pressing. Soon there will be scientists here, and then it'll be better if they don't find them here. They would probably spend half the night explaining why they are not both sick. After consulting each other, they decided to leave them a piece of paper describing their actions and an explanation of what they came to. There was little they could do. When Fronde's keen ears caught the distant hum of the helicopters, they hurried away, consoled that the patients who had been able to inject glucose were in better condition. Now they had to think about how to cross the sanitary cordon unnoticed.

Meanwhile, Never's group didn't even know they were being contacted. The phones of all three were silent, as if the museum in which they were located was inaccessible to cellular signals. The curator left a long time ago, the door locked behind him, the guards drank beer in the booth in the parking lot, and it could be taken for granted that no one would disturb the place until morning. So far, nothing has happened in the entire castle, and the only thing the group could ever complain about was the feeling of undefined danger, which they perceived as a product of their own imaginations. After all, the museum was no different, at least outwardly, from other similar institutions. Old paintings hung in it, valuable pieces of jewelry were exhibited in showcases, and sculptures stood in the corridors. It is not surprising that such an equipped and at the same time poorly guarded structure attracted thieves. Although, when they finally finished...

"Do you think it will happen to us?" whispered Oggy, looking around the dark corridor.

"I doubt it. Just don't touch anything of value," Never answered soberly. "Anyway, let's take what Leland told us about the first two thieves at face value. I don't believe this story about turning blood into lead, it seems too ridiculous, although it may contain some truth. Something undoubtedly killed the third thief, we just don't know what. We are not stealing anything, we don't even have any intention to."

"Your reasoning is correct if this thing is really just defending its territory. Because what if it's not?" Gerard asked, holding back the chattering of his teeth. From the moment he walked in, he had a feeling stranger than ever before. Fear dominated over everything else, but there was no sign of the feeling to which he had long been accustomed to – the vague horror that lived its own life and clung to him like some kind of nightmarish octopus. The darker it got, the worse the feeling became. His comrades did not seem to succumb to this mood. They looked carefully in all directions, looked at the portraits and old armor, even exchanged humorous remarks, but he... he could not adapt to their light tone. He was silent, cringing, as if trying to defend himself from an expected blow, and became more and more gloomy. Finally they noticed it. They had to notice it.

"What's wrong, my green-eyed fellow?" Never asked anxiously.

"Whispers," Gerard muttered without looking up. "I've been hearing them for a while now. Like in the horror movie *Village of the Damned*. Fronde brought me to see it one time... in the movie, at the beginning, there are such whispers and then a shadow envelopes everything... and then people fall asleep, wherever they stand, and all the women become pregnant and give birth to monsters."

"What do you care? You won't get pregnant, so you don't have to worry about giving birth to a child with white hair and telepathic abilities," laughed Oggy, who has also seen that movie.

There was a noise from somewhere nearby, and Gerard screamed in horror, covering his head in his hands.

"Geez, you're so nervous! Will you calm down on your own or do I need to slap you across the face a few times?" Never asked with disgust, shrugging his shoulders a little. "It's just our buddies. Gladiator crashed into one of the cabinets, that mountain of muscle never looks where he walks. How did you get here?"

"Through the door. Their locks are terrible," Fronde replied. "Why does he look like a crumb of misery?"

"Don't take him to see horror movies anymore. He claims to hear whispers, like in the *Village of the Damned*."

"It's not impossible. After all, there must be some kind of force that we don't know about, it is logical that someone who is a medium, like Gerard, would have contact with it."

"To hell with your logic," the actor moaned.

"How do you know that he is a medium?" Oggy asked curiously.

"Just look at him. I have met many spiritualists and I know what a real unbridled medium looks like. Whatever it is, Gerard can feel it, and he can hear it…" Theo spoke more and more slowly, as if he had just realized what those words meant. It was clear from Nevers's face that he understood that too.

"Do you think this thing is capturing people's minds?" Gerard asked anxiously.

He was truly scared to death, and it was obvious that he might lose his temper. Never took him by the shoulders and shook him hard.

"Pull yourself together," he said emphatically. "Horrors like *Village of the Damned* are based on the belief that the human mind is so easy to take over. That's not the truth, do you hear me? People are more immune to hypnotic manipulation than the authors of such nonsense think. Scientific experience has shown that even under hypnosis it is impossible to force a person to do something that he would never have done in a sober state. Understand? He can only be persuaded to do what he has nothing against. In short, a decent person will not kill anyone under hypnosis, or mutilate himself, or perform sexual acts contrary to his morality. These are facts. In addition, even the best hypnotist will not be able to hypnotize someone unwilling to cooperate with them. Let alone when we're talking about a theoretical non-human being, whose brain waves should be completely different."

"Then why do I still hear these whispers?"

"What are they saying? Concentrate and try to understand them."

"I'm scared."

"Big deal. Sit down and concentrate, go on."

His whole body trembling, Gerard obeyed him. He sat up with his feet on the floor and closed his eyes.

"No, I don't understand," he said after a moment. "It's saying something, but in a completely unfamiliar language, and it doesn't resemble any language I've heard. But there is more. Whatever this thing is, it doesn't seem to have any clear form. I would venture to say that this is a kind of astral being. I know this sounds ridiculous..."

"That doesn't sound ridiculous," Theo said thoughtfully, stroking the monkey curled up on his shoulder. "Van Vogt's *Mission Interplanetary* depicts an amorphous creature named Anabis. It's very dangerous because it feeds on death. It can live only when living beings die around it. Bad analogy, because what is here doesn't kill all of the time, but only under strictly defined circumstances. Gerard, you don't understand this whisper, but can you pick up the intonation? It's not aggressive, is it?"

Gerard hesitated, and a nervous shiver ran down his slender shoulders.

"No," he admitted. "I would say it's troubling, but not particularly hostile. Unless I'm misunderstanding it."

"I don't understand why such a being cares about these trinkets," muttered Gladiator, lasciviously looking at the exhibits in the windows.

"Don't touch anything," Never warned him. "That question is really important though. Why does it attack those who try to get anything out of here? Because it still hasn't even tried to pester us. Gerard, concentrate once more, and you, Yanek, touch the glass."

Gladiator obediently moved his large hand to the lid of one of the display cases.

"Stop!" Gerard shouted. "It's getting mad!"

The fair-haired highlander took his hand off the glass, as if burnt, and Never rubbed his forehead with the back of his hand and walked slowly down the corridor.

"So it seems that it is in fact about the exhibits," he said after a moment. "It has nothing against us, but does not want us to take anything out of here. I also think that as our green-eyed man does not understand its words, so as well that thing doesn't understand what we are talking about, and cannot read our thoughts. If it were otherwise, it would know that we are not thieves. Something is starting to dawn on me, but I still need to think about it more. Gerard, why are you making that face?"

The actor did not answer immediately. His narrow elven face was concentrated, and his eyes glowed with emerald light like lanterns. At that moment, he looked like an angel or an inspired saint.

"There's something there," he whispered. "Down below."

"Down below where?"

"Down below are dead people," Gladiator chuckled.

Gerard jumped up from the floor and, hypnotized, walked down the hallway, while the intrigued friends following him. Reaching the stairs, the actor ran along them until he reached the basement door.

"It's here," he said, trying to open the closed door.

"Hold on, hold on," Fronde pushed him aside and took out his wallet. "You have to have a method for this."

He carefully selected a lockpick and, whistling lightly, set to work. After a while, the lock on the door creaked and opened with a long groan, as if a rope had broken in it. Theo walked in first and, groping for the light switch, turned it all the way. The friends' eyes saw a view as if taken from a B-class horror movie. The floor of the room was a mosaic of an inverted pentagram surrounded by other, smaller symbols. The walls were covered with bas-reliefs depicting satanic versions of biblical events, and under one of them was some kind of altar with a stone bowl. The air was filled with an unpleasant, deadly odor.

"Satanist temple," Gerard whispered, reflexively touching his chest. The insignia of the pentagram that was once placed on him was still visible.

"Satanists' or whoever else's, does it matter?" Oggy shrugged indifferently. "People have fun in different ways. Fronde, where did you get that pet?"

"What pet?" Never looked up from the contemplation of one of the bas-reliefs and looked at Fronde.

It was only now that he and Gerard noticed the monkey huddled on Theo's shoulder.

"What? I took her from a contaminated laboratory. If you don't like it, too bad. For once I'll do what I damn feel like," Fronde said indignantly.

"As if it was ever different. You always do what you want, that's not new. Yanek, couldn't you stop him somehow?"

"But why? If he wanted to take care of his relative..." Gladiator grinned.

Oggy looked at the monkey with kindness and curiosity. The monkey looked at her calmly, very sadly and did not protest when, after a slight hesitation, the girl reached out and gently stroked her shaggy head.

"What kind is this?" she asked. "Not colubus, not macaque..."

"Cotton-top tamarin," Never said authoritatively. "We'll talk about this later, now we have a more serious matter on our minds than a monkey. Three unknowns: the guardian's connection with Nuntia, this basement and the bloodthirsty astral placed here. Is it all connected, and if so, how? And what do wasps and a mysterious disease that killed so many people, and only in this corner of the world, have to do with all this?"

"It's probably good that it's only here. I'm afraid to imagine what would happen if it spread across the country, or perhaps throughout Europe," Theo winced at the thought.

"Exactly. Interestingly, no one outside the village was infected. What is the situation in the village? Because on the way, we entered the store and dragged out the saleswoman to confide in. She told us some interesting things."

"It was rather boring where we were. Lots of corpses, but a few dozen survived. On Dea's advice, I gave them glucose because it turned out that the disease was affecting the pancreas or something like that... Scientists should be there now. I don't know how we got out of here. Dea said that a cordon was set up shortly after our arrival, but it must be doing a poor job since it didn't stop us. Our doctor will probably think we did some piece of work to get through them so easily."

"The best piece is a piece of meat," Oggy interrupted. "Fronde, does this disease also affect animals?"

Theo shook his head.

"Well, the least I can say is that I have not seen a single sick animal in the entire village," he added.

"That does not exclude the possibility that they can be carriers. Your cute little monkey could move these things to pristine regions," Gerard said soberly.

Never shrugged.

"I don't think so. If this disease was carried by animals, then people would get sick in places far away from here. After all, rats and birds know no boundaries. No, no, this is some dirty business. I would venture to say that this is not an accidental leak. Someone infected this village on purpose."

"Are you kidding?" Theo asked weakly.

"Do you think it's time for jokes? Because I don't. I've thought of something, but it's too early to talk about it... listen, faith, let's explore this Cave of Evil properly. Perhaps we will learn something about Nuntia, although I cannot believe that this organization is simultaneously playing Satanists and hunting vampires."

Whatever lurked in the museum upstairs did not mind them digging into the basement. Gerard couldn't sense its presence now, even as he focused his supernatural senses as much as possible and listened to pick up even the quietest whisper. He was all the more frightened when suddenly a thin, half-childish voice began to sing summertime. The singing was soft, but clean, it seemed to come from all directions at once, and what was significantly different about it, is that everyone heard it.

They stood motionless, each of them in their place, as if cut into a stone mosaic. It would not be an exaggeration to say that in their entire long life, nothing scared them more than that soft, innocent voice, so childish that it would be difficult to tell if it belonged to a boy or a girl. In addition, there was something amazing about the sound of this voice – not because of the timbre or pitch, but because it was a sound completely separated from any physical body. The source of every sound can be traced if your hearing is reasonably good, and here it was not possible. The singing did not come from any particular place, but it existed, it was just there, lingering like some unthinkable being, consisting only of notes. It didn't give the impression that it was paying attention to the people who so unceremoniously invaded this underground. But when it began its lullaby, childishly imitating Janis Joplin, it got colder in the basement temple, and the light from the ceiling lamps dimmed. Shadows in the recesses of the reliefs were drawn more and more, revealing forms that had not been seen before – images of some incredible creatures, caricatured faces surrounded by bundles of tentacles instead of hair, what they could not even name, who looked at them as if they were alive. A greedy, gluttonous creature, some kind of hellish cephalopod. All five of them realized that they were seeing something that was not in fact there, and yet they trembled with fear. Despite all the logical arguments, they could not help but feel that what they see now was, as before, only hidden from their eyes, hiding in anticipation, waiting for a chance. One thing they thought surprisingly unanimously: who knows whether schizophrenic people are really as crazy as people say they are? However, this thought quickly faded and disappeared from their heads, as if it were clouded with fear. The cold snap became unbearable, and the walls, covered with reliefs, began to glow with a gloomy light, as if heating up from the inside. Gladiator, closest to one of the walls forced himself to reach out and touch the stone surface. He immediately pulled his hand back, hissing in pain. There was a burn on his fingers, and the walls were hot, like in a blast furnace, but this did not affect the heating of the entire room. And suddenly it all ended, as if it had never existed. The basement turned into an ordinary basement, unsuccessfully stylized as a cheap temple of the followers of Satanism... or maybe voo-doo, because now they noticed in the corner, next to the dominating altar with a large bowl, cages with white and black roosters inside.

"Please, let's get out of here," Theo muttered, his teeth chattering. He was still trembling, although the atmosphere was already noticeably warmer.

"We will, we will," Never calmed him down. "But we'll come back here. What is happening in this basement needs a closer look."

"Do you think this is a hot spot?" Gerard asked, surprisingly calm.

The Indian shook his head slowly, and then made a gesture that meant it was likely.

He has already dealt with 'hot spots'– places where incredible things happened. The most famous of them on the European continent was located in Delphi, in the ancient temple of Apollo. Salem was one such place in America. Although the 'hot spot' cannot be identified, its influence has spread throughout the city. There were many more of them, scattered all over the Earth. Scientists stubbornly denied their existence, but they could not do anything about the fact that people, regardless of race, age or education, left such places and often received psychiatric treatment after spending the night in a house that was placed on a hot spot. In truth, such houses were few. They were erected during periods of inactivity of the hot spot, which could last a hundred or two hundred years, and were demolished when dangerous things began to happen.

Some of them, however, were hundreds of years old, and no one destroyed them, because they were either too valuable, or constituted the historical heritage of the area, or the strange owner did not agree with this. It seemed that the museum was one such structure, the Gates of Hell, as the occultist called such places, somewhat exaggerated. This name was adopted in many countries and in many social circles, although it had little to do with reality. It was more a reflection of human fears than an adequate term. "We are facing something we don't understand, something which could be deadly," said Never. "Science cannot explain these types of phenomena, so it denies their existence. However, the fact is that next to our well-known material world with Euclidean geometry, Einstein's law and the hydrogen bomb, there is a world that, from our point of view, is terrifying. Sometimes a creature from this world enters our world, and then people see Bigfoot, Chupacabra or bloodthirsty goblins. Sometimes the short circuit is large enough to cause more serious anomalies. I'd rather not even think about what happens to the person who is drawn into that world through the disrupted shield, but history mentions saints who went to hell and for the rest of their lives, despite fervent prayers, could not sleep peacefully."

"You talk and talk, while the peasant harvests plums, as they say in Podhala," Gladiator, the least agitated of all, began rummaging in the corners of the basement, not waiting for the end of his commander's tirade.

"We were already in a haunted hut, you know, the one from which I stole that beautiful pendant. We were almost killed. Are you not satisfied with that experience? Do you want us to get into trouble here, too?"

He found a photo file and started looking through it. They showed some kind of landscape pictures, panoramas of cemeteries and pictures of different phases of the moon. There was even a complete series of eclipse images, extremely accurate, no doubt taken with the best equipment. Only two photographs showed people: in one, Fronde was flirting with a blonde girl, and in the other, some young man walking down the street.

"I wonder who that is," Highlander held out the photo to Never, who stared at it and was speechless. With a sudden movement, he turned the small card over and looked at the marks on it.

"Photographed a month ago," he said. "Gerard, look at this. Do you recognize him?"

"Vandis! No doubt," exclaimed the actor, barely looking at the photo.

Theo snatched the photo from him, but he soon handed it to Oggy. They both recognized the tall figure in ecru-colored pants and shirt, straight shoulder-length hair and an unspeakably calm face half hidden by mirrored glasses. There could be no question of a misunderstanding. It had to be Vandis.

"Vandis? Kyrie eleison, what kind of name is that?" asked Gladiator, his words in his native highlander tongue.

"A name like any other," muttered Theo, who had already learned a little bit of Polish. "Everyone needs some kind of a name. The thing is, we saw his death with our own eyes... right?"

"Maybe we don't even know what exactly we saw," Never spoke slowly. When the first amazement subsided, he was most struck by the fact that those who used this basement, for some reason, kept a picture of Vandis here. They probably knew about his superhuman origins and may have wanted to use him for something.

"We have some puzzle pieces that don't fit together with the rest," he finally sighed. "Fronde, stop staring at everything like a fool. Take some photos and let's get out of here. We need to get to our point of meeting with the agent before dawn, where we will calmly think and prepare a plan for further actions."

Reducing everything to a purely scientific question somewhat dispersed the atmosphere of horror. The friends quickly fussed about collecting samples for the agency's lab and documenting anything they thought might be important, then finally turned off the lights and left. Theo locked the basement door with the master key, trying not to indicate that outsiders entered the basement, after which they climbed back upstairs with relief. After what they experienced in the basement, the mysterious creature in the museum seemed overall harmless to them.

"We won't learn anything else here," Never said, as soon as they were in the corridor. "I propose to get out and go to Bratislava. However, before that, I would like to conduct a small experiment."

He took a tangle of sturdy rope from his pocket and tied it neatly to one of the smaller drawers that contained a set of official stamps from two hundred years ago. Then he threw the tangle through the bars in the half-open window.

"Come on," he briefly said to his friends, without bothering to explain to them the reasons for his behavior.

Surprised, they followed him. Never went outside, picked up the thrown rope and kept walking, untangling it so that he had enough of it.

"Get on the ground," he ordered in an undertone, and when they all fell to the ground, he pulled hard on the rope.

They did not hear the rumble of the broken box, they were too far away, but they heard the shrill howl of the alarm. Almost simultaneously, light flashed in all the windows of the museum – not electrical light, but an eerie, blue-white, giving the impression of a self-luminous fog peeping out despite the closed shutters. The fog pulsed, turning into some kind of eerie branches that looked as if something inside the muse was spinning and moving through all the rooms in an uncontrollable rush, trying to reach an invisible enemy. The sound of the alarm clock was accompanied by an inhuman howl. For a moment, the entire castle seemed engulfed in flames, but as soon as the alarm ceased, everything else instantly calmed down and returned to normal. Not a single glass fell, nothing was shattered, and only the guards, who in shock jumped out of their booth and shivered on the pavement, frozen in fear. They dared not check again what happened in the haunted museum they were supposed to guard.

"Sorry, maybe that's a stupid question, but what exactly were you trying to prove?" Gerard asked in a trembling voice.

Never dropped the rope, no longer needing it.

"This thing doesn't really pay attention to people," he said. „And it's not interested in the exhibits either. It's simply afraid of high tones and, I'm guessing of noise overall. The sound of the alarm causes a blind fear in it, perhaps the consequence of this is murderous madness. No wonder that once upon a time, 'evil' was restrained by the ringing of church bells, using wooden hammers and choral, very loud singing. That's why it chose a museum as its headquarters. It's quiet there, the music is off, and people don't even raise their voices. I believe that such things also linger on the cemeteries for the same reason, hence the stories about amazing phenomena in various necropolises."

"And what does the voodoo temple in the basement have to do with it?" Gerard asked.

"Probably nothing. Or I'll put it another way: the temple was built because someone wanted to use, as they thought, the devilish forces hidden in this place. Meanwhile, our indistinct friend does not pay attention to the litany, nor to talking in backwards, nor to the sacrifices of roosters, but some ceremony brought something into the basement that is no joke. Or maybe they simply opened the Gates of Hell, whatever that even means."

"Well, did you think hell ceased to exist just because of the era of space shuttles, the Internet and digital TV platforms?" Theo asked aggressively.

"What I think doesn't matter. What matters is what we find as we continue to delve into this issue."

Never walked up to a large clump of bushes, raised one of them and revealed a small car hidden beneath them.

"What? I asked the agency to bring it here," he said at the sight of the astonished faces of his friends.

"Impressive foresight," Oggy muttered.

Vampire League - Book IV: La Vie Dans Le Noir

The car was so small that they could hardly fit into it, but it fulfilled its role and before the dawn came, the friends drove to one of the suburbs of Bratislava, where a branch of the VASP agency was located. The agent on duty with the *Bela Vitos* badge on his chest gave them the keys to the service apartment where they were supposed to spend the night without asking any questions. It was about time, because everyone's eyes were becoming glued shut and they couldn't stop yawning.

"Wake up, sleepyheads!" Never shouted as he entered the living room. Since there was only one bed, Oggy took it, and the men slept stretched out on a fluffy oriental rug. At the voice of their commander, they jumped up, and Gladiator, who did not really liked being woken up, threw a boot at him and growled something unflattering in Polish.

"I dreamed that I was running naked across the Place de la Concorde and singing a song about Madelon, who had a kitten," Gerard said semi-consciously, rubbing his face with his hands.

"How happy would your fans be..."

"What kind of song is that?" Gladiator asked.

"When Madelon unbuttoned her bra / so the kitten, poor thing, had what to suck / we ran with the whole gang..." Theo mumbled and fell silent, because the awakened tamarin jumped on his shoulder, where she obviously felt safest.

Never gave the monkey a banana and a few nuts.

"Eh, you, unsophisticated Tarzan," he sighed with pity. "Don't you remember that animals need to be fed? I had to do it myself."

"I don't suffer from insomnia, like some people," Fronde said offended.

"By the way, I found some information about our keeper," the Indian began, not paying attention to him. "The guy is divorced. Ten years ago, he lost his only beloved child in a car accident, and after the misfortune he became so peculiar that his wife left him. Today he lives in a hippie commune near Medjuno.

"Curious that she didn't..."

"Whatever the case may be, but in my opinion, we should talk to this lady. Her name is Eva Radovic, we know where she lives, so it shouldn't be hard."

"I'm hungry," Gerard said grimly and went to the bathroom, where after a while the noise of the shower sounded.

"Me too. Let's clean up and get some food, then we'll go visit the keeper's wife."

Waiting for friends to finish bathroom procedures, Never sat at the table and on a piece of paper counted out in points, what kind of image could be drawn from the current state of the situation.

Known:

- The type of being in the museum and the method of dealing with said being
- The cause of coma in people infected with the mysterious pathogen
- Location of an unknown cult
- The true motive of the fertilizer research station

Unknown:

- The cause and identity of Agent Leland's killer
- The location of the missing agents or their corpses
- The cause of the contamination of the entire village
- Cause of serious reduction of the outbreak's area

- The role of mutant wasps in all this
- Nuntia's links to a voodoo cult
- Nuntia's future plans

"I guess I should add the conventional *what's next?*" Never mumbled to himself, putting a question mark at the bottom of the page. That was a very good question. The activities of Nuntia became wider and wider, and ordinary people found themselves on the field of destruction, the peasants from Bratislava, whose luck ran out in front of all the gods. This was already truly unsettling, as it meant that these Vampire Hunters would stop at nothing to achieve their goal. Never had a sudden realization at that moment. He hastily wrote on the back of the page:

"Wasps as a biological agent that carries microbes. Artificially programmed with short life expectancy to eliminate the threat of disease outside the restricted area. The unusual coloring was to make observing the insects easier. For these reasons, none of the naturally occurring species were used."

On reflection, he added:

"Most likely, the goal of the biologists of Nuntia was to create a virus that could only attack vampires, but it underwent an unplanned mutation and became dangerous to humans. The release of wasps into the village was an attempt to prove the harmlessness of the resulting viruses. Neither mutation nor aggressive behavior of wasps, whose venom was unexpectedly toxic, was foreseen. If they had assumed the effects that it had, the staff of the station would've been able to protect themselves, and yet the attack of the disease took them by complete surprise."

Pleased with himself, he folded the card, then included it in the set of samples which Fronde took, and wrapped it carefully. He then went downstairs to the duty room.

"Please send this package by express to the laboratory of the central agency," he said, placing the package on the table in front of Agent Vitos. "Just make sure it doesn't get lost, or I'll rip your legs off."

"Don't worry, it won't," the agent reassured him.

When the Indian returned to the apartment, everyone was ready and waiting for him, wasting their time with some quarrel. They were always ready to argue about any topic, just to have a little fun.

"Everyone calm down. We're going to Medjuno, and before that we need something to eat, so let's get some order and discipline," Never said firmly. "Let's go downstairs."

"I can go downstairs, but I have no discipline. Maybe you should use a whip?" Fronda asked innocently.

"It would be useful to whip out the stupid jokes out of your head. Really, in my entire life, I have never seen an idiot like you, "Never said agitated and added a few more unflattering epithets. Theo didn't owe him anything. They almost got into a fight, but Gladiator suddenly grabbed them by the necks and banged their heads against each other.

"Shut up. Someone's outside," he hissed angrily.

Instinctively, the friends fell to the floor, then crawled to the window and looked carefully. In front of the agency building, right next to 'their' car, a motorcycle was leaning against a lamp, and next to it was a man in a long black coat. He was clearly waiting for someone.

"One guy. What could he possibly do?" Gerard muttered.

"Better be careful. I'll go out, and if everything goes well, I'll call out for you."

After saying these words, Gladiator, without waiting for the reaction of his friends, left, and after a while they heard him running down the stairs. Then they saw him leave the gate and walk resolutely towards the motionless figure under the lantern. After what seemed like an eternity, although in reality it was only two or three minutes, the highlander turned and waved his hand towards the window.

"Follow behind me," Never commanded, and all four of them rushed to the door in such a hurry that there was a little fight. Having finally agreed who would be in first, they found themselves on a dimly lit street, where both men were waiting for them.

Gladiator's interlocutor was a little taller than average, slenderly built, with dark hair. The most noticeable fact up close was that he must have been very young – there was no stubble on his smooth face, not even a trace of it. Smooth skin, clear eyes and this unique expression on his lips, an expression of hidden insecurity, typical only for adolescents.

"This is Goran," said Gladiator. "An envoy of the WVO, the World Vampire Organization, and a local expert at the same time. He's here to help us."

"How can such a kid help us?" Oggy asked surprised, on whom Goran immediately made a bad impression, for some reason. Maybe because she didn't like ponytails, even on girls, and even more so with boys. She was also irritated by the overly ostentatious skull earring.

"A chicklet! I can't believe my eyes, a chicklet!" Never said overjoyed. "I have never seen one in my entire life! Man, who did you in like that?"

"Chicklet? What are you talking about?" Gerard asked in curiosity.

Never explained to him with restrained excitement what he meant. It turned out that although it was not possible to solidify a child, in the case of adolescents, such an opportunity existed, although it was very risky. If the process was successful, then such a captured teenager was called a chicklet. His chances of survival were slim – people of such an immature age do not have enough stamina and experience to survive in a hostile world. Too often they revel in their newfound power and make fatal mistakes, and that's exactly what the Vampire Hunters are waiting for.

"That's all true," agreed Goran. "I was lucky and had good caretakers, so I survived. Many others are less fortunate. Listen, I have to take you to the organization's headquarters. The boss of the local group wants to talk to you."

"The boss?"

"Yes. Her name is Bozena. It's about Nuntia and Van Helsing's activities."

"We really don't have time," Never hesitated. "But all right, we'll go with you. But how will that help us in our investigation?"

"Because Bozena can provide you with our documentation so that you don't have to do tedious work in the field. You think we don't know why you're here? We also have interviews."

"Congratulations."

"All right then, shall we go?"

Never shrugged and nodded reluctantly. He didn't want his plans to be disrupted, but he himself had to admit that contact with the local group could pay off. Also, it was always a good idea to get to know and negotiate with a new community. You never knew when something like this could come in handy.

Bozena Sovova didn't look like the head of a group of vampire. She didn't even look like a vampire. She was short, decidedly plump, with short curly hair the color of freshly peeled chestnuts and a beautiful smile on her round face.

"I'm glad you took the invite," she said cordially, shaking the friends' hands like they were old acquaintances. "I have long since wanted to talk to you, but there was no opportunity. So, once I found out that you guys were investigating the museum..."

"The word already got out?" Never interrupted her in a submissive voice. "You can't hide anything from anyone nowadays. It's not even worth trying."

Bozena laughed heartily at this remark.

"I found out because we were observing the musem," she explained. "We're also trying to deal with Nuntia as best we can. To that end, we spy on them using the most modern methods. The keeper is an important figure in Nuntia, so it should come as no surprise that we look at him too."

"And you didn't try to figure out what's going on in there? I mean, in that museum?"

"And what do we care, love? Let humans worry about that. We have more serious concerns. For example, Nuntia. Over the past year, its messengers have killed fifteen of our people. We had to wage a merciless war with them just to make them back off slightly. I know we are not angels, but Nuntia are not saints either. When they're hunting a vampire, they don't care how many people they'll eliminate along the way. They believe that this is the inevitable price humanity has to pay."

"How do you know that?"

"How? We have one of them here. We are chemically interrogating him. It's better than electroshock or more traditional methods, but care must be taken not to overdose."

Fronde stared at his new acquaintance, but said nothing. He considered chemical interrogations extremely disgusting, since they did not give the person any chance of defense. Gerard winced in disgust, too, and Never raised his eyebrows in cold interest.

"Can I talk to him?" he asked after a moment.

"Why not?" answered Bozena. "Do you want to ask him something?"

"That's exactly right. I'm not expecting him to be well informed, but he may know something. And it's important that he doesn't lie to me."

Bozena looked a little surprised, but without saying a word, she led her friends into one of the rooms. Never went to a separate part of it, closed by screens, alone, the rest remained in the main room, looking at the computers placed there. They didn't really feel like looking at someone who was being forced to confess, even if it was for a good reason, and they were ashamed of Never, who was clearly not bothered by it. They looked gloomily at the computer screens, where some graphs and diagrams unknown to them were blinking, when a girl they didn't know entered the room. At her sight, Fronde nearly dropped the palmtop which he was just observing, and his ears, visible from under his newly trimmed hair, turned with frightening force it the color of a ripe tomato.

She wasn't just pretty. She was dazzlingly beautiful, of impeccable beauty that is rare amongst humans, since flaws can be found in nearly anybody. She had something of Raphael's Madonna – an idealized image of beauty and innocence, fragile tenderness and sweetness, concentrated in the expression of brown eyes, shaded by incredibly long eyelashes. She was such a wonderful phenomenon that even Oggy looked at her with calf-like delight, without envy. But that wasn't why Theo looked like he had been hit in the head with a club from the Museum of Human History.

"Catherine," he whispered when he was finally able to speak again.

"Phew," Gerard sighed with relief. "I was worried that lightning struck our dear Fronde. So you are his master? Damn, he didn't say you were so pretty!"

The girl opened her beautiful eyes wide, and Bozena made a sound intermediate between a snort and a giggle.

"Sorry, you must be mistaken," she said cheerfully. "This isn't some Catherine, not even a vampire. It's just Hyde, a Greek girl from Cyprus. Our... well, protege."

"Is she to be solidified?"

Bozena somehow reluctantly shrugged her shoulders. For a moment she looked like she was carefully choosing her words, then she waved her hand and explained:

"Nobody really has the courage to do so."

That didn't explain anything, of course.

"The PAS factor?" Gerard took a guess.

"If only that. Aplastic anemia."

"God, such a beautiful girl with such a terrible disease," Oggy sighed. "But vampire blood is the cure for everything, right? Once you become a vampire, you recover."

"That's how it looks in cheap horror films" Never said, coming from behind the room screen. "In reality, it depends, but when it comes to anemia, it's dangerous for the master, not for the adept. During initiation, the master could die, because the adept suffering from any form of anemia cannot control their first appetite and temporarily gains monstrous physical strength. Better not to risk it. Fronde, stop with that dumb look. I'm not letting you take that risk, you hear me?"

"I hear you."

"Darling, I'm very sorry, but there isn't much to learn from your witness," the Hindu man said to to Bozena. "He lacks the ability to speak."

"What?"

"He's dead."

Everyone except Hayde, who said a "Good Night" to Bozena and left, yawning with exhaustion (it was after midnight, after all), rushed behind the screen.

"How could this happen?" Bozena said with disbelief, looking at the corpse.

"Judging by the color of the skin, cyanide or carbon monoxide," he said, "I'm not a pathologist and I don't have time for detailed tests, but I would take the risk and say that he wouldn't be able he to poison himself with his hands tied to the handrails. You'd smell chad, so my guess is cyanide. You have a traitor at the base."

There was silence. The friends have already forgotten about Gusto, but now his image appeared in their memory as vivid as ever. He worked for the Van Helsing Institute, so is it possible that he offered his services to Nuntia as well? They lost his trail a long time ago, they thought he was dead, but either it was him or the Institute trained a successor.

"Have you perhaps been joined by someone of our blood, old and very educated?" Theo asked.

"Yes, the head of the research department said that they had found cooperation with Dutch scientists," the Czech woman said. "But I don't even know who it is. The research department lives its own life."

"What are you investigating?" Gladiator asked interested.

"Ah, nothing too fancy, a few biologists are working on a replacement for human blood that could meet our needs. They don't have any results yet."

"Contact them and say that if this scientist is Gusto Vanderbelt, he is a Van Helsing Institute plug. And if he gave a different name, make sure they somehow check if he has six toes on both feet," said Never. "If so, then that's him for sure. We're going back to our business, that's what they pay us for. We have to find the wife of our keeper."

"There's no need for that. Talk to the keeper himself, we have his address."

"Then why didn't you say so sooner? You, women, would put even a saint out of balance!"

"Don't yell at the girl or she'll start stuttering," Gerard reminded Never. "Why did you say 'judging by the color of the skin'? I thought you identified cyanide by smell. Bitter almonds."

"Not when it's an injection, Mr. Smarty-pants. And then the skin would be pink, not pale or bluish, because cyanide damages red blood cells in the same way as carbon monoxide. It also gives off the characteristic petechiae... but we have no time for lectures. We have to go."

"Maybe I'll stay?" Theo offered with obvious negligence. "I'll find out if Gusto actually works here, and all that..."

"Especially 'and all that'. Go ahead, do what you want."

Never went out and deliberately slammed the door so hard that the sound of it echoed. Sometimes he couldn't understand why Theo was still as reckless as a teenager after so many centuries, especially when a woman was involved. Any persuasion was a waste of time. Better to focus on the ongoing investigation and wait until Fronde regains his sanity, because in that state he would be useless anyway.

They didn't even drive very long. The keeper of the haunted museum lived relatively close, in the oldest district of Bratislava, in an old villa surrounded by a neglected garden. To get inside, they had to break in, as no one answered the persistent call. They were immediately struck by a terrible mess inside. The inside of the villa looked like it hadn't been cleaned in years. Empty cans and bottles, old newspapers, pieces of stale bread scattered everywhere, and the once beautiful furniture was covered with a thick layer of dust. From the dozen or so light bulbs in the crystal chandelier, only three were lit. In their dim light, the friends saw the keeper. He was sitting at a large table with his head resting on it, next to an overturned bottle of gin. Before they even approached him, they knew that he was dead.

"Murder or suicide?" Oggy asked with a dim whisper while Never examined the corpse carefully.

"Neither," he replied. "I would venture to say that it was a heart attack, most likely from drinking. In any case, our questions will no longer interest him. Let's do a quick search and we're out of here. I'll look over here, Yanek on the second floor, Oggy in the attic, and Gerard the basement."

"It's nasty," objected Gerard, but Never glanced at him, and the actor, cursing under his breath, went to look for the entrance to the basement of the villa.

The search was rather difficult since the friends didn't know what they were looking for, and in the mass of garbage it was difficult for them to understand what was important and what was not. After three hours of hard and dirty work, they finally left the house and stuffed whatever they found into the trunk of their car. In addition to hard drives from two computers, there were four folders of papers and a huge box with some documents mixed with old photographs.

"We'll have to look at all this later," Never grunted, closing the trunk. "Let's get back to the museum. I want to take those sacrificial roosters from there. No one is going to be looking into the basement now. Why do the birds have to starve? Ultimately, a rooster is also a man."

"If you say so. Just don't complain later that Fronde is sentimental, because you are also not lacking in that aspect," said Gladiator with sympathy. For him, roosters were only meat for broth.

"We're going to a museum when we're so filthy?" Gerard groaned.

"You're not going to an audition for a parade," the Indian muttered, sitting down behind the wheel. He didn't enjoy being dirty himself, but he felt that sometimes there were more important issues than personal concern, such as this one. After all, he wasn't going to the haunted museum just because of a few roosters, anyone could have done that, for example tomorrow.

He didn't want to share his thoughts with his friends yet. If the theory he thought of was correct, then the basement should be 'clean' by the time they get there – and that was what he wanted to test. He had already guessed the truth and, while searching the keeper's desk, came across key evidence: a photograph of a ten-year-old girl and a death certificate. He already knew everything, although he did not yet understand how a great organization could allow one of its bosses to be such an emotionally unstable person. Moreover, he did not rule out that no one from Nuntia knew about the keeper's 'other face'. This quiet, unremarkable man could actually be a cunning fox who reached the pinnacle of virtuosity in hiding what he wanted to hide. He was not afraid of what haunted his museum – on the contrary, he tried to take advantage of it, regardless of his safety. It that aspect, one could even feel some respect for him.

"What are you muttering about?" Gladiator asked aggressively, and Never realized that he expressed his last thoughts aloud.

"Nothing," he replied. "Just trying to figure all this out. Oggy, call the Fronde and tell him where we're going."

"I tried already. His phone is off."

Never cursed in Sanskrit – judging by the length of his speech, it must have been a very flowery curse.

"Then inform Bozena Sovova about it," he ordered after a while. "It's better if someone knows where we are going."

196

"Better yet, let's not go there at all," muttered Gerard, who had clearly decided to be gloomy today. Either way, he really didn't want to go there, and the sight of the already familiar, and in fact, very pretty castle made him flinch. It was quiet around. Even if there were night guards somewhere, they didn't show themselves. Friends easily burst into the museum and went down to the basement, lighting their way with flashlights. The door was not locked. From behind it came a terrible cold, which made them tense up. Only after a long time did they force themselves to open the door and look inside.

Meanwhile, Fronde didn't even consider looking for the mysterious poisoner. He reasonably assumed that the local vampires would know who to suspect and where to find him much better than he did, so he didn't get in their way and immediately set out to find Hayde. Reliable as always, psycholocation told him which of the many rooms belonged to the young Greek woman. It was locked from the inside, but Theo has dealt with more complicated locks in his lifetime, and got it open within a minute. Casting a wary glance to see if anyone could see him, he tiptoed inside and closed the door behind him. The room was small and nicely decorated.

Moonlight falling through the window flooded the bed and the girl lying on it. Hayde slept stretched out on a blanket, dressed in a silk nightgown, breathing calmly like a baby. Theo smiled fondly and sat down next to her on the bed. He touched the girl's smooth naked hand with his open palm. She took a deep breath and raised her head with a low shout of fear.

"Shh, it's just me," he reassured her with a whisper. "My name is Theo de Bonneville. They also call me Fronde. You're Hayde, aren't you?"

"Yes," the girl stammered, brushing her hair from her face. "I've heard about you. I saw you in the computer room today. What are you doing in my room?"

"I'm here to give you what you've been waiting for."

Waking up, Hayde sat up and stared at him with her glistening eyes.

"Aren't you afraid?" she asked. "So far no one made up their mind to do it, and I have less and less time…"

"I don't scare easily," Fronde assured her.

Suddenly, Hayde wrapped her arms around his neck and pulled him closer, until through the thin linen of his blouse and silk shirt, he felt the warmth of her body on his. For a moment he lost his breath. She was so close, so young, so beautiful, and so innocently sensual that he felt a sudden embarrassment.

"We don't need to start right away," she whispered in his ear.

He said nothing. There was no more need for words when her parted lips touched his greedy mouth and everything suddenly ceased to matter.

….."Ready? Theo asked as they lay side by side, exhausted and happy.

"I am. What about you? You can still change your mind," answered Hayde.

Fronde smiled and kissed her softly on the cheek. After a while, his mouth sank lower and his sharp teeth cut through her delicate skin, revealing the source of life essence. He drank slowly, listening to the girl's breathing, her heartbeat, and with difficulty forced himself to finally tear his lips away from her neck. Then he propped himself up on one elbow and dug his teeth into his right wrist. He hadn't done this for a long time, and never wanted to – truth be told, he didn't think he would ever want to solidify someone again, but today it was different. He brought his bleeding wrist to Hayde's mouth. Although he knew what to expect, he was surprised by the strength with which the girl held his hand. He had the feeling that someone was tearing open his blood vessels. He tried to push Hayde away from him, but she immobilized his hands with hellish force, literally biting into his right wrist. He could not, he was not able to fight her, overwhelmed by what had awakened in her under the influence of the first sip of immortal blood. He was beginning to lose consciousness when the door to the room opened and Bozena burst into the room, accompanied by another well-built girl. The two dragged Hayde away, who was howling in an inhuman voice, and then Theo must have succumbed to the blackout caused by blood loss, because when he regained consciousness, he was lying in a completely different room, on a white medical bed. A girl in a nurse's cap was bending over him and injecting something into his hand. Bozena was sitting next to her.

"Oh, you," she said pitifully when she saw Fronde open his eyes. "I knew you were the risky type, but not to this extent. You could have died, you know? We stepped in at the last moment. Your sweet face has turned completely gray. Drink. Don't be humble."

She handed him a bottle of blood. Theo drank it in almost one breath, which did not quench his thirst at all, and rushed for another one. He never even imagined that you could be this thirsty. Only after extinguishing the heat in the esophagus, he looked at his hand, tied with a white bandage, and tried to move his fingers. He grimaced in pain.

"She bit you by the tendons," Bozena Sovova proceeded his question. "You won't be fully fit for a while."

"Doesn't matter, I'm lefthanded anyway. What about Hayde?"

"She's fine. She fell into lethargy. We'll take care of her now, and put on some damn clothes, pervert. Couldn't do without it, huh?"

Theo sat up and, moving his wounded arm with difficulty, began to pull on his pants.

"I could, but you know how it is, it would be of different taste," he replied. He still felt weak and would like to sleep, but looking at Bozena, he realized that she had something to say to him.

"Your friends told me on the phone that they were going to the haunted museum," the Czech woman sighed, seeing his expectant gaze. "Then contact with them was interrupted. I am, well, not particularly relaxed."

"Worried," Fronde corrected her automatically. "I am, how I should put it, forced to ask you to let me borrow one of your vehicles. I have to get there as soon as possible."

"I'll go with you. I'm not entrusting you with my Opel right now. We will also take Goran, he won't cry for any dumb reason," Bozena said categorically and ran out.

"If that is to be my destiny. Women have always given me orders, and I guess that's how it'll be until the end of the world," Theo grunted in mock displeasure while glancing at the silent nurse.

Bozena returned after a long time, dragging the sleepy and desperately yawning Goran behind her.

"You said you were in a hurry!" she shouted angrily.

"I'll be ready in a moment," Theo hastily pulled on his sweatshirt and followed them into the hallway.

The short walk to the parking lot wore him out like a marathon run. When he finally got into the gray Opel, he could hardly breathe, felt a tingling sensation in his side and felt as if his head was about to burst. For a long time, he gasped for air, like a diver who had been underwater for too long and could not speak.

"You did yourself in good, pal," Goran, watching him from under his eye, shook his head disapprovingly. "You're lucky that you're still alive, you damn madman."

"I know. If you were as old as I am, you would know that sometimes it is worth risking your life for somebody else."

"Blah blah blah. You have a crush on the chick, that's all."

"Stop it, you two," Bozena interposed. "Tell me, Fronde, what in the hell are they looking for in this museum? You've been there before, haven't you?"

Theo shrugged.

"I have no idea," he replied wearily. "Maybe the keeper told them something, although I have no idea what…"

He suddenly broke off and hit himself on the forehead with his palm.

"I'm so stupid! I'm so blind!" he exclaimed. "The voice in the basement, my photograph, personal tragedy... I am a colossal fool!"

"That's not only conceivable, but also probable. But where did this conclusion come from?"

"It's simple: our keeper, at any cost, wanted talk to his daughter from the other world. For this, in the basement of the museum, he created something like a small temple of some kind of a dark cult. He probably thought whatever the scary thing in there was, it could help him, but I don't think he could handle it. However, he was a member of Nuntia, moreover, one of its bosses, and had access to all data. And among this data there must have been some critical information..."

"What would that be?"

Fronde didn't answer immediately. His painted face, visible from the rearview mirror, had a strange, indescribable expression.

"Have you ever read the story: *Oh, Whistle, and I'll Come to You?*" he finally asked. "It's from a collection of horror stories called *Ghost Stories of an Antiquary.* Sometimes, a person is gifted with the ability to summon a creature that is best not looked at. Anyone who knows about it can use it... Girl, step on the gas. Their lives are in grave danger."

Bozena, apparently, did not understand a word of this speech, but, without objection, increased the speed. The silver-gray Opel raced through the night streets of Bratislava until it passed toll booths, and after another ten minutes of crazy driving, it pulled up outside the haunted museum.

There was no sign that anything unusual was going on inside, although... maybe there was? Eerie, barely perceptible cold-blue flickers crawled over the surface of the Gothic windows, and the perceptible smell of ozone wafted through the warm stagnant air, as if right before a summer storm. Despite this, the grass and bushes next to the descent to the basement were covered with brittle frost, crackling underfoot.

The wide-open door was no longer the entrance to the underground temple, but a window to another dimension – a dimension of boundless, inexpressibly menacing white with blue and yellow-red reflections. This whiteness had a strange quality: it blurred the contours of everything it enclosed, and Theo couldn't be sure if he really saw his friends in depth, or if it was just an illusion.

"Don't follow me in there until I give you the signal," he said to his companions, who, without a word, agreed with an impatience that didn't reflect their courage. They had never experienced anything like this before and would prefer not investigating it up close.

Fronde crossed the entrance, which was covered in snow and ice. Now that he was inside, he could see a little better and noticed his friends pressed against something that was most likely a wall, although at that moment he couldn't be sure. They were motionless, like ice sculptures, but he felt life smoldering in them, and silently breathed a sigh of relief. He didn't have time to approach them – something else was currently more important.

"I'm here, Cyrotte," he said in an undertone.

Some five meters away from him, the air thickened, changed color. As if from a nightmare, a black, tar-like figure emerged from within, its head framed by flaming hair. They were covered with red-black coat, curling restlessly, twisting as if they were alive, wrapping around the slender neck, slender shoulders and a beautifully sculpted head. Behind them was the form of a young girl. Fronde shuddered against his will. This child was even more terrifying than Cyrotte – at first glance, normal, but upon closer examination it seemed that she was made up of parts that didn't fit together at all. Theo felt weak at her sight, even though he was used to such things.

"He's dead, Cyrotte," he said through his tightening throat. "He's not going to feed you anymore. You have to leave. Please, don't hurt my friends and spare this place. Enough bad things have happened because of you. If you need one last victim, I'm right here."

Cyrotte took a step forward. Her bare feet left perfectly symmetrical, iron-burned footprints against the cold white background. She did not take her ruby glowing eyes from the vampire before her, and her gaze was focused and greedy. Theo, panting, removed the bandage from his right arm and scratched the fresh wound with his nails.

"Take my blood," he whispered in a barely audible voice. He fell to his knees, losing strength when an inhuman force pressed on him, which he could not resist no matter his efforts.

Cyrotte stopped. She reached out and touched the bleeding wound with her fingers and backed away. She slowly collected the blood with the tip of her tongue, still staring at the man kneeling in front of her. The solid white color suddenly burst into flames as sharp as spilled gasoline. It lit up in the blink of an eye and so suddenly that Bozena and Goran, looking at all this, were not even frightened, it went out, and with it everything that could be considered unusual disappeared. The basement was again just a basement, and anything that made it a satanic temple melted into a shapeless mass covered with a thin layer of slag. Freed from the chains of terrible cold, the friends tried to get up from the brick floor, still bitten by the frost. Bozena and Goran rushed to their aid. Fortunately, the cognac was with them, so they poured it down the throats of their new friends, massaged their icy limbs, and slowly made them stand up on their own.

"I don't understand any of this," Never grunted when he finally managed to hold back the chattering of his teeth.

"What was all that? A collective hallucination?" Goran asked incredulously.

"A hallucination would not be the reason for such a mess," Oggy snapped back.

Theo, still kneeling on the floor, gazed at him with eyes that had no pupils or whites, just a shimmering black color that stood out sharply against his snow-white face.

"The keeper summoned a Cyrotte and demanded that she return his daughter to him," he said slowly. "To remain here, she needed someone's death, so he released the experimental wasps, leaked the virus, and killed Leland, who took him by surprise at the research station. He performed several dark rituals to bring the child back, but he didn't realize that Cyrotte couldn't resurrect anyone. However, it is able to create frames using parameters taken directly from the memory of the 'supplicant'. It was the keeper's memories of the deceased child that created the ghost that we saw here. She lived a life dependent on what was imprinted in the mind of this unfortunate man, and after his death she began to crumble, like a statue made of unbaked clay in the rain."

"So many people had to die just so he could have his illusions a few moments longer..." Oggy whispered in horror.

"I wonder if Nuntia knew of his obsession," Gerard was still shaking like a leaf in the wind and rubbing his shoulders.

"My guess is no. They are vampire hunters, not Satanists. Fronde, are you okay?"

Never rushed to his friend to support him.

"He had a difficult night," Bozena explained to him, "first Hyde, and then this mess here. I swear my heart dropped to my heels as soon as I saw her. What the hell was that?"

"You don't want to know. I have no idea how Fronde knows her, and I don't want to know, but this is the second time that we're saved thanks to his acquaintance with this devil. She, like most women, has a weakness for him."

"Not me. Hey Theo, open your mouth and have a drink, it's good for you."

Bozena poured Fronde some brandy and stroked his cheek. Theo swallowed the alcohol and opened his eyes, which now looked normal, human.

"She'll kill me one day," he said with deep conviction.

"It's your own fault. That you wouldn't even reject the devil, you must be some extreme erotomaniac," the Czech woman snorted, helping him to sit down. Fronde moved her hands away and stood up, holding onto the wall. He was still terribly pale, but he was much more awake.

"It's not like that," he said. "I really don't why I am at the mercy of this lady. Maybe it's that relationship of mine? Just kidding. It's just that Cyrotte spares some people, me being one of them. Perhaps she is impressed by the fact that I'm not afraid of her, or maybe it's the aura."

He looked around the ruined basement. Now there was nothing magical about it, it looked like one big trash can. Terrified roosters, almost all black, crawled over the heaps of rubbish and slag.

"Look at that, the broth is walking on two legs. What are we going to do with them?" Gladiator asked. With a decisive movement, he took a bottle of cognac from Goran and drained it to the bottom in one gulp.

"We'll let them free. Outside, they can easily find something to eat until someone turns them into the broth you mentioned."

The friends began to catch the roosters, which clucked desperately, trying to escape them, as far as they could on their little feet. Never, chasing them around the basement, suddenly stopped and began to listen. Everyone fell silent, noticing the unusual expression on his face, and then heard a faint meow coming from the far corner of the basement. Never went in that direction and returned after a moment, carrying the little bundle with great care.

"It's a child," he muttered with a completely stunned face. "It's at most three days old, cold, wet and probably hungry. By Rama, how did it get here?"

"We probably won't find out," Gerard said. "The keeper is dead, and Cyrotte left. Fronde could summon her I'm sure, but that seems like a bad idea. He risks his life every time."

"What if it helped the child? It's so cute," Oggy said in surprise, taking the crying newborn from Never. "Is it a boy or a girl?"

"Check that yourself, if you like, but we'll talk about that later. In the meantime, let's get those damn chickens out of here and head to the base, because dawn is coming soon.

And only after half an hour of intensive cooperation of all those present, they managed to persuade the birds to leave the basement, and only then were they able to leave. Goran was driving the Opel, next to him was Bozena Sovova. Both were silent. The child, wrapped in Gladiator's shirt, slept, snuggled against Oggy's chest, who looked pleased. Never and Fronde, on the other hand, whispered nervously to each other, looking anxiously at the child. Vampires are not known to be suitable for caring for an infant, regardless of gender. Although there have been cases when a vampire kidnapped someone's child and raised them as their own, all such stories ended fatally, most often by being found.

Vampire life is incompatible with parenthood, even when it comes to adoptive parents. Friends would like to return the child to his mother, but they did not know where to find her and even who she was. They didn't even know who was responsible for placing the child in the temple, but it was probably not the keeper.

Cyrotte, on the other hand, was not involved in kidnappings. Apparently, they missed someone else, maybe not even just one person, but a whole group of Cyrotte worshippers. It must have seemed to them a revelation of Satan. Judging by her appearance and demeanor, it was hard to blame them. So, a sect, possibly uniting members of Nuntia, and it was scary to think what rituals were performed in that basement...

"Why are we going to the hospital and not to the orphanage or the police?" Goran finally asked as they stopped at a traffic light.

"Because the child requires medical attention," Oggy said. "Besides, no one is going to question us at the hospital, and the police or the shelter may. After all, we still don't know anything about this kid, and if we were interrogated, strange things might come to light."

Bozena shook her curly head, muttering something to herself in Czech.

"You know what?" she said after a moment. "You better get back to your own place. My people and I will investigate the case to the end and take care of the Nuntia here. It shouldn't be too hard to send the corresponding services on them, and we will try to ensure that there is a sufficient amount of relevant evidence. They are dangerous people. They should not be allowed to continue their experiments."

***

"That was a good, well done operation. I'll give you some time off now," the general said and hung up.

"Great," snorted Oggy. "We did the hard work and he's the won who'll win the laurels."

"The philodendrons too," Gerard agreed. "It's too bad, but that's just how it is. Do you know Tygier's condition?"

"Dea says there have been no changes. Wait, this report from the central lab is really interesting," Never took a sip of his cocktail, put the glass down on the table and began flipping pages covered machine-printed letters: The mysterious virus that infected those people was entirely artificial, created by technology much more advanced than the mainstream world. It attacked the pancreas, causing a rapid overproduction of insulin. It had an interesting property: it was killed by direct sunlight after only thirty minutes.

This is why it did not spread. Now about the wasps. They were not wasps, but a mutant strain of African bees. This was only established by DNA testing. The mutation was cleverly programmed because the gene that determines the colors has been changed. A side effect, unforeseen by Nuntia's biologists, was an increase in aggression and a shortening of the life of the bee to ten days."

"Working days?" Gladiator asked.

"Shut up. Now here's where it gets interesting. Those bees were conditioned. They were supposed to attack living objects, not emitting any smell. It was unfortunate that the conditioning didn't work and the insects that were supposed to kill vampires (since you're probably aware already that a few hundred stings of these little monsters can kill any of us) attacked humans. I guess you could call it an accident at work, but not necessarily. Nuntia operates on two fronts. On one hand, they fight with vampires, on the other, they create things that can be used on people. For what purpose? Apparently, in the documents we delivered to the headquarters, there are some that suggest that this organization wants to somehow connect to the apparatus of power. The VASP agency is preparing an official report for the European Union on this matter. Of course, it will not talk about vampires, but about the threat of modern fascism."

"That's heavy," Fronde muttered, continuing to massage his sore wrist. He was still feeling the effects of Hayde's bite, and his fingers were recovering very slowly. The monkey sitting on his shoulder ate tangerines, looking at the friends with large, trusting eyes. They were getting used to it.

"Heavy or not, we've done our part on this matter," Gerard said grimly. "Let the agency worry about the rest. Since when were vampires promoted to the commando saving the world from destruction?"

He lay down on the couch, tucking a rolled-up blanket under his head. Since their return they lived in a rented cottage, incompletely furnished and rather dirty. They felt like a stranger in it, but still better than behind the walls of the agency, since they could run away at any moment.

"Don't be so overwhelmed, your poor child. Did you get Superman complex?" Gladiator laughed unpleasantly, continuing his daily dumbbell exercises.

"Saving the world or not, whatever, we've done our part. I wonder how the baby is doing."

"I called Bozena," Theo said a little indistinctly, as he was just tightening the bandage on his wrist, helping himself with his teeth. "Weird thing. The baby has disappeared from the maternity ward in central Berlin. How it ended up in the museum near Bratislava is hard to say. In addition, despite a meticulous examination of the surveillance tapes, the police did not discover the manner in which it was kidnapped. Maybe it's better not to know?"

Never smiled sarcastically, squinting his golden eyes in the process.

"Life's not an Agatha Christie's crime novel," he said emphatically. "Not everything can be solved. What's important is that we're all alive, the situation has been brought under control and that the child has returned to her rightful mother. I just want to know how many such babies haven't come back... I don't think we'll ever know."

"That's for the better," Oggy shuddered. She still couldn't get used to what they discovered in the course of their work – not so much paranormal phenomena, but what seemingly ordinary people are capable of.

"What about Gusto? Did they capture him?" Gerard suddenly remembered and lifted his head from the improvised pillow to look at Fronde. No one doubted that Gusto was behind the poisoning of a member of Nuntia captured by Bratislava – he fit the description of a 'Dutch scientist' perfectly. The renegade vampire was still dangerous.

"So far he's been able to slip through," Theo replied, stroking the tamarin on the back. "He's smarter than they think. I have a feeling we'll meet him again."

"He's not the only one I'd like to meet again," Never finished his drink and took a small card out of his pocket. He set it on the table, leaning against the vase. It was a picture of Vandis, taken from the basement, as incomprehensible as most of the phenomena they dealt with there. It was incomprehensible how Nuntia came into possession of this photo, how Vandis could have lived after he had died in their hands, and the most incomprehensible thing was that the photo was changing. Vandis's figure faded slowly.

It couldn't have been a flaw of the emulsion, since the entire background was untouched, only the detective's image blurred, as if evaporating. They didn't include this photo in their file. They preferred the agency not to know about the existence of someone like Vandis, although neither of them fully believed that their friend from the U.S was still alive. However, the hope that this photo awakened in them was priceless. And it was only theirs.

In the ensuing silence, Never's phone suddenly rang. The Indian answered and listened for a moment, answering what someone said to him in monosyllables. Finally he turned off his cell phone and looked at his friends with a gloomy look.

"It was Dea," he said, "Lambdon Tygier died a few minutes ago."

Part 3

Posessed

"Why are vampires always portrayed so idiotically in movies?" Gerard asked one evening as they were leaving the theater.

"How do you mean, exactly?" Never looked at him with light amusement.

"I mean, they have such demonic makeup around their eyes, red lips, huge teeth and such a specific manner of movement. They emit some kind of growl, hiss, and they are all gloomy, like the night of St. Bartholomew. And notice, how in the movie they always attack from the front, but in real life they don't. You even taught me how to sneak up behind people's backs yourself."

"Well, there's no way for directors of cheap horror flicks to know that," Theo laughed. "You should understand, kid that people cannot believe that a vampire differs from them only in their diet. The rest of the differences are irrelevant. Look at me, for example: I am over six hundred years old, and I still remain who I was before, only more educated than I was.

Someday I will die, but before that happens, I will remain human. I have human weaknesses and human virtues... a movie about me would be just boring, without the demonic smiles and bloody orgies. Who would watch that?"

"On the other hand," Gerard clearly didn't want to give up, "think how wonderful it would be to be able to fly, climb walls like a lizard, or slide into a room through the keyhole..."

"Have you read the works of Saadi Gulistan? He is a Persian poet. He described in detail how one woman betrayed her husband through a keyhole... a very large one, of course."

"Fronde, your brain has degenerated a lot," Oggy said indignantly. "How can you boast about reading filth like that?"

"Filth? My dear, Saadi Gulistan's works are a world-renowned classic, like that Brantome whom I knew personally..."

"I'd like to note that such classics aren't worth shit."

"I guess Gerard has a point," Never listened to this quarrel completely inattentively, busy with his own thoughts. "The film and the book image of a typical vampire is, rather, the embodiment of the human dream of a superman. Obviously, that's a dumb approach. In one book, vampires shouted every two pages that they were the new gods of humanity... by Brahma and Vishnu, I have never laughed so much in my life. What gods, from a bunch of unfortunate madmen?"

"Terrible," Fronde agreed with him.

"Although, if you think about it, I knew one such person of our blood, who tried to pretend to be the god of death. Wore a black cloak, painted over the upper and lower eyelids with dark henna, drew his nails to almost two inches long, but it eventually ended badly..."

They walked through the lantern-lit streets, heading for the nearest park. They didn't want to go back to their cottage, and they looked for an excuse to wander a little more. They tried not to get used to rented apartments, didn't show their presence in them, not changing even a single piece of furniture, hanging a picture on the wall, or anything else. It was safer that way.

Since they no longer resided at the agency's headquarters, they managed on their own and moved frequently to make them harder to find. They were in constant contact with the agency, as well as with Dea, who remained at the headquarters. She could afford it because she was little known, like Conan. Lenore left the agency, summoned by some old friends, Lambdon Tygier is dead, and an outsider might think that even if there were vampires in the organization, they have long since left.

Only General Dagwood and his closest associates, who were fully trusted, knew that the Tau squad was still active. It was better that way, although Gerard complained that they were living like stray cats again, and Oggy turned into a dog every time they moved and could not regain her human form for several days. In fact, neither of them wanted to move, and only Jen was indifferent, as long as she was with Theo.

"Frondy, dragging this monkey around everywhere will eventually get us all in trouble," Never spoke in a bad mood, but he could not help but notice that his friend fell in love with the little tamarin like his own child. He has always loved animals, and woe to anyone who he caught being cruel to animals. However, he usually understood that having a pet of his own was dangerous for the undead. This time he was deaf to the voice of reason.

"I will not leave Jen to the mercy of some bastards, no matter what our problems are," he said, and ended the discussion.

There really were no problems with the tamarin. She rode in a cat carrier, registered as a cat, was polite, clean and without objection, she ate what was bought for her. He had to admit that everyone cared about her, not just Fronde, and sometimes too much. For example, Gladiator secretly treated the monkey with halva or chocolate, which Never strictly prohibited. The Hindu was the only one who knew monkeys and knew which diet was right for which, but Gladiator was difficult to keep track of.

"That last case won't give me peace," Gerard said, kicking the pebbles in the road. "We've never encountered one that was this dark. There is no anchor point."

"Don't like losing?" Never laughed. "My dear Gerard, you can't always win. We had only unknown people at our disposal. We can't even tell if this... Roget we were told to look for exists. We only have a testimony of a disabled boy and some strange events. Nothing more. Well, it didn't work. VASP will assign us another case soon, perhaps from day to day."

They walked through the park, which was currently empty, listening to the rustle of trees. In such places they were always comfortable, not to mention the fact that it was easy to 'hunt' there. Supplies were still their Achilles' heel. Despite supplies from the agency, they still had to find victims among drunks and various derailed people, because in order for a vampire to stay in shape, they must not starve. Although the hunger tolerance of the 'children of the night' is phenomenal compared to the pure humans, it comes at a price. Even a one-year hunger strike will not kill the undead, but a two-day hunger will lead to a significant decrease not so much in physical strength as in intellectual abilities. Friends could not afford it, so they took every opportunity to eat.

"These parks are like a small restaurant. You can find everything here, including the girl and the client," said Gladiator as they gathered again after a successful hunt.

"Someone is following us," Oggy said, bouncing merrily up the path.

"I know, I noticed it too," Never replied, wiping his mouth with a napkin. "One man, strong build, definitely a man, young and athletic. I bet it's Conan."

They stopped, intrigued. They did not have to wait long before the grim giant appeared before them.

"You're lucky we're used to you," Theo said cheerfully, looking happily at his enormous figure. "If you surprised some old man in a wheelchair like that, he would have a heart attack at the sight of you."

"Why are you following us, coach?" Gladiator asked.

"We've got a problem," Conan said shortly.

"We can see that," Gerard nodded. "Otherwise you wouldn't be here. But what's the problem?"

"It's a big one," Conan sighed and ran a hand through his disheveled hair. "The agency doesn't know we're here."

"We?" Never was surprised.

"Yeah. Me, Dea and Stasiek Zakrzewski. But I guess we're not going to shout our secrets in a public park. Come with me."

"Drop the sticks, come with us," Gladiator quoted. "What are you staring at? This is how the demonstrators cried during martial law. To militia officers. In ZOMO they threw tabloids, because there was nothing to discuss with these hammers. Strikes, demonstrations, Radio Free Europe were entertaining, and a flower cross was erected in front of St. Anne's Church. I hear the times weren't that bad, but there was nothing to eat."

They became lost in thought.

"All times are bad," Theo finally sighed. "All of them. I already know a thing or two about this. Only in retrospect does something seem better than another thing."

"Don't philosophize, Fronde. You're right, yes, but it all seems silly to you, I don't know why, Never spoke in a tone of good advice. Lead, Conan. In any case, we now have nothing to do."

"We could go home and clean," Oggy muttered unconditionally. "Awful dirty in there."

Wherever they lived for more than a few days, it was a terrible mess as none of them were eager to clean. Somehow, they didn't feel such a need. Only Gerard sometimes hinted that it would be a bit of a chore to smooth their current home a bit, but his words had no effect. Now, too, no one showed too much enthusiasm.

"Better listen to what Dea has to tell us," Theo said.

The others agreed, and followed Conan, who glided ahead of them like a tank of the latest generation. As it turned out, he and the other two rented a triple room in a nearby hotel, not hiding at all, as if they were the most ordinary people. Such nonchalance was dangerous, and Never shook his head disapprovingly but said nothing.

"There you are," Dea said as they entered. "We've been trying to track you down for two days."

"If it was easy, any dumb monkey-brain would find us," said Gladiator jokingly.

Dea ignored the remark.

"We quit VASP," she continued. "After the death of the general, it was the only reasonable solution."

"What?!" The friends exchanged stunned glances. They didn't expect such news.

Dea raised her manicured eyebrows slightly.

"Didn't you know? He had a stroke."

"Just like that?" Theo was clearly surprised.

"I don't know. He just had one, that's it. Is that so strange?"

"You don't have to shout," Fronde touched her hand apologetically. "It's just somehow hard for me to imagine... he was so strong. Go on."

"We covered our tracks as best we could." The three of us set up a detective agency, the papers were given to us by a full-time counterfeiter for VASP. He owed me a favor. We decided to do the same as you, but we got stuck right at the get-go. Talk, Stasiek, what are you sitting like a pole for!"

"Talk to a brick wall all you want, it won't respond," Gladiator remarked.

His brother ran a hand over his fashionably shaven head. Though similar to the Gladiator, he was shorter and much thinner than him, and at the moment looked even thinner. And very tired.

"You must know, I'm being blackmailed," he began. "This guy recently came to see me. He told me that he was a pedophile and that he didn't want to live like that anymore. That he knows who I am and who to report that to. And that he will, unless I kill him."

"I would do him this favor," Dea interjected viciously.

"He doesn't have the courage himself, and is afraid of hurting some child in the end. All in all, he's a total pervert. It's a shame that he can't be cured somehow... anyway, he stuck to me like tar, and while I was negotiating with him, suddenly he said that he knew who and how infected Tygier with AIDS."

"Then let him talk!" Gerard shouted, as if it would bring their friend back to life.

Doctor Zakrzewski smiled sadly.

"It's not that simple," he said. "He wants me to kill him as soon as he gives me the information. And what if the information needs to be completed or verified, then what? Besides, I did not become a doctor to kill."

"I think you're the only one," Gerard said maliciously.

"Why are you so anti today, Gerard? Stop latching onto everyone and let's finally find out what's going on," Theo suggested seeing that Dea was already getting ready to kick his friend in the right leg, to which she was closest.

"I talked with the guy and suddenly he said something that alarmed me," continued Stasiek. "He said that a girl who introduced herself as Nuntia called and tried to blackmail him. Apparently unaware that Nuntia was an organization and not a peculiar name. He is afraid of others, he is afraid of himself, he is a nervous wreck in general, and the fact that I am a vampire was revealed to him by an idiotic accident. And that wasn't something he got scared of."

"Go on," Never encouraged him.

"I'm in a dead end. In addition, our first serious client commissioned us to track this particular individual, because she suspects that he has abducted her daughter, despite the lack of any evidence of it. We want to find this child, but the trail given to us by the client leads nowhere. This pedophile would probably not do it. He hates himself for his inclinations, but Dea and Conan checked him thoroughly and he really didn't abduct the baby."

"Wait a minute," Never raised both hands defensively. "What do you guys want from us exactly? Should we do your part and do the guy in or help you with the investigation or take care of Nuntia? We can't do everything at once. And what about Tygier?"

"That's the thing. The guy gave the name Celia Bourdon. I checked. She is a Nuntia activist, a skilled biochemist, and as to the infection method... The matter was simple. That we didn't come up with it right away... she gave Tygier a bunch of immunosuppressive drugs, and then smuggled him a suspension of live HIV viruses in a portion of frozen blood. Probably for this purpose she ordered kidnapping him. They gave him the drug so he couldn't remember anything. He was supposed to be a guinea pig, but it seems then that Nuntia lost track of him."

"How does your pedophile know all this?" Theo asked distrustfully.

"He overheard it. When this girl called him trying to blackmail him, he was so shocked that he didn't hang up at all. She then called someone named Holger and talked about it. There must have been a short circuit on the line, because our pervert heard everything."

"*Tiens, tiens,*" Fronde muttered and bit his lips lightly, "I don't mean to be cruel, but this guy really needs to be taken out. That is not negotiable. That's one. Two, we already know that Nuntia has not stopped their experiments, so we must continue to search for their workplace, regardless of other tasks. What else do we know?"

"That a vampire infected with AIDS doesn't infect others himself," Dea replied. "Lambdon had an affair with two ordinary girls and with Lenore at a time when he wasn't feeling well anymore. All three affairs lasted quite a long time, and yet none of them ended up infecting the partner. I checked, and it can't just be a lucky coincidence."

"Always something."

"Look," said Conan. "We'll take care of the baby ourselves, but we ask that you distract Nuntia away from us. They're right on our tail."

"Sure, that's what we're good at," Never agreed. "It would be nasty on our part to put that on you."

"Stasiek, tell me where to find your pedophile," Theo asked doctor Zakrzewski, who was sitting with an expression as if he just swallowed a frog.

"Why the hell now?"

"Because I agree with Dea, and you are too thin-skinned to settle this matter. If the dude wants to move to the angels, I'll make it easy for him."

"Fronde, don't you have any morals?"

"I do, if necessary. I don't if it gets in the way of something. So are you giving it to me or not?"

The doctor took a piece of paper and wrote a dozen words on it.

"You damn Satan... have the address and piss off. I know that you're all right, but at least understand that I can't kill."

Fronde smirked, took the note from him, and left, closing the door behind him.

"He's going to do it?" Oggy asked, looking at Never questioningly.

"Of course. Theo hates pedophiles and woe to any he gets his hands on. He believes that people like them have no right to live, and frankly I agree with him."

"I won't say anything," Dea said gloomily. Never, will you take care of those jerks at Nuntia?"

"I already said yes. It could be some cut off group, we tracked the main organization with the help of VASP and Interpol, and they're far away now. Only remnants remained. Anything else, doctor?"

Dea was silent for a moment, staring blankly out the window.

"Do you trust the general's son?" she asked finally.

Never shrugged. He didn't quite know how to answer that question – Sheridan Dagwood looked like his father almost in every way, but instilled less confidence in him than the deceased general. He could have worked for him because the agency was paying well, but he knew he would have to be careful. And make sure that no one in the entire agency has even the slight idea of their current address.

"I guess I'd be careful around him," he said finally.

"I thought so. Something about him doesn't suit me either, though I don't know what. This is why I preferred to disappear, and before that I thoroughly wiped the agency's computers of all information that could be traced back to us or you."

"The erased information can be retrieved," Oggy pointed out.

"I used a virus developed by one of Stasiek's buddies. They won't, even if they work on it for the rest of time."

With a nervous movement of her hand, she ruffled her copper hair. She had cut it even shorter and looked more like a handsome boy, especially in the oversized sweater that masked her figure.

"So now we're dealing with the kidnapping of a child, the probable murder of the client's wife and Nuntia..." she finished in a lower voice.

"We'll take care of Nuntia, I already told you," Never said impatiently, and jumped up when dense darkness rose from the floor next to him.

"You brought him to your office!" Gerard exclaimed. He had almost forgotten about that extraordinary figure of their world that appeared and disappeared whenever it wanted.

"What's so strange about that?" Shadow hissed slowly. "After all, the profession of a detective is absolutely perfect for me. Should I speak in front of them, girl?"

"Do what you want," Dea sighed.

"The child has not been abducted. The father sold them through an illegal adoption agency," reported Shadow. "How you're going to prove it, that's your problem. Be warned that it will not be easy."

"I wonder if the mother knows anything about it," Stasiek mused.

"Unlikely. She wouldn't have hired us. And this son of a... oh well, we'll get him. Don't take it personally, friends, but you should get out of here now. We have to get to work."

"Okay, Dea. We'll be in touch," Never gave her a kiss and left, pushing his friends in front of him.

The fact that one of Nuntia's divisions was stalking Dea didn't surprise him too much. Even after they had caused serious trouble for the entire organization, she was still able to continue her work. They tried to paralyze 'that hydra' by hitting the management, but made a mistake. In this case, those who were 'at the bottom' were especially dangerous. They still believed in their noble fight for a genetically and ideologically better humanity.

Nuntia knew a thing or two about brainwashing. Its acolytes were convinced that by becoming vampires they were sacrificing their existence for the sake of a higher good. Their ultimate goal was to build a world in which only a person who has passed the racial and ideological verification would be allowed to become undead. They enrolled only those who conformed to the Nordic model, drawn from the insane works of Nazi theorists, and ruthlessly shared views on the purity of blood.

Eliminating generally small groups of activists was not easy, because first they had to be tracked down, then cornered, and then managed in such a way that the police would recognize these people as criminals or dangerous madmen. But they were good at it, getting better and better. They managed to drive their enemies into a corner, even when the situation was unfavorable for them. But the amount of enemies was constantly increasing.

They were a bit surprised when the insistent doorbell rang them the next day.

"Fronde went to pick up girls as usual and lost the key," Oggy growled, dragging herself out of the bed to open it.

As it turned out, she was right. Theo burst into the apartment furious and feverish.

"Where the hell is that Stasiek?! He screamed. "Just wait till I tell him! That fool!"

"Tell me what happened," Gladiator demanded, giving him a soothing punch on the back.

"What happened? What happened? It just so happened that this damn pervert made a fool out of him!" Fronde raged. "He didn't want to die, either way all he would need for that is a rope. He thought that if a vampire killed him, he would become a vampire himself, and then he would be free to let his sick desires loose and no one would do anything to him! I corrected him, you can be sure, but I still can't calm down."

He grabbed the bottle of cognac on the table and took a long sip.

"I was able to probe his mind," he continued, wiping his mouth with the sleeve of his shirt. "I don't use this trick every day, it exhausts me too much, but this time I forced myself to. What a freak, I'm telling you. Sometimes it doesn't pay to be a vampire at all, you know too much."

"All right, calm down," Oggy forced him to sit down and began to gently massage his neck and shoulders. "You're so tense. You can't get so worked up about every pervert, there are too many of them in the world. At least this one won't hurt anyone anymore."

"At least. Oh, I feel that our lives will get confusing now..." Theo muttered, much calmer, surrendering to her treatments with clear pleasure. The coming weeks would reveal that he was right after all.

*****

A terrible noise woke the three friends from their restless sleep. Oggy, curled up on Fronde's blanket, raised her head as well and growled, her ears shaking warily.

"An earthquake?" Gerard asked absently.

"Maybe it's the end of the world?" Fronde yawned with a vague hope in his voice.

"It looks like someone broke in through the window," Never said after some thought. "It's that home alarm, Yanek's idea."

The 'home alarm' consisted of a simple sheet of metal on the floor under the window, and several heavy pots on the windowsill. Anyone trying to get through the window would have to knock down at least one of them, and it gave an indescribable thud. In the cottage they rented, only this room had a window. The building was conceived as a photo studio, so it did not require more windows. It was very convenient for the friends.

"So, are we fighting or going back to sleep?" Gerard groaned, his expression clearly indicating that he would have preferred the latter.

"I don't know if there is anyone left to fight with. Our visitor probably escaped when the things fell," Theo rubbed his face with his hands and patted Oggy's head, who was cuddling up to him.

The girl had been in the form of a dog for two weeks and there was no indication that this would change. The periods she kept in human form got shorter and shorter, which worried everyone. They knew that their friend needed help, but didn't know how to help her.

"Maybe it's not a robber, and there's simply a fire?" thought Gerard.

"If that's the case, let's get back to sleep. We're not firefighters, are we?"

"Stop fooling around," Never interrupted them with disgust. "What if it's some loser from Nuntia, and not a petty thief, then what?"

Blissful snoring interrupted further reflections of the friends. Gladiator was somehow not awakened by the noise from the other room – it's unlikely that even a salvo of heavy artillery could do so. When the blond highlander fell asleep, he suddenly seemed deaf, because no sounds, no matter how terrible they were, could reach him.

"This one is so blissfully ignorant," Theo said sadly, looking at his sleeping friend with some envy.

Never reached for a decorative vase, took the decorative dried freesias, and poured the water on Gladiator's head. The effect was immediate.

"You degenerate linnet, marinated in the seven thieves' vinegar!" shouted the Pole, sitting up on the bed.

"Get up," Never ordered him calmly. "Someone broke in through the window."

"If he got in, he can get out himself," Gerard sighed, propping his head in his hands.

Oggy barked furiously, clearly trying to get their attention. Gladiator swore like a shoemaker, wiping his wet head with a sheet as their guest appeared at the bedroom door – the least expected of all guests.

"Vandis!" Theo shouted in amazement.

Indeed, in front of them was the mysterious detective whom they met in America. He looked exactly the way they remembered – tall and slender to the point of exaggeration, in ecru clothes and long hair, smooth as glass, cascading down to his shoulders.

"I'm so glad you're alive!" Gerard exclaimed impetuously, jumping out of bed and squeezing him hard.

"I'm glad you're alive, too," Vandis replied, responding to his hug. "You were not easy to find."

"Good thing you went the distance, then."

"Kyrie eleyson! Who is this weirdo?" asked Gladiator in an alpine dialect, looking at the blue-eyed newcomer with clear distrust.

"Let me introduce you, he's an Angel," Never answered. "A real angel, so try not to anger him."

"Angel…" Gladiator said surprised, with a dumb smile.

Vandis bent over to Oggy, who was jumping next to him, and touched her head between her ears. Almost immediately, the huge shepherd dog shuddered, and a tiny naked girl appeared in its place. Fronde threw her a shirt.

"Cover yourself, shameless girl," he said sternly.

"Tell that to your grandma," retorted Oggy, wrapped the shirt around herself and ran to the bathroom.

Meanwhile, the still sleepy Gladiator tried to get dressed, which, oddly enough, he failed to do.

"What the hell is wrong with my pants?!" he finally screamed angrily.

Never hit him on the neck with his open palm.

"You're trying to stick both legs in one pantleg, you dummy," he realized.

Gladiator turned around, and for a moment he had a fight with his pants, during which the highlander finally sobered up enough to correctly assess the situation.

"Logically speaking, this can't be an angel," he said, finally pulling on his jeans. "First of, he has no wings, second, I can see him, and third, I don't think any artist has ever placed an angel in sunglasses in their painting."

Never waved his hand at him and addressed the patiently waiting Vandis:

"I suppose you looked for us not to see our beautiful eyes, but for completely different reasons. What brings you to us, Angel?"

The detective didn't answer for a second. And only after a long silence did he speak again, his voice sounding weaker and somehow incoherent.

"I have a problem," he said.

"Speak freely," Gerard encouraged him. "Problems are our specialty. We are especially good at getting caught in them, we are world champions in that."

Vandis went to the wall and touched it with his hand. An enlarged image of a young man in black pants and a collared shirt appeared on the smooth surface. It didn't look like a projector image, but rather a three-dimensional, extremely clear projection.

"Meredith Johnson," said the detective. "He's a vampire like you, but he used to be a priest. He still considers himself a priest, which is logical that he was never formally deprived of ordination. He and his group are the Ghost Hunters."

The friends laughed because the lately fashionable *Ghostbusters* was their favorite comedy.

"It's no laughing matter," Vandis continued. "Paranormal phenomena destroy the lives of many people who have no one to turn to with their problems. Meredith has become an expert in such matters. His team works with him, or I should say, worked with him, whose members need not be mentioned now. It so happened that Meredith did not foresee in his work one thing, that Evil as such is neither an abstraction nor an invention of anyone's mind."

"What do you mean, exactly?" Fronde asked.

"That Evil doesn't like when something gets in its way. It must be fought skillfully and very carefully, and it is a job neither for humans nor vampires, who, after all, is just an immortal human. Meredith didn't recognize this. His companions who died paid for it, and now he himself is the prey of the Messenger. There are reasons why I cannot help him. But you can."

"We can?" Gladiator asked doubtfully.

"You can. However, you should be aware of the risks. Everything you have dealt with so far is a trifle compared to true Evil. Are you willing to help, or not?"

Never shrugged, not knowing what to think of it. Although he had heard more than once that 'something has stuck to someone', he didn't attach much importance to these stories. Evil in isolation from people was a purely abstract concept for him, and the fact that it could physically threaten someone was beyond his understanding.

Before he could find an answer, someone rang the bell.

"I'm coming, I'm coming!" Gladiator exclaimed angrily and, yawning strongly, ran into the hall. He still couldn't get rid of the remnants of sleep.

"Password," he tossed into the microphone at the door.

"The best chestnuts are in Place Pigalle," came the irritated reply. "Open up, idiot, or I'll knock your teeth off!"

"Ah, our little dove," the highlander, who liked Dea very much, was delighted and quickly unlocked the door.

"What are you standing there for, help me," the girl snapped, struggling with Conan's huge body. "This bastard must weigh a ton."

Gladiator propped up Conan on the other side, and together they dragged him into the apartment. He was half-conscious, bloody, and they could not drag him onto the sofa – he fell on the carpet.

"What happened?" Theo asked anxiously, bending over his friend.

"What do you think? We ran into Nuntia! You were supposed to take care of them!" Dea screamed angrily.

"We did!" Never said offended and began to examine the coach. "Maybe it's some new group. Or maybe it's not Nuntia at all. Don't yell at us. You have no right to."

"I don't care what I have the right to," Dea ended her statement with a long, unique patchwork of words.

"What happened to her?" Vandis asked Gerard.

The man looked at him in surprise.

"Nothing," he replied after a moment, as if that was enough to answer him. "She was born like this."

"We have to get him to Stasiek's infirmary," Never said, looking up. "He was shot with a small-caliber weapon, the bullet is stuck in the mediastinum."

"We're not going to take him anywhere. The ones who shot at us are sniffing around the area, we won't get far. In any case, it's a miracle that I managed to confuse them enough to not put you guys in danger."

"Then we have to remove the bullet ourselves."

"No, you've lost your mind! Since when am I a thorax surgeon?!"

"Your specialization has just changed. I'll get the tool ready, and you wash your hands."

Never always carried a well-stocked doctor's bag with him, although he was not a doctor himself – at the very least he did not have a diploma.

Dea took a deep breath, about to blurt out a set of invectives, but the fight was suddenly interrupted by Vandis who was watching them."

"Allow me," he said, and bent over the wounded giant. Reaching out, he touched his chest with an open palm. Conan gave a long groan. Vandis stood up and held out the small bloody object to Never.

Dea whistled delightedly.

"You, who actually are you, that you know such tricks?" she asked.

"An Angel," he replied in such a natural voice, as if he was announcing that he was an insurance agent."

The doctor examined him from head to toe, her admiration replaced by incredulous amazement. She turned to Never:

"An Angel, huh? Should I pray to him or maybe test his reflexes?"

The Indian told her everything he knew about Vandis, continuing to treat Conan's wound, making his statements as accurate as possible. Dea, who was an extreme realist, didn't believe, as Theo claimed, half of what she saw with her own eyes, let alone stories that sounded like pure fantasy. Never's words, even the ones most careful and measured, must have been impossible to accept to her. However, after a moment's thought, she nodded.

"If you say so," she said. "Let's say I'm buying this, and that's mainly because I don't have the head to argue right now. We all have a problem, because if what hunted us down was not Nuntia... that means we have a new adversary, and a very dangerous one."

"Let's not ponder about that just yet," decided Never, getting up from his knees. "We're not going to drag this damn elephant around, let him lay on the carpet. Fronde, Gerard, Oggy... Oggy! Get out of the bathroom, are you going to sit there for the rest of time?! All three of you, get out on reconnaissance. And may the hand of God protect you, that you don't let them get you."

"Close your beak, you old bastard," Oggy said calmly as she came out of the bathroom and ran a comb through her wet hair. "We know what to do."

"Speak for yourself," Gerard muttered, and without enthusiasm began to pull on his pants.

He had not yet had time to buckle up when a powerful explosion thundered, and the shock wave knocked down everyone present.

One of the walls of the house was reduced to rubble, and masked figures in leopard-print outfits and ready-to-fire weapons appeared in the gap. Never immediately realized that these people definitely did not belong to Nuntia. At least three of them were of very dark complexion, one was definitely African. Nuntia would never have recruited such people. So it was more likely a branch of the Van Helsing Institute.

He reached for the pistol, knowing full well that he would not have time to use it since the others were already holding them in their line of fire when Vandis blocked the path and raised both hands. A split second later, the others stopped, lowering their weapons. It was like a scene in a silent movie. Moments later, the intruders turned in unison like programmed machines and left, disappearing into the darkness of the night.

"I'm afraid you will need to get out of here as soon as possible," Vandis said softly. He was as motionless as ever.

"Of course we do. That much we know ourselves," Never growled. "Well, why are you sitting like toads in a ditch? Get to work with the rug. It will serve as a stretcher."

This was not the first time they had to leave the premises in the proverbial five minutes. Effective evacuation allowed them to get away from the threat in a short time, but did not solve anything. There was a wounded colleague with them, and they still didn't know where to go. The squad attacking them looked determined and well-organized, so it was best not to risk it by heading for any of the focal points they know. Everything indicated that after a period of relative peace, the regular hunt for vampires began again, and Poland, while still safe, was becoming a very dangerous place.

"Let me drive," Vandis said to Never. "I'll take you where they won't find you."

"The cemetery?" Dea asked incredulously.

The detective shook his head.

"No," he replied. "A completely different place, but it's not very far. I'll teach you something, even though I shouldn't. If you are to support Meredith, you must have some advantages."

"I don't understand. None of this makes sense," Dea sighed, checking how Conan was doing.

"Don't worry, we don't know much either," Theo said. "So far, only that Vandis has a friend who has been exposed to unclean forces. It's all about some sort of black magic or something... cool, right?"

"So cool that you can choke on it!"

"People call black magic anything they don't understand in this world," Vandis said. "When something incomprehensible happens to them, they willingly explain it by the illusions of their imperfect senses and step back, not even trying to understand what they are faced with. All in all, I suppose it is a favorable circumstance, otherwise it would lead to great misfortune."

"Are you going to give lectures now, or tell us something specific?" Dea asked crookedly.

He ignored the obvious irony in her voice.

"Now listen to me carefully: people are not indigenous to this planet. Especially since they only occupy one of its dimensions and cannot use the other."

"Slow down, bud," Gladiator interrupted. "I believe we have three dimensions, even I know that."

"I'm talking about spacetime dimension, not the geometric ones," he explained patiently. "You see, the Earth was once inhabited by creatures like Cyrotte, whom you already know, people like me, and many other species. A series of natural disasters left only a specimens, and no population survived enough to recover. You should know that in many ways their representatives were neither worse nor better than humans, but having lived millennia with the knowledge that they were the last of their own, they were demoralized. They hate people mainly because of their hateful immortality and the human reproductive capacity, which their immortality replaces. However, they can't just openly harm them. Instead, they resort to trickery, and you can see that they are good at it."

"How many of those dimensions are there?" Never asked, being the only one in the van who understood anything from this speech.

"As many as you can imagine," Vandis replied. "However, we are currently interested in six of those that are closest to yours... that is, the one in which we are now."

"Something else is close, too," Dea interrupted. "They're after us."

Indeed, the two cars were clearly visible in the rearview mirror as they tried to approach the van. These were definitely not police cars, as could be seen from the fact that their headlights were turned off.

"Will this lambo of ours be enough when they start firing their AK's?" asked Gladiator with the calmness of a professional soldier.

"It should last a few minutes," Gerard replied. "And they probably won't start to, because even the Polish police are not deaf."

"What do you mean *even,* you frog-eater fed with snails, Marseille and tortured in your backside?" the offended highlander tried to get up and straighten up menacingly, but hit his head on the roof and sat down again.

"I mean that I've lived here long enough to know how your police work," Gerard replied without a trace of insult. "And stop trying to get up, or the remains of your brains will splash out from under that scrap of linen of yours. Since when did the Polish police officers become untouchable?"

"Stop," Vandis demanded. "And hold on, because it'll start shaking a little."

They didn't notice what he was doing, but suddenly there was a sound like that of a broken string on a guitar, and the van swayed forward like a rocket. Everyone collided with each other, because, of course, no one had time to hold on to anything.

"You are carrying people, not potatoes!" Dea screamed, anxiously checking to see if the sudden action had hurt her patient. But the vampire's wounds heal quickly, and Conan was getting better. He was almost conscious.

"Where are we?" Fronde became worried as he looked out the window.

They were definitely not where they were before. Outside the windows of the van, there was a gloomy landscape, devoid of the slightest greenery, with a low-hanging white sky. It looked a little like a surreal photograph of the area after the explosion of an atomic bomb, especially since they could not hear the sounds of birds or even the hum of the smallest insects anywhere around, even though it was clearly daytime.

"No kidding, little angel. Where are we?" Gladiator asked menacingly.

Vandis slowly turned away from the steering wheel. Somewhere the last semblance of humanity with which he disguised himself was blurred. His face was like translucent porcelain, blue streaks on the temples, his black eyes sparkled with a thousand sparks, and his hair shone with iridescent reflections, as if lit up. The shirt and trousers he wore turned into a tunic and a white robe, fastened on the left shoulder with a strangely shaped buckle.

"Welcome to my world," he said softly.

Even his voice changed, became unearthly. Everyone was silent, numb, only Dea looked unperturbed.

"I see, I see, cool," she said finally. "But what the hell are we doing here? Conan needs medical attention, and I think we have a job in our own world."

"I don't need anything," Conan said weakly. "I'm better now. Soon I will be as delirious as before."

"Shut your mouth, I'm the doctor here."

"Don't argue," Vandis interrupted. "It's a serious matter, otherwise I would not have taken you here. I broke all the rules in order to do so, so please respect what I'm risking."

"What are you risking, now?" Oggy asked curiously.

"Don't ask. Let's finally get to the point, because while I am who I am, you cannot stay here too long. Listen:

Meredith Johnson is my special protégé. I have always helped him ever since he grew up and stopped being a child. I couldn't stop him from turning into a bloodsucker, that's true, but that can't be reversed anyway. It turns out that it's difficult to have any chances against Segovia, because he never plays fair..."

Never frowned at the hated name. Whenever it was mentioned in his presence, it always ended in big trouble, since Segovia was the kind of vampire who loved creating chaos. There were reasonable suspicions as to the sanity of his mind, and this was the main reason why the rest of the undead, especially Never, his own son, avoided him like fire.

Vandis didn't notice anything and continued:

"Meredith is, as he calls himself professionally now, The Haunted. That means, he is not alone. That which follows him has no name in any of the human languages. As for what it looks like when it doesn't turn into something familiar... maybe it's better if you do not know. The fact of the matter is that The Haunted is not only in danger himself, but also threatens literally everyone with whom he comes to contact with. Do you understand what tragedy it is for Meredith, who has helped others all his life?"

"Boo hoo," Gladiator muttered. The godly fear he experienced when he first met Vandis turned into irritation. That was not how he envisioned an Angel. And on top of that, he was seriously frightened. This place was so strange that he dreamed of only one thing – to get out of here as soon as possible.

Meanwhile, Winger continued.

"As an ordinary person, as a priest, and even as a vampire, he was a real blessing for those who needed help. And now he has to take care to stay as far away from people as possible. He's terribly lonely, and I'm afraid his psyche can't handle it. I have no one else to turn to. Only you have the courage to take on this business, but I want you to be fully aware of the risks before you agree to help me. And I won't be mad at you if you refuse."

Theo coughed in embarrassment.

"As if. We've seen enough strange things. The problem is whether we even have a chance to solve this case. We've dealt with unclean forces before, but what you're describing sounds a hundred times darker than anything we have dealt with," he replied, scratching his head. He was quite superstitious and, like in all his eras, believed in a material, tangible devil.

Vandis lowered his head as if wondering which words he should say now.

"Because it is dark," he said finally. "Not so long ago, people like you were considered the servants of what I'm talking about. I know that this is not the case, and if we're talking about IT... it doesn't care if you are human or vampire. It will want to hurt you either way."

Silence reigned in the van, in which only the steady howl of the wind outside could be heard.

"I have a question," Never said finally. "How are we supposed to fight something so powerful that it couldn't be taken care of for millennia?"

"I did not say that it's impossible. Segovia once fought IT, and in a sense even won, although it cost him constant madness. You should know that Segovia himself is very old, he is thousands of years old, and he probably remembers the time of Julius Caesar, and maybe even Akhenaten. Perhaps it is precisely the fact that he is mentally ill that allows him to soar on the surface of phenomena and accept all the changes..."

It seemed that he was somehow confused in his words. He stopped for a moment and only continued after a long moment.

"In any case, I will teach you how to hide here in the case of a hard-won situation. IT cannot gain entry here, but you also have to take into account the fact that you can only stay here for a short time, a maximum of three hours. This is not a place for humans. And not for vampires, who are, after all... human too."

"Well, no one has called us that yet," Dea snorted.

The Angel's speech didn't seem to make much of an impression on her, and her friends weren't too surprised. No wonder this girl was told that the devil himself wouldn't be able to handle her – it was not unreasonable.

"Take him to court for that," Gerard advised teasingly. "Listen, Vandis, I'm an atheist..."

"Mother of God!" Theo interrupted him. "How many more times are you going to say that?!"

"...and I don't believe in any devil. So explain to me rationally, what am I supposed to be fighting with?" finished the actor, not paying attention to him.

Vandis threw up his hands helplessly. It was obvious that he lacked the words to satisfy Gerard's demand, or perhaps the phenomena he was talking about were simply eluding verbal descriptions. After all, it is very likely that he was talking about things different from what constituted the content of the life of the human species, so different that this could no longer be. It is true that the human imagination is quite flexible, it shies away from what is truly unknown.

This is especially noticeable in science fiction films, where aliens take on familiar forms and are usually very human in their reactions, unless they are an amorphous and mindless jelly that devours whatever it finds on its path. People simply cannot imagine something that is truly alien, so they make copies of themselves. Sometimes such a copy has antennae, sometimes insect eyes or pointed ears, but usually it is still a person with their own virtues, vices and a whole attitude towards life. So how could he explain to people what a Dark Creature is, which from time to time leaves its abyss to torment those whom it picks?

"All you'll need to know is that you'll be dealing with a truly intelligent and almost infinitely powerful Evil," he said at last. "Until you meet it face to face, you won't understand what I'm talking about. So tell me: do you agree to help me?"

Everyone looked at Never, even Dea. He was the leader and, like the captain of the ship, always made decisions for everyone. They muttered, rebelled, but in the end they always followed his orders. And not only because his IQ was absurdly high – it's just that this demonic Hindu had an instinct for leadership and a certain innate authority which everyone unconsciously obeyed.

Never looked out a window with the terrible landscape. He didn't know what to say. Not a single vampire feels like a demon, nor a savior of the world, with the exception of unstable people. He feels like an ordinary person, whose fate has become more peculiar, that's all. Considering this, he hesitated on what to say.

"Why is it so disgusting here?" he asked for time.

Vandis followed his gaze and smiled pitifully.

"It's not," he said. "Your eyes are simply not adapted. They can only see what your brain can pick up. I see something completely different from you. But no matter, what is your answer?"

"We'll give it a try," Never sighed resignedly. "We can't promise anything, but we will try. After all, we are not new to this industry."

Vandis nodded in satisfaction. Without saying anything else, he started the engine and the van moved, and after a while it was back on the intercity highway. The chase was nowhere to be seen.

"That's rather impressive, if you ask me," Oggy muttered to herself.

"It's a pretty simple trick," Vandis said. "I'll give you the exofusion key... don't try guessing what it is. You can only use it once. And do not forget to use this escape route only in a state of extreme danger, when the UNINTELLIGEBLE literally grabs you with its claws."

"Damn, it sure would've been nice to be able to travel to another dimension every time the Hunters grab us," Never took a metal box from Vandis's hands. It contained a shining octagonal crystal.

"For the key to carry you, you must destroy it. As for your remark, it's... the molecular structure of living people is not adapted to this environment. It disintegrates quickly. Unfortunately, the one-time key is the only weapon I can equip you with."

"But tell us at least something about this place, about yourself..." asked Theo. His black eyes burned with unhealthy religious curiosity. Whoever this wonderful detective was, the medieval knight saw in him a real angel, a messenger from Heaven.

Vandis looked at him a little sadly.

"Very well," he replied after a moment. "I think in the end I owe you that."

He began to explain it step by step, and although his lecture sounded very strange, it seemed to everyone that it was burning itself with flaming letters inside their minds. It was not just a transfer of knowledge, but an aggressive invasion of their memory and recording in them every spoken word. They should never forget what he was saying to them now, although if they were to repeat it to someone, they would not even know where to start.

Conan, who had somehow managed to sit up, listened to all this with genuine horror in his eyes. Despite his massive form and formidable appearance, he did not like fights and military adventures, and now he also received a chest wound, and the last thing he wanted was to look for new bruises.

"I have a question," he finally said. "Do we have any chances against this thing?"

"Probably not," Fronde said cheerfully, thrusting his hands into his pockets. "And that's the funniest thing."

"Bite your tongue."

Conan rubbed his aching body with his hand. He felt that his wounds were closing under the influence of the self-healing factor recorded in the DNA of every vampire, but he still suffered from pain and stress.

"Damn, I'm not made for this," he muttered. "I never wanted to play an adventurer for hire. I know I look like an animal, but I'm not aggressive at all. And I'm not a Cimmerian."

It seemed he had no choice now, but Never, who was sometimes an elemental telepath, took pity on him.

"Dea, you'll take our athlete to safety and take care of him," he ordered. "You will also warn all the locals that a manhunt is imminent. If we fail, do not try to continue the action yourself, I forbid you from doing so. Promise me you won't."

"What if I feel like it," Dea said angrily. "Since when did you become my boss?"

"Give it up, she won't let anyone order her around," Fronde said before Never could reply. "The only thing you can do is ask her... and ask politely."

The Indian sighed resignedly. He never knew how to get along with women, and even tomboys like Dea scared him. He felt that they are capable of anything and are completely unpredictable.

"Okay, do what you want. But first, take care of Conan and warn all your friends... please."

"That's an order I can fulfil."

The van stopped in front of a small house next to the local police station.

"You can stay here for now," Vandis threw Never the keys and left. "This place is relatively safe, that's why I rented it. Nobody would risk a loud action right in front of the police. In the drawer of the desk, you have all the material related to the case, and spare documents. Good luck."

And before anyone could answer him, he disappeared into the darkness of the night. He didn't leave. He simply melted away, as if he never existed.

*****

Based on the documents, it seemed that Meredith Johnson was indeed somewhere nearby. When the friends got together at a meal and summarized everything they learned, they were sure of one thing: it was an extremely interesting personality. If he got into trouble, it was only because he insisted on helping others when he needed help himself.

"We act similar, too," Gerard remarked, reaching for a can of conserved blood.

"There is a difference. We were forced to do this by circumstances, and he does it voluntarily," Fronde skillfully prepared a cocktail for himself and others with the addition of gin and lemon juice, and then sat down in a chair with a glass in his hand. "Besides, we usually help others like us, and Meredith, from what I can understand, only humans. Am I right, boss?"

Never nodded his head in agreement. The documents left no doubt about that. Johnson's actions were primarily for the benefit of humans, rarely and only by chance did he help another undead in trouble. He was known among humans as an outstanding exorcist and an expert on the paranormal.

It was noteworthy that his actions never raised the Hunters' suspicions about him. In their records, he was not listed as a vampire or human. He knew how to disguise himself, even though in this area he was self-taught. The question was, then, how were they going to locate him? They knew that he was in Poland – they knew that he was somewhere in the area they were staying – but they did not know anything else. The photo didn't help much. After all, it's hard for them to simply go out with it and question the locals, as in a bad detective story.

In addition, as if that wasn't enough, Vandis warned them that Meredith was well versed in methods of appearance changing, and may not be very similar to that photo at the moment. All this combined meant that at first, despite a promising start, their searches became stuck at a dead end.

"Give me some advice, because I'm at a loss," Never said once when another plan to 'hunt down' Meredith backfired.

"You shouldn't have taken the money from Vandis, then we could have just thrown this case to hell and go on vacation," Gerard muttered.

"Shouldn't have this, shouldn't have that... you know very well that we're broke. Even Dracula himself would not have lasted long without financial liquidity these days. We do what we can, which isn't much, unless we organize ourselves into a gang and rob banks."

"Ask Oggy to knit balaclavas for us and we can get to work," the actor suggested.

"Stop fooling around, Gerard. I'm asking for constructive suggestions," Never poured himself some pure vodka and drank it in one breath.

He has been drinking more and more lately. This is the curse of most old vampires. Unable to cope with the changes taking place in the world before their eyes, they fall into alcoholism, gradually losing control over their lives. He himself was not yet that old, but due to the torrent of anxiety, he had problems with self-control. He hadn't told anyone about it yet, but he was secretly afraid that he would slowly start being burnt out.

Theo, who was looking at the whole situation from his own point of view, refused another drink. He has had enough and didn't want alcohol to confuse him. Being more sensitive to certain things than his colleagues, he felt that their search had already attracted the attention of the Dark Forces – whatever can be described with these words.

"We don't belong to the Dark Forces at all," he explained yesterday to Lilianna, a girl he had been seeing for some time. "We've never had anything to do with them. We are just people, like anyone else... well, with some minor differences."

She understood him well. She was very smart. Next to her, the aged Fronde felt truly comfortable for the first time in a long time, and yet he should have been on his guard. She immediately understood who he was, although she couldn't see him – she was blind from birth. But her other senses were so developed that he was unable to take her by surprise during their first meeting.

He was returning from a night hunt then. He walked the empty streets, well fed and complacent, singing frivolous songs to himself in Old French, when everything played out in a split second. Literally at the last moment, he grabbed the lone girl and pulled her aside. Otherwise, a drunken cyclist would have ran into her. He didn't see the white cane in her hand. He probably thought that she would dodge him herself, or maybe he didn't care. Drunkards were unpredictable.

They stood against the wall. He held the stranger in his arms, feeling the frantic beating of her heart, which slowly calmed down.

"Are you okay?" he asked. "Can you hear me?"

"I can hear you," she said. She was not as scared as he thought, because her voice was calm. She snorted slightly. "You smell different than people. Actually... I can't smell you at all... that's weird."

Suddenly she touched him with her hand, ran her fingers over his cheeks, hair and neck. Finally, the mouth and teeth. It didn't seem threatening, but it was. However, he succumbed to her satin touch, filled with a delicious shiver. Despite the darkness, poorly lit by dimly flashing lanterns, he could easily see her face and large, clear, blind eyes. Something took possession of him in the blink of an eye.

"You are a vampire, stranger. An undead," she said, not asked, lowering her hand. "How old are you?"

"More than six hundred years old," he replied before he could think.

"Would you like to walk me home?" she asked then.

She was not afraid of him at all, while he felt some sort of delicious fear. It was a dangerous situation because this girl could betray him, give him out... but he could not tear himself away from her. It was the first time in centuries that he felt something this strong.

She was of light build, with blonde hair, maybe not so much pretty, but fragile, frail like glass. He was so fascinated by her from the very first moment, that he could not tear himself away from her. He put everyone at risk – yes, he knew that, but he couldn't reject her. Although it seemed impossible, he managed to hide their relationship from others, at least for the first few days. However, Never, the most perceptive of them, immediately understood what was going on. He kept silent about it, although he looked at his friend with obvious concern, who realized this and was relieved to tell them everything.

"We have to be careful," Gerard said after a moment. "Now that Gladiator is looking after Conan and the company, we don't have as many assets as we once did. Our group practically broke up."

Dea asked to 'borrow' Gladiator for some time. Her agency took on investigating the mysterious assailants, which Vandis chased away, and she needed help. The blonde highlander was a logical choice, as he wanted to leave himself after a visit to another dimension.

"Don't hold it against me," he said bluntly. "I can fight anything that comes from here, but I'm not eager to put myself against demons and devils. What I've experienced is enough for me. Maybe I'll end up going to hell anyway, but I'm not that eager to go there yet. If even the angel didn't succeed, then I'm even less likely to, and honestly, I'm surprised that you're not going to back out of it as well."

They understood where he was coming from and were not going to stop him. Once again, there were only four of them, as in the beginning. In the midst of a difficult case, their strength was greatly weakened. Despite this, Never not only did not protest, but even encouraged his friend to leave. He knew that the task Vandis had given them was extremely dangerous, so the fewer the people that might be killed in front of him, the better. The Dark Forces didn't like those who interfered in their affairs, no matter who they are.

"The Dark Forces are ones that we simply do not understand. Better not to get in their way, but this time we have to do it if we want to save this priest," he explained to Conan, who visited them in a friendly manner.

"So be it," agreed Conan. "However, if I were you, I would be more careful with Fronde. Everyone has the right to their little secrets, but he is clearly hiding something."

Never followed his gaze or laughed.

"Come on, he always makes expressions like a monkey when he's love. Now he has a girl on his side, but this time he told us about it himself. She knows who she is. He doesn't know how to keep secrets, at least from women. And not from me, even when he tries to, because I can always guess what's going on. He makes everything so obvious."

"And you're saying so this calmly?" Conan looked at him in amazement.

"What am I supposed to do about it? This donkey is as truthful as the last idiot. Fortunately, women are infatuated with him, so the fact that their beloved is a 'child of the night' only excites them. And he uses that as much as he can."

He has long since became used to Theo wandering around like a cat and making friends that he usually talked about too late, but very colorfully. He got into serious trouble a few times because of this, but it didn't teach him anything. It was also true that he was very successful with the prettier sex. Not that Never wasn't. Or Gerard. Or the handsome highlander who was now part of their team.

Unlike vampires from movies and books, none of them led the life of a count or any other great lord. It would be dangerous. However, they easily entered romances, sometimes fleeting ones, sometimes more serious ones. People may not know who they are actually dealing with, but they are always happy to have a relationship with vampires. An aura of strength and prosperous health, usually filled with undead of both sexes, a pheromone of attraction secreted by immortal blood, and it all causes them to be unable to resist. The atmosphere of secrecy, which must be maintained, also does its job.

"I want to laugh when I read about a vampire who seeks the company of humans," Never said. "Even without that, we have enough problems with maintaining our anonymity."

He was undoubtedly right, because there were always Hunters to hide from.

That's right, the Hunters... they were still unable to explain from which wing their pursuers were coming from. So far, they managed to slip past them, but such luck couldn't last forever. The matter was complicated by the fact that they still didn't know who they were dealing with. Lilianne even asked Fronde if it's not all the same, but he explained to her that this was not the case. It would be all the same if they were absolutely sure that it was humans attacking them – meanwhile, the manner of action and the amount of knowledge of the attackers indicated the they were undead, which made the whole matter twice as complicated.

Nuntia started it. There was no doubt about that. However, it seemed that this squad did not belong to this organization, so what is it about? It looked like an attempt by one organized group to dominate the environment. Dominant or maybe... intimidate. But for what purpose?

"Let Dea take care of it," Never stopped the discussion. "We have to solve the case with Johnson because, hell, that's what they're paying us for. Oggy, tell me what you sniffed out."

The girl took a small notebook from the pocket of her dress and flipped through a few pages.

"The tracked person stopped at the *Golden Moment* motel outside the city, on the road to Szczecin," she said. "As far as I understand, he was conducting a private investigation into a local pimp, but I don't know exactly why. It's not about the ladies who work for him, because, as far as I understand, cooperation is mutually beneficial. It's also not about the motel owner, who has a passion for creative bookkeeping. It's as if our priest was waiting for something or someone. He has now moved to another motel called *Respite*, located three miles from here, and that's where he is now."

Never thought for a second. They could choose a risky action or follow Meredith from afar, as they were doing thus far. It was the safe option. Only that the current method of investigation has given them nothing.

"Pack up," he decided. "We'll give that motel a visit. We'll move in and see what happens."

"There will be trouble," Gerard muttered with confidence.

This was not the first time they were putting themselves in something like this. At first it scared him, but over time he got used to living on the edge. However, he sometimes felt nostalgic for the glory days and felt terribly alone.

"That's just proof that you've not yet become completely vampirised," Fronde consoled him.

"I didn't ask for it," he growled back, but he had to admit that this state of being had its advantages. Their life was like a colorful, not very coherent dream, and it certainly wasn't boring.

"Listen, I can go where you want me to, but first I'd like to take Jen to Lilka," Theo said. "If we don't come back alive, I want to make sure that someone will take care of the creature."

"And if we come back dead, imagine how worried you'll be then," Gerard finished ironically. "Hand her to the zoo, we'll all get caught because of her one day."

"Shut your mouth, you idiot comedian," Fronde said offended, gently scratching his beloved companion's neck.

After a stormy meeting, the friends agreed that they would pretend to be tourists whose car broke down. Such a cover story had two advantages – it explained their presence in a certain area and allowed them to stay there for as long as they needed. Thus, they established a course of action relatively quickly. Finding the motel was the hard part. They drove around for several hours before finally finding it, more by luck than anything else.

It was unusual in itself: a motel tucked away as if someone wanted to it to be hard to find? This contradicted the very idea of such a place. They were also not welcomed very willingly. The very beautiful, but tired receptionist looked at them incredulously at first, and then asked if they needed to stay here in particular.

"Our car has started to fail. Why?" I was never surprised.

The secretary reluctantly handed him the guestbook.

"Nothing," she said, avoiding his gaze. "Please write in. Make it readable."

They all took turns writing names from their papers, thinking only one thing: something with this motel was off. They could not clarify this thought – something simply didn't feel right.

It took them a while to figure out what it was. Despite the fact that the building was kept completely clean, dust swirled in the streaks of light and there was some strange smell, at first imperceptible, but later becoming more and more unpleasant. There was a shadow in the corner that seemed perceptible. There was silence on the second floor, where their rooms were, as if there were no one else in the entire motel but them. The sidewalk that covered the corridor looked rotten – the impression was simply absurd and vanishing on closer inspection, but at first glance extremely unpleasant.

"If Dea had been here with us, she would have called the Sanitary Inspection or the cleaning crew. I can already hear her voice: *Haunted or not, I don't care. I want this place clean!*" Fronde giggled, having nerves of steel.

"Oggy, what is this stench?" Gerard asked the girl, shifting nervously from foot to foot. "Somehow I can't identify it."

Oggy shrugged slightly. She couldn't name it either, even though she was an expert in this area. In addition, it annoyed her more than the others, and she could hardly keep herself from simply running out of this place.

The rooms they were given were decently decorated and reasonably clean, although they would not have been surprised to see age-old dust in them. It was hard to imagine how this place made its profits – hidden from the human eye and not very inviting. However, according to Oggy's discoveries and guestbook entries, Meredith Johnson has been staying here for a month.

They met him just after sunset as they walked down to the front desk to find out what was the matter concerning meals (they never neglected this ritual, allowing them to keep a safe incognito). He was just leaving: not too tall, thin, with dark hair over his forehead. He paid no attention to the new guests. He seemed to be absorbed in his own thoughts. They, on the other hand, looked at him closely, noting silently anything that might matter.

They noticed that Meredith was, first of all, terribly pale, that he had dark circles under his eyes and a bandaged left wrist. He was dressed in black, with a collar around his neck, but without any metal parts. He didn't even have a watch. This last revelation bothered Never, but he said nothing until Johnson was out of sight. Immediately after that, he dragged his friends into the small courtyard behind the motel.

"Listen, did you see that damn priest? He was not wearing anything metallic, not even buttons," he said in an excited whisper.

"So what?" Gerard asked, puzzled.

"Just that this guy is voluntarily risking protecting himself! Metal objects, especially iron ones, and weaken the influence of foreign forces on the mind. Don't ask why, that's just how it is. If someone followed by the Dark Forces voluntarily deprives himself of this protection, then you can start guessing uninteresting things.

"I see that you've become a fan of conspiracy theories," Fronde said sarcastically.

"So you think I am, of all people, fantasizing. What else has come to that genius costard of yours?"

Never looked at him with pity.

"You are hopeless as always," he replied. "But never mind that. I think I recognized that smell. The same one was in the morgue of the Medical Academy. Do you find that funny, too?"

Gerard silenced them both with a loud hiss and pointed to a side road visible from the courtyard. Some two girls were bargaining with passing men in leather jackets – not a word could be heard from this distance, but the meaning of the scene was too clear. The friends exchanged glances and rushed into the bushes. The girls quickly came to an agreement with the drivers and went with them to the motel.

"Let's go back, but officially, let no one notice what we are watching," Never whispered imperiously. "Line formation."

The friends dutifully dispersed in different directions, turning back at some distance to the silent motel. It was silent and dim, which became clearer the deeper the night outside. The receptionist was nowhere to be seen, and an extremely nasty guy with a cigarette in his mouth leaned against the front doorframe. At the sight of the friends approaching, he spat out the cigarette butt and stamped it with his shoe.

"Get out," he said shortly and without preamble.

"What do you mean, get out? We're staying here," Oggy said, giving him a puzzled look.

"Not any more. Get out."

"Who the hell are you?"

"Security. Get out of here now, pipsqueaks."

Fronde looked at Never and raised his eyebrows questioningly. The man shrugged.

"All right, knight. Show the visitor how we respond to such remarks," he said and sat on the low wall surrounding the building.

Theo eagerly rolled up his sleeves.

"If that's what you want, then go ahead, go in," the man muttered unexpectedly and stepped aside. Fronde opened his mouth in surprise. This was not what he expected.

"Let's go," unimpressed, Never got up from the wall, let his friends pass in front of him, and as he passed the man he suddenly turned and hit him on the neck with the edge of his hand.

"Are you crazy?" Gerard exclaimed.

"Quiet down, it's a professional secret, not everyone has to know," Never held down the sliding bodyguard. "Touch here."

He pointed to the man's neck. Gerard obeyed a little hesitantly and withdrew his hand as if he had burned himself

"You killed him," he gasped.

"You idiot. His blood wasn't circulating before either. Do you know what that means?"

Fronde flinched slightly, and Oggy's hair stood up suddenly, like the hair on a dog's back. Gerard looked at them questioningly, confused.

"He's a zombie," Never explained sweetly. "Look now."

The skin of the bodyguard he was holding was suddenly covered with brown-green blotches, his cheeks and lips sunken, and the stench of rot wafted from all around.

"The illusion fades as the subject loses consciousness," Fronde guessed. "Does that mean that the others...?"

"Could be. We've never dealt with zombies before, though I've heard of them. It's an extremely disgusting form of life after death... Hey, Gerard, don't you faint on me," Never let go of the corpse he was holding and supported his staggering friend.

He led him to a bench in the empty hall and sat him under a withering palm tree. Fronde hurriedly took a flat bottle of cognac from his pocket.

"Have some," he said. "It always helps."

"The living dead..." Gerard drank heavily and took a deep breath. He did not expect such revelations.

"You could call it that," Never agreed, sitting down next to him. "It's still unknown what causes the genesis of this condition. They can only 'live' for a while, and slowly turn into walking skeletons covered with scraps of rotting flesh. They eat the bodies of people they murder themselves, because they can only eat what has a human composition of amino acids and basically... is still alive. They are always hungry. To delay the breakdown of their own tissues, they drink preservative fluids – formalin, aldehyde and saline.

"Hence the smell," Oggy shivered. "It was not the usual smell of decay, but the smell of the dissecting room, as you noted. You mean this motel is a zombie's nest? What's Meredith Johnson doing here?"

"It's simple," said a dry, stinging voice behind them. "He's trying to work out the mechanism that creates these unfortunate souls and stop it."

They turned around. The man they were spying on stood in the doorway, staring at them unfriendly. Something vague swirled behind him. It seemed to be something that ordinary mortal eyes would not notice.

Never got up.

"We're here at Vandis's request," he said softly.

Meredith narrowed his eyes.

"I know," he replied. "Vandis Winger always gets involved in others' business. Don't make the mistake he did. You don't have his power or capabilities, you won't last long."

"Why? Is the thing that follows you going to kill us?"

The man laughed unexpectedly. His handsome face took on an expression of diabolical malice.

"Kill you? You won't be so lucky," he said.

From somewhere deep in the house came a muffled scream. The friends sprang to their feet and, ignoring Meredith, rushed toward the voice. As fast as they could, they made their way through the winding corridors until they reached a locked door.

"Shoulder to shoulder," Never commanded, wasting no time.

Under the pressure of three men, the door gave in, revealing a dark, musty passage. The scream rang again, this time much closer and more desperate.

"I wouldn't recommend it," Johnson blocked their way, as he had grown out of the ground. "They don't care, they'll eat you too."

"What do you care? Better worry about whatever that thing that is with you is. And get out of our way if you don't want to help."

"I am helping."

The darkness behind him deepened even more and rose like a wave of tar. It seemed like it was looking at them, although it was impossible to guess what it was.

"You're nuts. You're messing around with a devilish power and want to help? You won't help anyone, you will only harm them," Fronde cautiously took a step back.

"What I mess with is my business..."

Meredith didn't finish the sentence, because Never, ignoring his sinister comrade, unceremoniously pushed him away and walked along the corridor. Others followed, encouraged by the fact that somehow nothing was happening. However, after a dozen steps, they noticed that this was not quite the case. The light around them went out, as if it had been blown out. Black clouds swirled around everything, so it was impossible to know where and how to move.

"Oggy, lead with your sense of smell," Never ordered before anyone started panicking.

The girl growled like a dog and obediently moved to the front. Following after her, they quickly reached a staircase leading somewhere down, which was so steep that they nearly fell. They no longer paid attention to the rippling darkness – Meredith's companion was clearly from the same ward as the Shadow. It could scare a person to death, but nothing more. They could not understand why Vandis considered it such a threat, but there was no time to ponder it now.

The staircase ended in a dimly lit basement in which they saw a scene as if from a nightmare – several creatures devoured the tattered bodies of unwary drivers at a speed that seemed nearly impressive. In this insatiable orgy, the zombies looked more like corpses than living people, which they in fact wee. The signs of decay on their faces and hands reached down to the bones in some areas, and their torn clothes were smeared with a sticky, disgusting liquid. Even the healthiest-looking of them had an unhealthy blue-green hue, and his hair hung down like a drowned man's. The remnants of the old feasts were everywhere, covered with swarming larvae.

Fronde instinctively reached for the pistol, but Never hit him in the arm.

"You're crazy, knight. They can't be killed. They are below death, at least temporarily. Even if you cut them, they'll stick back together."

"T-then w-w-what are we s-supposed to do?" Gerard asked, holding back his chattering teeth.

"You ask that now? You shouldn't have entered here then, and now do what you want," Meredith reappeared next to them again, as if out of nowhere. He looked angry, and the darkness surrounding him now enveloped him like a large cloak with a life of its own.

"Why are you doing this?" exclaimed Fronde.

"Why does he do what?" Oggy groaned, losing her calm with fear.

"Can't you see? He's helping these monsters!"

"At least they're sitting in one place and bring here those that no one will miss anyway!" Meredith shouted.

"And who gave you the right to judge whether they won't be missed?!" Never continued furiously, who must have already guessed the essence of everything before and didn't like what he found.

Meredith stepped closer. He seemed to be walking on air, not on a rocky floor.

"I don't need to explain myself to you lot," he hissed slowly.

The ghouls, eating greedily, froze, and then, as if on command, their faces, which were at various stages of decomposition, to the new arrivals. Their sunken eyes, partially dry, flashed red.

"Ah, that's not good," Fronde muttered.

"You've done it now. They will no longer let you go," Meredith said grimly.

"It's about time they noticed us," Never didn't seem scared, he even sent a scolding look towards his friends, who were shaking as if from a fit of fever. "Look, priest, I understand your motives, but you screwed up."

"Not at all. Thanks to my actions, they are sitting here, and not bustling around the area! Do you know what was happening before I arrived here?"

The Indian put his hands behind his back. He was the only one who managed to maintain an ice-cold calm, which in such circumstances would be impressive if his companions even had time to look at him.

"So what, you think you're the savior of humanity? Did you hit your head? You are not helping anyone! People are still dying, only that you're playing judge, jury and executioner, deciding who gets to live! You're insane, do you hear me? You need treatment."

Meredith turned pale, and bluish circles appeared under her eyes. The darkness that was around his shoulders stretched and rose. Now it seemed that it was beginning to overgrow the vampire's skin with myriads of tiny filaments penetrating every cell of his body. The monsters backed away. Even they seemed to be afraid of what Meredith represented now – whatever it was.

"Now!" Never commanded.

His friends instinctively obeyed him before they could think. They lunged at Meredith and grabbed him, trying to overpower him. The man did not defend himself, did not even flinch, while they at first froze, and then they began to tremble like in a state of paralysis. They felt a shock, as if they had touched a high voltage wire. However, neither of them let go, their fingers desperately clutching Meredith's arms and clothes, who was still standing unaffected.

Never quickly crushed the fragile crystal he received from Vandis in his hand. There was a light around, so strong that everyone reflexively closed their eyes. Meredith twisted their arms with incredible strength, but they still held onto him tightly, as if their lives depended on it. A furious whirlwind howled around them, one which they've never heard before, and then suddenly something threw them to the ground with great force, making them all momentarily lose consciousness.

They were where Vandis had led them before – under a low hanging white sky, completely silent and motionless. They struggled to get up off the rocky ground and stood on wobbly legs. They felt drunk, their bones ached, and the lingering warmth in the air pressed onto them from every direction.

"You will all be destroyed!" Meredith shouted. "I will crush you like insects!"

He stood next to them, hovering about 15 cm above the ground, and the nourished pieces of dense darkness writhed around him like moving vines with thick stems. If they expected that transporting to this strange location would solve the matter, they miscalculated. The man approached them, spreading his wide, spectral tentacles that seemed to have a life of their own, attempting to reach the friends.

Never, with a desperate movement, threw dust in his face, which remained after the crushed crystal. Meredith jumped back with a hoarse curse. A crack suddenly formed between him and the group of friends, from which a column of gray-white smoke burst out. For a moment nothing was visible, then the smoke cleared and the friends saw Vandis. He looked different than usual. And it seemed that he was furious.

"Who told you to bring him here?" he exclaimed.

"You fool! Why did you get them involved in this?! Did you warn them that they would die?!" Meredith's voice suddenly became metallic, hollow, as if it was coming from the depths of a thick iron pipe.

"He forgot, it's hard to remember everything," Oggy snorted sharply. Unlike the men, this petite girl didn't look scared at all. She looked more furious than anything.

Vandis glanced at her briefly. He tried to pull himself together with an effort of will, but he still didn't look like an angel. More like a striga.

"Well, it happened," he said. "I will take care of him now, and you will immediately leave this place before the autolysis of your bodies begins."

"How are we supposed to just leave?! Gerard shouted. "We're not wizards, damn it!"

He was not yet finished when the ground, as far as the eye could see, began to split into uneven fields. Geysers of steam and sparks of silver burst from the cracks, covering everything around. Friends huddled together, afraid to be cut off from each other in this hostile place. Splitting stones rumbled around them until a hot whirlwind enveloped them and they momentarily became stunned.

When they regained consciousness, they were on the highway outside the motel. It was deep night and there was silence around, but compared to the silence of the mysterious world of Vandis, it was full of noises – you could hear creatures of the night, from time to time a car passed somewhere, the trees rustled soothingly. It was incredibly beautiful.

"What are we doing?" asked Fronde after a moment, not even trying to hide the fact that his teeth were clattering with fear, as if he was a newbie. He still couldn't figure out what was this 'other dimension' they were in just a moment ago, or who their friend, who called himself an Angel, really is, but he didn't really want to worry about that. The important thing was that they returned whole.

"I never want to deal with Vandis or any other member of his race again. Whatever they may be," Never muttered and looked absentmindedly at Fronde. "We have to pacify the creatures that the priest cared for. We must not let them terrorize the area."

"Pacify how? You said yourself that you cannot kill what is dead."

The Indian shuddered slightly and nervously smoothed his long hair.

"There is something that will destroy them," he said with an effort. "The only thing that is really omnipotent when dealing with such things. We need to burn this motel down."

"Is that necessary?" Gerard asked in disgust.

"Yes, it is, my green-eyed friend. Don't worry, they don't feel pain. Their nerve endings are dead."

"But they have awareness," the actor swallowed with effort. He looked like he was about to throw up.

"Yes... that's why it's so difficult. I numb at the thought that I could be in such a state myself. Theoretically, it's not impossible, but if it does happen, don't let me exist like that. It's hideous and without dignity."

"Don't be silly, it won't happen to you," Fronde shuddered again. "Or any of us. You're right, let's get a move on, we have to finish this and go back. I'd prefer if Dea could count on our support when Nuntia or anyone else sends their squads on her."

"It's not Nuntia," Fronde remarked, reluctantly following them. "I know it may seem like, but it really is a different formation. We don't even know if our blood flows in them for sure, maybe not at all..."

He shook his head. He disliked the idea of vampires fighting each other for supremacy as Hunters not only continued their activity, but also flourished. Never didn't pay attention to his last statement. It bothered him that the motel was not illuminated – previously, it at least remotely resembled an inn of this type. Now it looked like it had been abandoned for ages. Only the smell remained the same, which they could feel from afar, but it was much weaker, as if it was freshened. This could indicate that their worst fears had become reality and that the living dead, which no one was holding back anymore, had spread to the area.

"But this soon? Never said quietly in surprise. Something felt wrong to him.

"Let's investigate the building," he ordered.

His companions shuddered but made no protest. They themselves were aware that it had to be done, although their contract did not include fighting zombies. All they had to do was find Meredith, which they had succeeded, and free him from possession, which they had failed. It was difficult to free someone who doesn't want it at all, and the symbiotic bond between the former priest and IT was all too visible. Any help was beyond their strength, and either way, they only partially understood the complex nature of the phenomenon.

They also preferred not to think about what was probably going on in the mysterious world of Vandis right now. They didn't even know a basic thing such as the kind of laws of physics that operated in it. It was indeed a different dimension of reality, so different that it was beyond their understanding. It was only fortunate that it usually had no contact at any point with other ones. Especially with 'their' dimension.

In a deserted motel they found only the remains of the victims' bodies, some relatively fresh, others in a condition that could make even a seasoned pathologist sick. To their consternation, they also found an abandoned newspaper, which it seems one of the lured victims had with them. From the date on it, they found out that somehow four days have passed them – the action was on the eighth, the newspaper was from the eleventh, and after sniffing it, Oggy said it was undoubtedly yesterday's issue. This was clearly indicated by the smell of the printing ink.

"What the devil?" Gerard was surprised, who at times could not comprehend such manipulation.

"I've heard of similar phenomena, but only theoretically," Never answered him. "Let's not think about it too much, or we'll go completely insane. What is more important to us is something else: where did these creatures go?"

"Do we need to know?" Gerard asked with some hesitation in his voice. His face expressed a silent plea and Never shrugged in response.

"Have it your way, we don't have to," he replied. "But let's find out if our car is still in the garage..."

The metal barrack next to the motel was locked, but one of Fronde's lockpicks could easily handle the poor padlock. To the great relief of the four friends, their van was there intact. In fact, if they gave it some thought, it was suspicious in itself, as since the area around the motel wasn't well-known – car thieves were quite ordinary and common here – but they didn't think about that now. They only wanted to get out of this terrible place as soon as possible.

"Fronde, get behind the wheel," Never ordered, opening the door. "Destination: Warsaw."

"Yes, sir."

Theo took his seat hastily, waited for the others to enter after him, and started the engine. The van pulled out of the garage onto the highway and headed for the capital. They were all overcome with a feeling of unspeakable relief.

"What an unpleasant experience," Never said, stretching out with an involuntary grunt. All his bones ached, same as with the others. "Good thing it's behind us. I'm rarely ungrateful, but I don't want to see Vandis or his like anymore. Let them stay far away from us..."

A sudden cry from behind caught his attention, but a quarter of a second too late. A cold, damp, foul-smelling body rolled over him, wrapping its arms around him, and reaching his neck with its spread teeth. Only now did everyone feel the repulsive stench, previously disguised, just as the zombie's appearance, with some kind of illusion. Never was able to grab the attacker by the hair and pull him away at the last second, avoiding a bite. But this one did not give up, he pierced his shoulder with teeth, sharp and strong as wire cutters.

"There's another one!" Oggy screamed desperately.

"Fronde, don't stop, go!" Never screamed, struggling to break free from the zombie's grip. The living dead finally allowed himself to be pushed away, having previously torn off a piece of his body from his shoulder.

Oggy and Gerard tried to take down the second attacker, while Theo desperately scanned the area, trying to find something to help them. He knew what it could be and prayed that it would be there.

Finally, to his unspeakable relief, he saw what he was looking for and directed the vehicle in its direction.

"On my mark, everyone get the hell out!" he shouted. There was no time for explanations, and no one needed any either way. They were accustomed to acting as one body, and in times of extreme danger this was an invaluable skill.

"Now!" Fronde called, opening the van door.

Never, with movement as quick as thought, wrapped the seat belt around the attacker's neck, Gerard and Oggy tucked it under the back seat, and all four jumped out of the car almost simultaneously. The van crashed at full speed into an abyss at the side of the road, exploding at its bottom in yellow-orange flames.

"Did they have time to jump after us? Anyone can confirm?" Oggy asked with tears in her eyes, hugging Fronde.

"I don't think so," he said, putting his arm around her. "But we are left without a vehicle. And far enough from home."

"We don't have a home. We're free birds," Gerard said, kicking a rock.

This may not have been what he wanted in his life, but he was beginning to get used to it. Beginning to... considering how many years he had already lived the way he lived, it sounded almost humorous. Decades passed since he was placed in a coffin dressed as Cid, and he still felt almost human. He still felt like the same Gerard who portrayed characters from classic plays and movie heroes.

"Let's go on foot, per pedes apostolorum. Dawn will come soon, we have to find shelter," Never stopped and suddenly hit himself on the forehead. "I should have thought about it in advance! What else are mobile phones for?"

He took his phone out of his pocket and dialed a number. He listened for a long time to the signal, then a sharp displeased voice said:

"Who's this with a goddamn death wish to wake me from my first sleep?"

"It's me, dear," Never answered as affectionately as he could. "We got stuck without a car somewhere on the highway. We need transportation."

"You'll need an ambulance when I get there! Dea was clearly in her usual bad mood. "Do you know where you are? Find the some road sign and read it. Then call me. Give me some accurate directions, you good for nothing man, before I change my mind, because a good dream is still worth more than your miserable faces."

Fronde continued to stare into the abyss. The stench of a burning van and burning human remains was unpleasant, but a certain thought was even less pleasant.

"There were only two of them," he whispered. "Where are the others?"

Oggy shook her head helplessly.

"Are we doing anything?" Gerard asked.

Never turned off his cell phone with a firm motion. He folded the retractable antenna to avoid breaking it.

"We are not the saviors of humanity," he said firmly. "We're not playing Supermen. Let people solve their problems on their own. We're waiting for Gladiator to come pick us up, because I doubt that Dea would do us such honors and come personally. Then we go back to... the base and take an inventory of our assets. Then a discussion and free conclusions."

"What conclusions?" Fronde looked at him in amazement.

"We'll see. For now we have to get back. So we're sitting here and waiting for our transport."

"What would you men do without women to get you out of trouble," Oggy involuntarily muttered.

"We wouldn't get into trouble as often," Never answered her, but without his usual carelessness.

He rubbed his sore arm, which was still bleeding. Oggy tore off a piece of linen from her dress and bandaged his wound as best she could.

"I hope you don't get tetanus or an infection," she said anxiously.

"Or that the zombie didn't give you some disease," Fronde chuckled.

"A vampire with an infection. That's out of the question, dear..." Never hissed slightly when Oggy squeezed his arm a little harder than she intended.

"Don't be so sure. We already know that we are threatened by at least one human virus – HIV. A zombie bite can have unpredictable consequences," said Gerard, who has read many horror books in his time. "Does anyone know how they reproduce?"

"In any case, not like how you think. What an idea..." Never raised his eyes to the sky with an expression of silent pity. "You should stop grumbling, all you've been doing lately is complaining."

"Whatever you say, not everyone has an innate predisposition to Prince Dracula..."

Gerard didn't finish and jumped back, when the motel receptionist suddenly appeared in front of him. Despite the scare, he was a little surprised, because the girl looked completely normal. Now her skin currently had a healthy pale hue and smelled not of a corpse, but of the *Celebre* perfume. She also appeared to be shorter than in the motel, but at the time they only saw her sitting in the reception area, so they could not correctly assess her height. Now they remembered that they hadn't seen her among the feasting zombies, so was she not one of them? But in that case, what was she doing amongst them, and how did it happen that they did not harm her?

"Where is Meredith?" she asked. There was a vague threat in her voice, but it mostly sounded with dismay.

"He's gone," Never said, stepping forward. "I don't recommend looking for him. Who are you?"

The girl stepped back and pointed her index finger at him.

"What did you do?" she whispered accusingly. "Why did you get involved in something that did not concern you?"

Gerard involuntarily raised his eyebrows.

"You know, Raja, that's a pretty good question," he said, looking at Never, who glared at him in response.

"We do that all the time. We get paid for it," he replied. "How about the young lady introduces herself first?"

The girl nodded slightly, not taking her eyes off him.

"You will regret your curiosity and arrogance," she promised grimly. "You'll see."

Then she turned on her heels and disappeared into the woods, leaving them speechless, a little confused and very bewildered. For a moment they thought about following her, but in the end they decided not to.

"She must the priest's partner," Fronde said after a moment. "I hope she doesn't bother us, because I've had enough for one experience. I suspect that we've screwed up the matter, Vandis stuffed us into a mess and wasn't completely transparent with us."

"You don't say," Oggy muttered grimly, looking at her hands with some displeasure. Her nails, possibly under the influence of stress, turned into dog's claws, and despite repeated attempts, she was unable to reverse this transformation.

Never waved his hand helplessly and sat a moss-covered boulder.

"No matter," he sighed. "Let's wait for the transport and pray that the Hunters don't track us down in the meantime. They would have us all on a plate. What if that beauty works for them?"

"Now you're starting to get paranoid. Of course not. Her scent..." Oggy hesitated for a moment. "There was something familiar about her scent... but it had nothing to do with the Hunters. I will think about it later, right now I'm too exhausted."

She sat down at Never's feet and laid her head in his lap. He stroke her tousled hair lightly. Others joined them as they sat on the cool grass. They were all exhausted, physically and mentally, and it seemed like the disgusting creature had sucked all their energy out of them. Sometimes they forgot that even vampires weren't indestructible, and now they realized this with brutal clarity. There was nothing else they wanted, other than lie down and sleep.

"Oh well," said the Indian, looking at the already slightly gray sky. "We'll think about it tomorrow... someone will come pick us up soon, then we can rest in hiding. We've overdone it a bit lately... we've overworked ourselves, and that's not a good idea. After all, we are just human..."

After this observation, there was silence. For a few minutes all they could hear was the chirping of birds and the buzzing of insects, then the air suddenly thickened and a thin familiar figure emerged from within.

"I really thought you were professionals," Vandis said reproachfully. He looked as flawless as when they first saw him – dressed in clean and neatly ironed ecru clothes, glass-smooth hair, and dark glasses. However, this time they looked at him with a different gaze, and experienced fear in spite of themselves. He tied their legs and arms, blocked their breathing.

"What the hell did you expect? What do you want from us now?" Never gasped without recognizing his own voice.

Vandis smiled with endless sadness.

"Nothing," he replied. "Nothing else. You wouldn't understand anything I'd say anyway."

"Try us," said Fronde. "What is all this for?"

He shook his head.

"The world is not what it seems. No world is. People are fragile creatures, but... the most..."

"The most what?"

"The most beautiful."

"You've got to be kidding," Never snorted. He began to slowly recover.

Vandis was still smiling.

"Some hate you, others love you. There are those who long ago decided to give some of you a substitute for immortality or true power. So that you're not so incredibly vulnerable. This is where it all started."

"What started?" Oggy lamented. She pressed closer to Never's thigh, not taking her eyes off her interlocutor.

"Interference. Someone meant well, but... infected your world. Your dimension along with its Newton's law, Riemannian space and Euclidean geometry. For thousands of years, my compatriots and I have been trying to fix this, but something is still interrupting us. You believe that these attempts are supernatural occurences."

"This is too much," said Gerard. "I'm about to lose my mind."

"Bullshit. Be quiet, Gerard," Never finally got up and, pushing Oggy away from him. "Vandis, or whatever your name is... what happened to that obsessed priest? Why did you care so much about him?"

Vandis stepped closer. The Indian instinctively stepped back.

"He was a gate. The gate through which the alien beings passed. I could not close this passage myself, as he did not allow me to get close enough. I thought that opening an immediate point of contact would suck in what has possessed Meredith, but it was too strong. It took him with it, and with him you. I managed to send you back, but I advise you be very careful from now on."

"Why?"

"Even a short stay in another world causes irreversible changes. You may have acquired new skills, lost old ones, or walked out with a damaged mind. Hence, the key I gave you was one-time use. However, I do not wish to deceive you. You may have acquired the ability to spontaneously step through. If so, please don't abuse it."

They exchanged glances. This was not what they expected. They didn't know what to think about it, and they felt as if suddenly the ground beneath them slipped through.

"We're not going to," Never said slowly. "But since you've said so much, tell us how to protect ourselves."

Vandis shook his head slowly.

"I don't know that," he replied. "If you have acquired this power, it will manifest itself suddenly. Just be careful. That's all."

From afar came the noise of a motorcycle. Someone was approaching. Instinctively, they looked in the direction of the sound, and when they turned back, their interlocutor was nowhere to be seen. He disappeared as if he never existed. All that he left behind was a feather lying on the rocks – a lonely, crystal clear feather, sparkling with the colors of the rainbow.

www.ingramcontent.com/pod-product-compliance
Lightning Source LLC
Chambersburg PA
CBHW050125030726
47505CB00007B/2046